The Salvation Project

A novel

Joe Rothstein

For Bruce and Carolyn, and our many pleasant beach times together

Joe

Copyright © 2019

ISBN: 978-0-99769-992-0

Library of Congress Control Number: 2019915996

Cover by Akira007

Published in the United States of America

Published through Gold Standard Publications

Washington, D.C. 20008

Author website: www.joerothstein.net

For Sylvia, and our wonderful, love-filled years together.

The Moving Finger writes; and having writ,

Moves on: nor all thy Piety nor Wit

Shall lure it back to cancel half a line,

Nor all thy Tears wash out a Word of it

—Omar Khayyam

1

Two corridors radiate from the mosque's large open prayer hall. In a room connected to one of those corridors, a man in a blue linen suit paces. Another man, dressed more casually, tan chinos, red-and-white plaid cotton shirt, sprawls on a sofa. The only sound is the amplified voice of the mosque's imam, his afternoon sermon crackling through speakers attached to the room's ceiling.

The room is spartan. A simple three-drawer work desk. A straight-back wood desk chair. The sofa, pine, built low to the ground in traditional Ottoman style, softened by kilim cushions. Two metal filing cabinets. Metal folding chairs. A few wall hangings with Islamic sayings, notices of coming mosque events, all written in Arabic. Little here says privilege.

The ceiling speakers go quiet.

"Sounds like he's finished," says the man on the sofa.

"About time," replies the anxious man, still pacing the floor. The afternoon service already had begun when the two men arrived. An usher escorted them to this room, the imam's private office. Javier Carmona, the man in the blue linen suit, does not know why he is here. An hour earlier he had completed a business deal with his friend, Tahir Badem. A very important deal. A deal that promised unusually large profits. After they signed the papers, Badem insisted that Carmona go to this mosque and meet with its imam, Musa Kartal.

"What business do I have with an imam?" Carmona asked.

"Urgent business," said Badem. "I would not ask you otherwise. I have a car and driver waiting to take you there."

Now he is here, chauffeured by the man sprawled on the sofa. All of this is quite annoying to Carmona. He is the chief operating officer of a major international conglomerate and has no time for foolishness. Compounding his annoyance, his companion is an incessant chatterbox.

"So, I understand you are from Mexico. I've never been to Mexico. I hear it's a beautiful country. But dangerous, yes? Cartels? Gangs? My friends have gone to your beaches. One friend went to Cancun. Wild, he said. Very wild. American girls there for something called 'spring break.' Do you know what is spring break? We have no such thing here in Turkey. The way my friend talks, spring break is when the girls take off their clothes and run naked around beaches and hotels. My friend often exaggerates, but sometime I must see for myself."

Before Carmona responds, the office door opens. The imam appears. He's younger than Carmona expected. The imam's coal-black hair frames his unwrinkled face, a beard trimmed so neatly one might think he had just arrived from a visit to a hair salon. His knee-length white tunic is spotless. This is a man who obviously values his appearance, even as he shuns symbols of finery. He moves with energy, grasping his visitor's hand as he would an old friend.

"*Asalaamualaikum*, peace be upon you, Senor Carmona. Thank you for waiting while I shared my thoughts at prayer."

"Tahir Badem said it was most important that I meet with you."

Imam Kartal motions for Carmona to sit in one of the

room's metal folding chairs. Carmona's annoyance rises. As the chairman of Groupo Aragon, one of Latin America's richest and most important conglomerates, he is not accustomed to being offered only a stiff folding chair. If he is about to be solicited for a major contribution to this mosque, there are better ways of doing it.

The imam nods to the man on the sofa, a signal for him to leave the room. Now Imam Kartal and Javier Carmona are alone. The imam takes the seat behind the desk. His eyes lock with Carmona's. He remains silent for a moment, studying Carmona's face, ascertaining that he has Carmona's full attention.

"Tahir is one of my oldest and trusted friends," said Imam Kartal. "His business is much like yours, isn't it, Senor Carmona? Power generation, energy production, agriculture, entertainment—so important to your country and the Americas. Tahir is the same here with Fertile Crescent Industries."

"Yes," said Carmona. "Tahir invited me to Istanbul to talk about business arrangements between our two companies."

"I know," said Kartal. "The first contract will be for the importation of significant amounts of your agricultural products."

Carmona and Tahir Badem had shaken hands on such a deal just an hour earlier. Carmona, a man not easily surprised, stared wordlessly at Imam Kartal, for the first time since being summoned to this meeting allowing discomfort to replace annoyance.

Kartal smiled. "Senor Carmona, I must confess that I am responsible for your new business arrangement. I asked Tahir to find something sensible for both of your companies, an arrangement attractive enough to bring you personally to Istanbul so that you and I might have this talk and others in the future."

Kartal's surprising disclosure transformed Carmona's discomfort into a spike of anxiety. For decades he had used the power of Groupo Aragon to manipulate others. Few knew how to leverage power better than Javier Carmona. Seldom had he felt it being used against him.

"Then let's not drag this out," replied Carmona. "Why am I here?"

"You are here to help us take control of the United States, Senor Carmona."

Take control of the United States? Carmona's expression, until now animated, froze with these words. A preposterous suggestion, obviously. Perhaps the imam's attempt at a little humor, worthy only of a wry smile in response. Or, perhaps not. The words inferred knowledge of events in Carmona's recent past, events he had no interest in revisiting. He forced himself to suppress his increasing sense of alarm.

"Really now," he said, "that's why I'm here? To help you take control of the United States?"

The imam nodded.

"And who is 'us'? The church, or whatever you Muslims call it?"

"No, Senor Carmona. Not the church, or a caliphate. I am representing a project to save humanity. For want of a better term, we call it the Salvation Project."

Carmona's anxiety dissolved into amused relief. "Take over the United States? Well, Imam Kartal, no offense, Groupo Aragon is in many businesses, but we have no particular expertise or interest in salvation projects. We leave that work to others." Carmona looked at this watch. "So not to waste any more of your time or mine, please excuse me. I have an airplane waiting to return to Mexico."

Carmona rose to leave.

"You will help us," replied Imam Kartal. "Let me explain why you have no choice." From the top desk drawer, Kartal retrieved a large envelope and handed it to a now standing Carmona. Carmona reluctantly took the unmarked envelope. Inside were a number of photos. He withdrew one, then, quickly, another. His head jerked reflexively from the photos to the imam's dark eyes, staring coldly at his. Carmona instantly recognized the photos and the threat they posed not just to his position with Groupo Aragon but to his continued life on earth. In fear and wonder, he involuntarily sank back into his seat.

Kartal's expression changed from one of captor to confidante. With a calm, beatific smile befitting a servant of God, the imam said simply, "You see, we really do have much to discuss."

2

For long flights, Groupo Aragon's Gulfstream G550 could be arranged to comfortably sleep as many as eight people. On this trip, from Istanbul to Mexico City, it carried only two passengers, neither of whom slept.

Javier Carmona had no intention of sleeping. He struggled to keep his mind focused on the trap in which he now found himself. Hours had passed since those shocking moments in the Istanbul mosque. Decades of intense deal making had taught him to say little when he was not in control. Be aware of all factors. Give away as little information as possible. Keep your emotions in check. Quickly sort through all options. Carmona knew how to deal with crisis. But the photos of the dead priest had blown away reasoned reaction. Why wouldn't it? The priest was the brother of the president of the United States. Carmona's personal security chief, Bernard Soto, had committed the murder. Carmona ordered the execution.

Carmona had not wanted to kill Father Federico Aragon. Federico was the grandson of the late Miguel Aragon, Groupo Aragon's founder. For many years, Federico trained to inherit control of the company. But when he became aware that price fixing, money laundering, bribery, and illegal drugs were unrecorded Groupo Aragon profit centers, Federico, who did not have his grandfather's appreciation for the value of illegal business, fled to a Jesuit monastery.

That would have been the end of it. Then, improbably, Federico's sister, Isabel, born in New York, raised in Los Angeles, heiress to Miguel's fortune, was elected president of the United States. Isabel Aragon Tennyson, "Tenny," as the world knew her, was not inclined to forgive Carmona for continuing to direct a massive illegal enterprise, one that defiled the proud Aragon name. From her first days in the White House, she had begun using her considerable powers to squeeze the Mexican government into destroying Carmona. To survive, he conceived a conspiracy to impeach Isabel and remove her from office. That would elevate the vice president, Roderick Rusher, a trusted and cooperative friend, to the Oval Office. Carmona enlisted powerful allies in US business and finance who also were being pressured by President Tennyson's reformist government. It was a brilliant effort: deep research into her background, cleverly forged documents, witnesses paid well to perjure themselves, an extensive media campaign to weaken her public support. After extensive televised hearings, the US House did impeach the president. The US Senate was days away from voting to remove her from office.

The conspiracy was on the verge of success. But somehow, working as a visiting priest in some of Mexico's poorest communities, Father Federico Aragon became aware of Carmona's role. Fellow priests helped him accumulate evidence to expose it. He was about to testify before Congress and reveal all he knew. What choice did Carmona have? The priest had to be stopped.

That was months ago. How had an imam in Istanbul been forewarned the priest was about to be murdered? How did he get those photos? Bernard Soto was so reliable, so careful. Who possibly could have been at the scene of the murder to take the photos without Soto's detection? In the wrong hands, those photos would lead to Carmona's arrest for murder. He would be convicted, and Isabel would see to it that, he, Javier Carmona, her brother's murderer, would be executed, with or without a trial. Of that he could be certain.

Against that prospect, Imam Kartal's demand had seemed surprisingly benign. "We want your research files on President Tennyson," Imam Kartal said.

"For what purpose?" a shaken Carmona had replied.

"Senor Carmona," said the imam, "I do not believe you are in a position to ask many questions at this moment. But let me assure you that we share your interest in removing her as president. We admire the extensive research you commissioned trying to accomplish that, and we hope to deploy that information in ways that allow us all to succeed. A more complete discussion of our interests will have to await another day and another meeting. For now, we would like to examine your files."

And so, Carmona had been dispatched to the airport. Waiting to board the plane with him was a man who introduced himself as Melek. Melek said he would accompany Carmona on the flight to Mexico City, retrieve the files, and immediately return with them to Istanbul.

For nearly the entire trip Melek remained silent. Silent, but awake. Carmona was thankful for the silence but intimidated by it as well. He was under surveillance. Carmona had arranged surveillance on so many others— associates he considered unreliable, rivals for power, competitors, politicians, common criminals temporarily employed to do work for which only they were suited. He could not recall a time when his own moves were being monitored.

Carmona had planned so carefully, carefully enough to escape prosecution after the conspiracy was exposed. But now he realized he had made one foolish mistake. He had not destroyed all of the incriminating evidence he had collected and fabricated against President Tennyson. Why not? Because of his own vanity. Because he was not used to failure. Because of the hope he might find another opportunity to use it. How did the imam know the files still existed? Obviously, they had people following Soto.

Who were these people? His old business friend Tahir certainly was part of it. Who else? Years of showing up at Davos, working at the highest echelons of the energy, agricultural, and banking worlds, Carmona knew almost everyone important to know. He mentally sorted through his contact network for possible candidates. Take control of the United States? These people clearly were delusional. But they also were diabolically clever. In many ways they were his kind of people. Why not play along? It made sense. Their goal, among other things, was his— to remove Isabel Aragon Tennyson from control of the US government and to replace her with a more compatible president. They needed Carmona's help to defeat her. He needed them now to survive. The more he considered his situation, the less threat he felt.

Carmona was so deeply engrossed in these thoughts he failed to realize the flight had come to an end. The Gulfstream's wheels touching down on the runway at Toluca, Mexico, startled him.

A pleasing, familiar breeze greeted Javier Carmona as the airplane's door opened. Toluca was nearly nine thousand feet above sea level, above the foul air that so often blanketed the Mexico City basin. The terminal here was about thirty miles from Mexico City, but it allowed private aviation to operate without the traffic and control complexity of Mexico City International Airport, Latin America's busiest.

Bernard Soto was waiting at the foot of the stairs to the tarmac, the door of Carmona's black Lincoln Continental open, a welcome safe harbor after the insecurity of the past few hours. Carmona was now back in familiar territory. His territory. His security chief. The imam's man, this Melek person, would be the one adapting.

Soto steered the car onto the Toluca–Mexico City toll road. Hours earlier, Carmona had informed Soto that he and his guest would be going directly to Mexico City's Tepito barrio. Soto knew what that meant. The instruction was a surprise, but Soto was not one to question an assignment.

Many tourist guides said this about Tepito: "Don't go there." Its picturesque open-air street markets were compelling, but its stalls were filled with stolen and counterfeit goods, and the streets were patrolled by thieves and gangs. Police occasionally conducted raids and had been known to demolish tenements that hid illegal drugs and other contraband. Mostly, though, the law had ceded this barrio to the lawless. In Tepito, an area where Groupo Aragon retained many operatives and could safely conduct whatever business the law might otherwise not permit, Javier Carmona stored his most secret files, including his extensive research about Isabel Aragon Tennyson, president of the United States.

Bernard Soto had no safety concerns steering an expensive car through Tepito's dangerous and narrow streets. He was a familiar figure here, often hiring the lawless for lawless work. Soto paid well, and because he worked for Carmona and the powerful Groupo Aragon, he also was universally feared. A winning combination for survival. He maneuvered the Lincoln past the skeleton wearing a pink dress that resided in the Shrine of Death, one of Tepito's major attractions, and turned onto Panadero Street, stopping at a nondescript tenement that was locally known as Soto's place of business.

Waiting at the door was Chub Cabrillo, the building's night guard. Soto entered, exchanged words with Cabrillo, and motioned for Carmona and Melek to follow him. A narrow hallway led to a locked room that Cabrillo quickly opened to reveal a wall of vaults. Carmona walked to one of the vaults and entered a set of complicated combinations. Thirteen bolts unlocked the vault's half-inch 10-gauge steel door. As the others stood by, Carmona sorted through the safe's contents, found what he was looking for, and emerged with two large boxes.

"This is what I have," Carmona said to Melek. "Our years of research on President Tennyson. Everyone she's ever dealt with and slept with. Every bank account she's ever had. Dossiers on all those close to her. I wish you more success than I had in trying to bring her down. I would like nothing more than to have you succeed."

Melek silently sorted through the contents of the boxes. Digital storage discs, photos, recordings, government documents, and other papers.

"There are no copies elsewhere? No other memory sticks, CDs, hard drives, microfilm?"

"No," said Carmona. "I've been most careful. I've destroyed everything outside of here that could be traced to us."

Melek closed the boxes and motioned to Soto and Cabrillo to each take one. "Shall we go?" he said.

Carmona was only too happy to see the last of Melek, who was booked to return to Istanbul on a flight later that night. They headed back down the narrow corridor, Carmona in the lead.

Suddenly, Carmona heard a pop, then another. Then the boxes crashing to the floor. Behind him, the bodies of Chub Cabrillo and Bernard Soto slid lifelessly down one of the newly bloodstained walls in the narrow corridor. Melek still held a Glock 43 semiautomatic pistol.

"Good God!" shouted Carmona. "Don't kill me!"

"Why would I kill you?" asked Melek, holstering his weapon, seeming genuinely surprised at the question. "The imam says we need you."

"But Soto. My God, Soto! Why?"

"To save your life."

"Save my life? I had no more trusted ally than Soto."

"You killed the brother of the president of the United States. You don't think she knows that and will use her many assets to make you pay for it? The president commands the FBI, the CIA, the Navy SEALs. She has enormous power over Mexican authorities. You had your Mr. Soto fire the bullet that killed her brother. A grave error. It was just a matter of time until the president's gentlemen paid a visit to your Mr. Soto and invited him to discuss his whereabouts the night of the priest's death. After a bit of persuasion, he would have told them, and then, you would have become one of the most notorious assassins in Mexican history. With Mr. Soto gone, there's no one for them to talk to."

Horrified, barely able to walk or speak, his body now an uncontrolled vehicle of fear, Carmona managed to seethe the words, "There's you."

Melek laughed. "Yes, there's me. But I'm a professional. I leave no room for error."

He motioned to Carmona to head to the door.

Carmona's legs had turned to rubber. Urine involuntarily poured down his leg. He fought to remain conscious and gasped for lack of breath.

"How do you think we will get out of this hellhole? It's not safe to walk these streets."

"Three cars are waiting outside. One to take me to the airport, another to take you wherever you want to go."

"The third?"

"My associates in the third car will make certain that your friends on the floor are never seen again."

An hour earlier, disembarking from the Gulfstream, Carmona had felt the comfort of alighting on familiar soil, protected by his trusted security chief. Now, all he felt, for the first time in his entire life, was uncontrolled terror.

3

Under most conditions, the drive south on Interstate 380 from Cedar Rapids to Iowa City takes about half an hour. But not on this stormy January day. Gusts up to twenty miles an hour whipped snow horizontally into windshield wipers struggling to provide visibility. Only the faint suggestion of red taillights ahead interrupted the late- afternoon darkness. A crawl, a stop, then a few hundred more yards of forward progress. The blizzard showed no respect for the presidential motorcade wedged into the convoy of trucks and cars sharing the highway.

Aboard the president's campaign bus, aides were frantically working to salvage the event at Iowa City's Hancher Auditorium. Nearly two thousand supporters would be attending. Good media coverage was assured. It would be, that is, if the campaign bus arrived more or less on time, and if the trailing press bus did, too, and if those thousands of supporters could slog through the deepening snow to fill those seats.

While her campaign staff struggled to reschedule the remainder of the Iowa City events, Tenny was arguing her case for a new vice president.

"Fish," said the president. "I want Fish."

"I love Fish," said Ben Sage, Tenny's long-time political consultant. "But two women on the ticket? Two glass ceilings to break? And she's from Alaska. Even if she helps you carry Alaska, that's only three votes."

"That didn't stop McCain from picking Sarah Palin."

Ben laughed. "Do you really want to use that analogy?"

Despite the fact that she was president, Ben could spar with Tenny as he would an old familiar friend. They were indeed friends, a relationship formed decades earlier when Ben lured her into running for Congress and guided her development as a charismatic political force. She would have felt naked in a political campaign without Ben. But the selection of a vice president was more than a political decision. Tenny felt that keenly now, after the events of the past few years.

Tenny had wanted Alaska congresswoman Sheila Fishburne to share the ticket four years earlier, the first time she ran for president. Instead she gave in to the political expediency of selecting Virginia senator Roderick Rusher. Rusher had been her chief competitor for the Democratic Party nomination that year. Ben and others argued that Rusher would help her carry states she otherwise might lose, and he likely did make the difference between winning and losing in November. But he was tied to Wall Street, the oil companies, and others Tenny had spent her political career fighting. When that campaign ended, so did the smiling platform scenes of her and Rusher together. During the years they shared the White House, there was little personal contact between Tenny and her vice president.

And then, the betrayal. Rusher had been in league with those plotting her impeachment. When confronted with recordings of telephone conversations and other evidence he could not deny, Rusher agreed to cooperate in the investigation and resign rather than face further disgrace and prosecution. That was a month ago. Now Congress was waiting for President Tennyson to nominate a replacement. She knew who she wanted— Congresswoman Sheila Fishburne of Alaska.

"Ben," she said, "you talked me out of this four years ago, and I'll give it to you—you probably were right. This time I'm not budging. Fish doesn't have a big national profile, but she's so dynamic. Once the spotlight hits her, the country will love her style, her irreverence, her independence. I trust her like I trust you and few others in this political world. Most important, her main mission in life is mine—to bring down the greedy bastards killing capitalism and making so many people's lives so miserable. I need a partner as committed to that fight as I am. And that's Fish."

"To fight, you have to get reelected," said Ben. "Impeachment left you with a lot of scars, and not just the ones on your body from the explosion. You've seen the poll numbers. Scary."

Before the Senate vote to remove Tenny from office, and unrelated to the impeachment effort, members of a right-wing militia group had engaged in a plot to assassinate her and came close to succeeding. They set off an explosion that destroyed portions of the hotel where she was the featured speaker. Many died, and Tenny suffered extensive injuries. This campaign trip to Iowa was her first public outing since she was discharged from the hospital.

"Isn't there anyone else you trust the way you trust Fish?" Ben persisted.

Tenny considered the question for a moment, then smiled at the irony of it. "Yes. Yes, there is. Hal Thompson."

Hal Thompson. The former governor of California. Hal Thompson, the mentor who guided Tenny in her transition from rich liberal do-gooder to street-smart patron of Southern California's hungry and homeless. Hal Thompson, once her lover in a long-ago affair, an affair that the opposition turned into an X-rated campaign against her when she ran for the US Senate. Both her career and Hal's were nearly derailed by that campaign. Naming Hal as vice president would reopen that sordid scab and almost surely would lead to her defeat.

"Fish or Hal," she said coyly. "You decide."

Ben knew she wasn't serious. Along with her sense of mission and Thatcheresque steel, Tenny had a playful inner partner who could emerge at unexpected moments. Tenny was a passionate woman. Her prepolitical life left a trail of lovers, some of whom became household names during her impeachment trial as the prosecution tried to destroy her character. Hal Thompson as an alternative was not a choice, just Tenny's little joke. He shook his head and smiled.

An aide interrupted.

"We've just passed the Coral Ridge Mall, Madam President. Should arrive in ten minutes. Looks like you're going to have a full house at the auditorium. We'll be ready for you soon."

"Stall—I need at least a half hour," Tenny replied. "On a night like this, no one will mind if I'm not on time. I've an important phone call to make first." She turned to Ben. "Ben?"

Ben started to say something, then hesitated, knowing he would not win this argument. He threw up his hands in mock surrender.

"We'll make it work," he said.

4

"Great Cooks and Tough Cookies," Tenny and Sheila Fishburne had named their group. They were high-energy women newly elected to Congress in the same class, and with similar ambitious legislative agendas. They had enlisted two-dozen other congresswomen, anointed themselves co-chief cooks, and turned the heat up high enough on the congressional leadership to demand a place at the table when important deals were baked. For Tenny and Fish, it was a bonding that tightened with their growing political influence. Now, years later, Fish was near the top of the congressional political ladder, often mentioned as a future Speaker of the House.

Tenny had expected Fish to resist giving up congressional power for the amorphous role of vice president. Resist she did, but Tenny was not to be denied. She played all the cards in her strong hand. Their years of personal friendship, their trust in one another, their similar policy views, the scars Tenny endured during her first White House term that needed healing, the gender breakthrough of an all-woman presidential ticket, the symbolism that would inspire American Indian, Inupiaq, and other minorities. All powerful motivators. It would be a Tenny-Sheila ticket. Two women. Two divorced women. One, Mexican American, a direct descendant of the Spanish conquistadors who arrived in the Americas shortly after Columbus. The other, an Alaskan who could trace her indigenous native roots to the once existent land bridge between Asia and the American continent. The greatest test ever of presidential ballot diversity.

Tenny enjoyed a moment of satisfaction when Fish finally agreed. Then, something she had not expected. Not exactly buyer's remorse. No. Selecting Sheila Fishburne was something

Tenny needed to do. But Ben Sage was right; this wasn't the smartest politics. Tenny suddenly felt the need for validation. From her small office in the back of the campaign bus, Tenny called to her personal secretary, "Please get Secretary Sanchez on the phone for me."

Carmen Sanchez was Tenny's lifelong security blanket. When Tenny was ten years old, newly arrived with her family in Los Angeles from Mexico City, it was Carmie who Americanized her to fit seamlessly with her new classmates. Carmie was the maid of honor at Tenny's wedding and the shoulder she leaned on a few years later after two heartbreaking miscarriages and a shattering divorce. Carmie introduced Tenny to Hal Thompson and the social service network that formed her first political base.

Now Carmie was her secretary of commerce, her invaluable eyes and ears into Wall Street and the business community, and, though it would sound odd at her age and position to openly admit it, her best girlfriend.

"She's agreed," said Tenny. "Just wanted you to be the first to know."

"How many Alaska roads, bridges, and airports did you have to promise her?"

"Don't be cynical. I just told her I'd kill myself if she didn't do it."

"Well, you know how much I love Fish. She'll be a great vice president. Is Ben convinced?"

"About her, yes. About getting reelected with her on the ticket? Not really."

"She is a wild choice. But then I've hardly known you when you weren't either thinking wild or being wild, or both."

"Excuse me, but didn't they used to call us both the 'wild ones'?"

"Of course. And we loved every minute of it. But during all the years I spent on Wall Street, I learned to wear sensible shoes."

"Oh, Carmie. Thank God you are sensible. You've saved me from myself so often."

"Well, let's talk about that. Are we on a secure phone line?"

"Who knows anymore? They tell me it is."

"Fish being on the ticket is one thing. You being there is even more risky. What do your doctors say?"

Tenny didn't reply right away. She long since had laid aside questions of her health. Only her doctors and Carmie knew the full extent of her injuries.

Carmie broke the silence. "Sorry to bring up such an unpleasant subject, but if you don't, I'm the only one left to do it. We both know that you have no business running for reelection, and if you're going to bail out, do it right now, before you screw up the whole campaign and let some jerk sneak through later and get elected."

"I'm running, Carmie. Case closed."

"You are unless your body tells you you're not."

"My body's fine."

"Sure it is. It just survived an explosion that by some miracle didn't kill you. Your chest was crushed. Your lung collapsed. Your leg was broken. Your body has so many scars it looks like a railroad yard map. And God knows what it did to your head."

"I survived."

"Let me remind you, your souvenir from those guys who

wanted to assassinate you was a thing called acute respiratory distress syndrome, and according to the mortality tables, that's not a good thing to have. Especially in the world's most pressure-cooker job."

"To hell with the mortality tables. I'm listening to my own body. It's telling me I'm not young anymore. A few creaks here and there. My broken ribs and leg are healing fast, and neither bother me much anymore. My head's clear enough to know that you shouldn't be worried. I'm not."

"Okay, so I won't, and I won't bring it up again. I'll just die a thousand deaths if you do."

"I know, Carmie. That's why I love you."

"And I love you. Now let's see what we can do about getting that beat-up wreck of a body of yours reelected."

5

"Carmona, you and I are much alike. We identify problems and opportunities and deal with each rationally. No rational person can look at the way today's public leadership is organized and fail to see we're engaged in a process of slow- motion species suicide."

Carmona did not know what to expect when Tahir Badem had summoned him to Istanbul, but he assumed the call was the tightening of a leash, an invitation that could not be refused. The memory of that night in the Tepito barrio—the bloody walls, the sudden transformation of life to death, the cold precision of Melek's planning, the casual indifference he displayed as executioner—all were indelible images that in weeks since had consumed Carmona's waking moments and sleepless nights. From the first sight of the photos Imam Musa Kartal handed him that damnable day at the mosque, he had lost control of his own destiny. Istanbul now and forever would be synonymous with danger. He did not know why he was here. He did not want to be here. But he knew the choice no longer was his.

Now, he, Badem, and Kartal were alone in a conference room of Fertile Crescent Industries, a company Badem ruled as chief executive. Badem was standing at a whiteboard, addressing Carmona as a lecturer would a student.

"Tell me, Carmona, how you came to be the leader of one of the world's most powerful businesses. Were you elected to that position by the workers? Or the customers?"

Javier Carmona shook his head, not knowing how to answer such a ridiculous question.

"No need to answer. That would be folly," said Badem. "You rose to the top of Groupo Aragon the way I did here at Fertile Crescent Industries. We were both ambitious. We did our homework to understand what our business and corporate structure required. We formed alliances with important coworkers and customers. We managed to outwit rivals, sometimes fairly, sometimes not. We earned our power. And through our competence, our organizations thrive even with fierce competition and in uncertain times. We know how to lead them. You agree with my description of your rise to power? Carmona?" Badem prodded, demanding his full attention.

Carmona was finding it difficult to focus. The question of his own security weighed heavily on his thoughts. None of his trusted people were allowed in this meeting or even this building. Imam Kartal's piercing eyes had flashed unmistakable pleasure weeks ago when he so casually handed over photos documenting the murder of the priest, brother of the president of the United States. Now, seated near him, Kartal was again watching him, carefully, a folder filled with papers at his elbow. What was in that folder? Even more compromising evidence against him? More photos? A tighter leash?

He became aware of the room's silence. Badem was also watching him, waiting for Carmona to respond to his question.

"Of course," Carmona finally replied. "The way you describe our success could be said of most who gain similar business power."

"Precisely," said Badem. "Necessity requires it. If the competition for business leadership was one of smiling faces, pats on the back, and pretty speeches, neither you nor I nor most business leaders we know would ever win the contest for leadership. Competence would be subservient to charisma. The marketplace would descend into stalls of unpredictable chaos. Yet, this is how most of humanity manages its most important affairs and why we are on the verge of global catastrophe."

"That's a very bleak view of the future," said Carmona.

"Bleak?" said Badem. "Not at all. It is reality. It is reality to anticipate inevitable wars as food and water grow scarce and tens of millions of people become refugees because of climate change. It is reality that someday, somewhere, we will atomize one another with weapons almost anyone can now possess. When people like you and I see real problems, we act, Carmona. We devise solutions. As you did when you tried to remove President Tennyson."

"And I almost succeeded."

"My dear Carmona, I never expected 'almost' to be a word in

your vocabulary. We do. It gets done. Success leaves no space for almost. You expected to bring down the most powerful person in the world using the services of an undisciplined army of druggies, blackmailers, murderers. My compliments to you for getting as far along as you did. But for a project of that difficulty and importance, true professionals are required. And frankly, your project was based on a goal that was unworthy of you, enriching yourself and a few others. A needless gamble for someone as successful as you are."

"Well, tell me what your game is if it isn't just money."

Imam Kartal, who had been quietly listening to this exchange, rose and walked to the conference room's whiteboard. With pen in hand he began writing a list.

"When we first met, Senor Carmona, you asked whether this would be a religious undertaking. That would be quite foolish. Religion? With all of its fantasy and denial of reality? A leadership based upon religion? Not likely."

"It was a reasonable assumption given that you are a religious man."

Imam Kartal laughed. "Senor Carmona, eighty percent of the world population is religious. Our mission could hardly succeed if we did not ride that wave ourselves. Ride it to control it. I have my army of believers. I can lead them anywhere. A billion and a half Muslims pray daily to Allah for deliverance. Two and a half billion Christians, half of them Catholics, the most strict and structured organization on the planet. The faithful of all religions already have ceded their identities to those like me who claim certain powers and wear certain garments. Recall your history, Carmona. The priests to the pharaohs, the cardinals to the kings, shamans, rabbis, Hindu sadhus, mullahs, from the start of known human history to this very day, we, the religious leaders, control the politics of tribes, peoples, nations. The religious want to be led. They are the most easily led people on earth. So, yes, I wear the cloth."

Kartal turned to the whiteboard and pointed to the list he had written:

artificial intelligence
robotics
genetic editing
nanotechnology
quantum computing

He turned back to Carmona. "Do you see what all of this has in common?"

Carmona pondered a few moments. "Well, science and technology, of course. But these aren't my strong suits."

"Precisely. Not yours. Not mine. Nor hardly anyone's. Even those who spend their lives in these fields have difficulty understanding one another. As we speak, scientists are in laboratories creating new forms of life by manipulating DNA. They are creating incredible materials rearranging individual atoms. They are teaching machines to learn far more and more quickly than we humans know and could possibly learn in a lifetime. Miraculous things are being discovered, and the only commonality is that you and I and hardly anyone else in this world understands the science, the potential benefits, or the threats."

Kartal walked toward Carmona and stopped only when he was so close, he could peer down into Carmona's eyes, as God would to a disciple.

"And we expect a political system that depends on hundreds of millions of people, people who know little or nothing of science, and certainly not in the depth where science has taken us today, we expect those people to decide how all of this will be managed? It's folly. Folly! Whatever benefits the democratic system may have had in organizing nations, it has no relevance to the realities of today. Democratic societies cannot even deal with the obvious consequences of a warming planet. We are only one false radar image away from the launch of a nuclear war that would end human existence."

Kartal turned away from Carmona and returned to the whiteboard. "You ask what our so-called 'game' is if not money?" In large underlined letters Kartal wrote:

S A L V A T I O N!

"Not salvation from your Christian fire and brimstone, or the Jews' angry god, or a seat in Muslim's Jahannam, but salvation here on earth. We must gain control of events before they destroy us, before some fools create disease in a laboratory that known medicine cannot cure, or a malicious life-form appears that's superior to humans, or we kill one another because a warming earth destroys our oceans and our soils and forces tens of millions of migrants to battle one another for survival, or doomsday weaponry spells doom for all of us."

Kartal returned to his seat while Carmona pondered all of this. "And so, you plan to take control of the world?" Carmona was trying not to betray his opinion of what he considered a ludicrous plan.

Kartal and Badem looked at one another. There was much more to say. The imam's slight nod, almost beyond perception, signaled Badem to continue.

"We are members of what you might call a 'project,'" said Badem. "There are many of us. Eventually this will be a ruling alliance. Are you familiar with Plato's *Republic*?"

"Only familiar enough to survive an essay once in a university philosophy class—quite long ago, obviously."

"I suggest you reread it. Not that we intend to develop the philosopher kings that Plato suggests, but rather read it to see how appropriate his thinking is to the crisis we face today. Even in Plato's time, few were able to grasp true knowledge and reality. Common people, Plato argued, required guardians, those able to understand the complexity of life and who had the wisdom to rule for the general good.

"Some years ago, a number of us accepted the reality that science was beyond the reach of commoners and its control not trustworthy solely in the hands of the scientists. In the face of this we formed an alliance to change the way we govern. Not for power or wealth, but to rule in a rational, humane way that extends the benefits of knowledge to everyone while minimizing the risk of self-destruction. Such a system obviously cannot rely on the collective decision of tens of millions of commoners who lack understanding of the world beyond their immediate lives. In other words, events have made democracy obsolete. Just as in earlier times, events made the notion of the 'divine right of kings' obsolete. And colonization of poor nations by rich ones obsolete. The times, not history or philosophy, dictate the system. A new order is needed."

"Hasn't Putin already created one for Russia," said Carmona, "and the Communists in China. And the Catholic Church has never taken votes on how things should be done.".

"Quite true," said Tahir. "But each controls only its own sphere. We know the consequences. The rivalries. The suspicions. The jealousies of power in their systems. There's seldom been a time when those with dictatorial power to control wealth and territory haven't been at war with one another, when there have not been victors and losers."

Badem drew circles representing Russia, China, Germany, England, Spain, Turkey, the United States, the Catholic Church, Islam.

"You see," said Badem, turning to Carmona, "all at one time or another power centers. Ultimately, all in conflict. Conflicts over resources, or religion, or the egoism of their rulers. Humanity has survived all of that, not because it had the wisdom that allowed it to survive. No, humanity has survived because the means to destroy were limited. That's no longer true. Now there are many ways humanity can annihilate itself. Without intervention, it's only a matter of time, and likely a short amount of time, before life as we know it is extinguished."

"Against that probability," Badem continued, "imagine that the power to make decisions about war and peace, the use of weapons, application of scientific advances, and other issues that affect all of humanity is ceded to a superior body. A body comprised of those uniquely suited, through knowledge, temperament, and experience, to make such decisions. That possibility has been created through technology. Google has no borders. Facebook has no borders. With artificial intelligence, not even language is a barrier to global decision making. Imagine a world order that recognizes these realities. Not a world order based on skin color and ethnicity, as Hitler envisioned, or wealth or economic systems, but one based upon informed rationality. A power center of what we call 'Project Managers' who govern wisely and benignly. Allocating resources fairly. Seeing to it that no one goes hungry. Everyone shares the fruits of progress. A system where no one fears war, for there's no reason to fight. A self- sustaining system, mimicking nature. You asked, 'What's our game?' This is our game."

Tahir motioned toward his crude circles on the whiteboard.

"We already have in place the people, the resources, and the plans capable of taking control of smaller nations that are dominated by the power of the United States, Russia, and China. In fact, it's the smaller nations living in the shadow of the dangerous giants that are most anxious for the existing world order to change. The key to change is to take control of the United States. How do we do that? The United States military is too powerful to be defeated by any enemy. Its economy is too strong to be compromised by any other nation or group of nations. How do we gain control? By exploiting its most obvious systemic weakness—the way it selects its leadership.

"We have that opportunity now. Competition for the presidency, the defeat of a president you already helped weaken. That's why you are here, Javier. No one is more informed than you about the vulnerabilities of President Tennyson. With your help, we will replace her with one of our own. And once we have control of the United States, the other dominoes will soon fall."

"What about Europe?" Carmona asked.

"Europe is too fractured to be a problem. We will control Europe the way Europe always has been controlled—through alliances that ensure that no single country can withstand our power."

"I have to say," said Carmona, "I admire your ambition. A monumental project for so few of you."

Imam Kartal spoke up to correct him. "Our ambition. Ours. You are one of us now, Senor Carmona. And of all people, you, with such deep roots in Mexico, should know what a determined few can accomplish when confronting the many. Cortés conquered tens of thousands of Aztecs with just a few hundred soldiers and missionaries. That changed the course of your continent for the next five hundred years.

"We asked you here not just to inform you of our plans but for you to provide us with information we need to defeat Madam Tennyson in her election. We've read your research, and we have questions. We already have our candidate. Now we must make certain he wins."

Kartal opened the folder that Carmona had eyed with deep dread. "It's time to begin."

6

Zach Bowman stood backstage staring in amazement at the TV monitor. CNN was broadcasting one of his rallies live. On stage, New Hampshire's Republican governor was rousing an already raucous banner-waving crowd, setting the fuse for an explosion of cheers and made-for-TV idolatry the moment Zach appeared. Zach Bowman, to the surprise of most everyone involved, including Zach himself, was the hottest candidate now racing down the presidential track.

Just two months earlier, Zach had been resigned to what seemed for him to be a political dead end. It had been a neck-snapping up-and-down ride. The up was weeks of intense national exposure as chairman of the Judiciary Committee, presiding over House impeachment hearings. The case against President Tennyson was shocking: a Mexican American president guilty of helping murderous cartels launder immense drug profits and tampering with border law enforcement to allow those cartels to smuggle drugs and guns. There even was graphic testimony strongly suggesting she had whored her way to wealth and power. The case against Tenny seemed so solid. With Zach leading the way, the House of Representatives had impeached her. The US Senate, based on the evidence produced in the House investigation, voted to remove her from office. Then, the down. An amazing turn of events. The vice president revealed it was all a scam, the product of falsified documents, manufactured emails, and a lot of perjury. The Senate rescinded its vote, and the public redirected its wrath to Zach and his staff for being duped. Zach appeared to be destined for the political grave he had dug for Tenny.

Until the phone call.

The invitation to visit with Gilbert Adonis came as a surprise. It would have at any time, but this was just weeks after the dramatic end of the impeachment fiasco. Zach had met Adonis before, at receptions and in other large groups. Handshakes. Nods of greeting. Nothing remotely personal. Nothing that would have prompted an alliance just when Zach's political story seemed to be ending in a much-reviled one-act flop.

Adonis owned a full-floor apartment overlooking New York's Central Park in a building endowed with a swimming pool so large it could host the Olympics, balconies with square footage that would rival many entire New York apartments, concierge service, cars and drivers on call, even an indoor dog walk and employees to do the walking. How many millions did such an apartment cost? Forty, fifty, sixty? What difference did it make? When numbers reach this altitude, the financial climate is so rare few mortals can relate.

Gilbert Adonis was big money. Huge money. Adonis just seemed to be one of those fabulously rich people whose wealth was difficult to assess, even for those who made a living keeping track of the wealthy.

Zach was escorted to the balcony where Adonis already was seated, reading a financial spreadsheet. He rose to greet Zach, shook hands, and dove right into it. Gil Adonis had little time for verbal foreplay.

"Have you considered running for president?"

It was just the two of them, facing each other forty stories high. Zach hardly had time to admire the view. He was still intoxicated by the experience of being alone with a man whose wealth was legend. Zach smiled, searching quickly for an answer. He defaulted to the politician's first reflex: dodging commitment.

"That would really be presumptuous of me, at my age, and with so many good people already running."

"Don't bullshit me," said Adonis. "I know you've talked with people about it. Do you want it or not?"

Adonis was not a patient man.

"Well, sure, who wouldn't want to be president? But the way things turned out with Tennyson...."

"The way things turned out with Tennyson is this—to a whole lot of people you're a hero. You did everything you could to nail her."

"But then I didn't. She got away. My poll numbers took a hit."

"What numbers?" said Adonis. "Democrats, independents, socialists. They don't vote in Republican primaries. I make it my business to take polls. I can't afford to be surprised. What's happening is that plenty of Republicans love you for trying. Most think she's guilty as hell and that she got off because she blackmailed Rusher, or that the CIA helped her, or something else. Hell, it makes no difference. They hate her. They want somebody who'll keep going after her. Who better than you?"

Zach looked at him, somewhat bewildered. That's not how the media was writing about it. In fact, he was taking a lot of heat from his home state Pennsylvania newspapers for putting the country through the impeachment ordeal on such shaky evidence. But Zachary Bowman had not reached this level of political importance and power by being timid about his own ambition. If Gil Adonis saw him as presidential material, why argue?

"I'm glad you see it that way, Mr. Adonis. I'm not convinced myself that she's innocent."

"Gil, damn it. Gil. I hate that mister shit. Yeah. My information is real, and I'm hardly ever wrong with my opinions. Zach, you're presidential material, and now's your time."

"I'd love to. But it's late to build an organization. The Iowa caucuses are just two months away. And the money."

"My business is making deals, Zach. Here's the deal I'm offering you. The money will be there. Whatever it takes. All legal. You want to go, we go together. For the last year or so my friends and I have been building an organization to take her out. Not just the money but a network of serious political contacts, pros in polling and media, foot soldiers, the works. We've been putting it together for somebody. I just don't like the somebodies already running. I like you. Did you read the thing I sent asking you to come see me?"

"I did. Those questions about what I would do about all those issues?"

"That's it. What about it?"

"I don't think we have a difference between us on any of

them."

"We don't have, or you don't think we have?"

"We don't."

"You want the White House job? You get there and you've got to make quick big decisions, like I do all the time. Only your decisions will be bomb the shit out of them or not. Or cut their nuts off or not. Or send them to jail or not. Yes or no. No time for maybes. So, if you're presidential material, make a decision. I'm offering you this deal now. In or out? There's no tomorrow. Want the White House job? This may be the only chance you'll ever have to get it. Want it and we start right now. I'll pick up this phone and we're rolling. What'll it be?"

That was almost two months ago. Adonis wasn't exaggerating. It was like he added water to a pot of extremely fertile soil and a whole campaign took root overnight. Suddenly, key players in Iowa and New Hampshire were supporting him. Bad stuff was showing up about his opponents. He was getting good press. Writers who published his obituary weeks ago now talked about his resurrection. Crowds began appearing wherever he went. The crowds and the polls meant more media traveling with his campaign. The more press exposure, the better everything else became. It was an incredible high. His energy level climbed with it. People around him, people he'd never met before, were working with him on what to say, how to say it, things he would never have thought of on his own. He was being molded, and he loved it. He was growing into the role of presidential candidate like an orchid in a hothouse.

Now he was in Manchester, days away from New Hampshire's primary election, thousands waiting to cheer him on. Cameras out front to showcase Zack-love to millions of potential voters from coast to coast. New Hampshire's governor gave one last roaring endorsement to "the next president of the United States." Zach Bowman ran to center stage and embraced the governor, a man who until yesterday he had never met but who knew a winner when he saw one.

7

The US Constitution doesn't require a president to appear personally before Congress to address the state of the union. Some haven't. Thomas Jefferson sent his messages in writing, to be read aloud by congressional clerks. Jefferson believed the image of a president delivering such a message bore too close a resemblance to the king of England's address to the British Parliament.

Most presidents in the modern era, however, relish the majesty of the moment. Members of Congress, Supreme Court justices, the nation's military leaders, and foreign ambassadors respectfully assemble to await the president's arrival. That arrival provokes rock star imagery, with a prolonged entrance during which generally staid members of Congress lose their cools and thrust speech copies toward the president for autographs and compete with one another to share a television moment. Once at the podium, the president speaks for an hour, more or less. An hour when the TV screen hugs the president's face as closely as a partner on the next pillow, capturing every blink of the eye, every gesture, every smile or smirk. The message is one of character and body language as well as spoken content.

During her first two years as president, Tenny had delivered electrifying State of the Union speeches, setting in motion astounding legislative victories. By her third year, feeling invincible, she reached even higher. But the political dynamics had changed. A Congress that already had done much balked at taking on new controversial challenges. The conspiracy being waged against her had taken root. Her popularity crashed. Impeachment followed. A once friendly and compliant Congress had become weary of her demands, tired of her drama. Borderline hostile.

The President Tennyson who spoke to Congress this year was markedly different than the President Tennyson of earlier years. Knowing she could not expect many legislative wins in an election year, she didn't ask for many. Knowing the residual sensitivity of many of the legislators who had voted to impeach her, she offered words of reconciliation. Tenny always performed well in important and tense situations. Tonight was no exception. The longer she spoke, the more Democrats stood for her applause lines and cheered with genuine enthusiasm. The more bipartisan she became, the less hostile the Republican reaction. Altogether, the speech would be deemed a winner. Not the call to arms of her past addresses but rather a call for healing and unity. A message that she, the Congress, and the nation needed after the wrenching events of the past months.

Her speech delivered, a hundred hands shaken, Tenny slid into the waiting presidential limousine. Her lifelong friend and secretary of commerce, Carmen Sanchez, was in the back seat waiting to join her for the two-mile trip to the White House.

"Was that you up there or was that your docile twin?" asked Carmie.

"Don't think it was easy to look out on that scene and say, 'never mind' to all those ingrates who voted to impeach me."

Tenny closed her eyes and let her head sink into the back cushion. The motorcycles, vans, and all that comprises a presidential motorcade began to roll.

"Was I convincing?"

"The soul of forgiveness and understanding. You're going to get great press."

"And no action."

"That's pretty much what you asked for this year, isn't it? Peace, harmony, healing, a breather from all the ghastliness of last year."

"I'll make up for it next year if I win. Those bastards will never know what hit them. We're going to make them squirm with every vote. This year we punch our ticket for another term. Next year we turn everything upside down."

"Ah, now that's the Tenny I love. Fish got a really strong ovation. I thought you handled that perfectly."

"You know, everyone on the Hill really loves Fish. She's the ideal partisan. No question about her progressive politics, but she knows that to get things done we need to listen and compromise and deal. That's why the vote to confirm her as vice president went so easily."

"Now we just have to make the rest of the country fall in love with her. Did you watch Bowman during your speech?"

"Watch him? Couldn't miss him. Preening like a peacock. I'll bet he's on every TV channel now telling the world what's wrong with me. When I was walking into the chamber, I saw him angling toward me to try to shake my hand or hug me or anything to get us together on TV, towering over me, young and trim, contrasting with me and my cane. I kept my back toward him and stayed busy with other people so he couldn't get into camera position. Pete Callum was escorting me down the aisle.

He did a good job keeping Bowman away. Pete's got sharp elbows."

"Do you think Bowman might actually win the primaries? Wouldn't he be the easiest to beat?"

"No one will be easy to beat."

8

"You know, as long as I've been at Georgetown I've never come here."

"Best pizza in town. Beer's good, too."

Father Bob Reynolds took a long swallow from his mug. "That *is* good. What's it called again?"

"Farmhouse Ale. It's local. In fact, the microbrew was started by a guy who used to work right here at Pizzeria Paradiso."

"Interesting. There're so many good microbrews these days I can't keep track. I look at these menus and seldom see a familiar label."

Ben Sage hadn't seen Father Reynolds for months, not since Bob played a decisive role in stopping Tenny from resigning as president the day Federico was murdered. Reynolds and Federico had been classmates at the seminary. They had taken their vows together, seeding a lifelong friendship and unquestioned trust in one another. Reynolds became Federico's conduit to Ben and to Tenny's impeachment defense team.

"I was really happy to hear from you, Bob. Lucky I happened to be in DC for a few days for the State of the Union speech.

We're on the road mostly with the campaign."

"She did well with that speech. Hit just the right notes. How's the campaign doing?"

"Fine. No doubt about the nomination. Not sure about November, though. She's carrying a lot of baggage and scars."

"And physically?"

"Well, she'll never be what she was before the explosion. She needs a cane, although she hates to be seen with it. That hurricane inside her has lost some energy. Sort of like downgrading from category five to maybe three. No more round-the-clock schedules. Her doc told me to be careful with her. You know, you can't have the horrific trauma she absorbed in the blast without your body becoming more fragile. But there's nothing wrong with her mind. And she's still hell-bent to bulldoze a lot of earth if she gets reelected."

"I'll pray for her. We'll all pray for her."

They both took long swallows of beer. Bob set down his mug and decided it was time.

"This isn't entirely a social dinner."

"It seems like it never is anymore when you and I get together," said Ben. "What's the bad news?"

"I wish I could tell you," said the priest. "I wish I knew more. I just got back from Rome. Spent two weeks there. Not sure that you know this, but the Vatican has a very robust intelligence operation."

"Really? Saints and spooks? What's that all about?"

Bob couldn't help himself. He laughed loud enough to turn heads at the next table.

"Saints and spooks. I'll have to remember that. My friends will enjoy the comparison."

Ben smiled at his own joke. "So, tell me. I'm so naïve about these things. I've never worked a campaign outside the US."

"Oh, I could give a whole semester course on the topic," said Bob. "It's been going on for centuries. The Vatican's always been a hotbed of international intrigue. Our priests and bishops and papal nuncios are all over the world, reporting in constantly on political and economic developments and just about everything else. We've got our own foreign office and diplomatic corps. Besides all the conventional spy stuff, we have the confessionals. It's like our own internet. People tell their priests more than just their sins."

"I wouldn't know about that, either," said Ben. "Never been there, and I try to keep my sins secret."

Bob lifted his mug, winked, and clinked it against Ben's. "No comment," he said. "But trust me, the confessional pipeline is full of news. And besides all that, we've got the Knights. You ever hear of the Knights and Dames of Malta?"

"I've always wondered about them. Aren't they part of some kind of secret order?"

"It all started a thousand years ago as sort of a hybrid, part the pope's army to protect Christians from persecution and part early-day Red Cross to provide medical care and help for the poor. That help mission's still really important. The Order of Malta actually employs about twenty-five thousand doctors, nurses, and other medical people and operates in more than a hundred countries. Last I heard they had almost a hundred thousand volunteers. Disaster relief. Epidemics. Just general all-around assistance to people who need help. The EU, UN, and a lot of countries pay to support it. They do a lot."

"And I guess what you're about to tell me is they also hear a lot."

"Exactly. Their work puts them in contact with people in local governments, some who have very sensitive jobs."

"What are they hearing?"

"Okay, this is what I'm supposed to tell you. In a number of countries, many of our contacts are government people who always have been open and friendly. Lately, many have become hypercautious about what they tell us. There seems to be an unusual repositioning in key jobs. Files that always have been open to us are often getting shut. That sort of thing. If it was just one country, well, things change. But it's happening in a number of countries, and that's what's creating a buzz that's caught our attention. It seems coordinated."

"And your people think this has something to do with our election?"

"The top people in our intelligence service think so. They're concerned enough that they instructed me to tell you."

"Why me?"

"Because you're close to the president. You talk to her frequently, and she trusts you. They think you're the quickest way to alert her."

"Alert her about what?"

"I don't know."

"That's ridiculous. She'll think I'm nuts."

"I know it sounds vague. But the church hasn't survived this long without being fine-tuned to detect trouble. And the people who manage the intelligence that comes through Rome are concerned enough to have me alert you."

"Why don't they have your spook tell our spook over a drink at their favorite bar in Rome?"

"I don't know," said Bob. "I'm just the designated messenger. I sense, though, they don't know who to trust."

Ben bowed his head until his forehead rested on the table, where he mock-banged it twice.

"Shit," said Ben. "I thought I was done with conspiracies. Why can't we have an election that's just an election? Speeches, ads, debates, grassroots organization— that's what I know. I'm out of my league with this cloak- and-dagger stuff. Not that I doubt what you're telling me, Bob, but what do I do with it? Go to the attorney general and say, 'I've heard on good authority that there's an international conspiracy to corrupt our election. I have no names, dates, places, or facts, but strange things are happening.'"

"I agree. It's hard to say what we're warning people about."

"And I assume that you don't want to go with me to discuss this with anyone."

"No," said Bob. "The church isn't partisan and doesn't get involved in political campaigns."

"Swell. What do you suggest?"

"For tonight, have another one of these good beers."

9

Where to go with this? Ben Sage stood at his office window, aimlessly watching traffic on Pennsylvania Avenue, three blocks from the White House. There was much for him to think about. Real things, not vaporous hints of conspiracy. Imminent decisions needed about the presidential campaign's scheduling and finances. Next week's filming of a new round of commercials. How much to budget for upcoming primary campaigns in South Carolina and Nevada. Ben could not focus on any of it, not with the concentrated attention he always applied to decision making while wearing campaign armor. It wasn't working this morning.

If Ben had not recently been at the center of one deadly conspiracy, he would weigh Father Bob's warning of another for what it was: supposition based on little more than random observation. If only. Both he and Bob Reynolds had lived through months of murder, assassination, and betrayal at the highest levels of the US government. Conspiracy had become more than just an ugly word. It was an experience that birthed new and powerful neural reflexes. The prospect of another conspiracy rang internal body alarms he never again thought he would hear. What to do with this warning eluded him.

Certainly not go through official channels. If the information were more solid, the Italians would have passed it on to US intelligence agencies. Using a backdoor delivery service indicated how tentative this was. Father Bob and Ben, not Italian intelligence, would be the ones looking foolish if the alarm was needless. If the information turned out to be important, the Italians could claim credit for spotting it first. They had tossed this hot potato to Bob, and now it was in Ben's hands.

He had slept little last night, egged to consciousness by these questions, torn by the decision of whether to ignore the warning or pass it on. Ben was so numbed by the mental conflict he failed to hear the office door open behind him.

"I didn't know we'd won a contract to count cars."

Lee Searer, Ben's political consulting business partner, gibed Ben for vacantly staring out the window, then he laid a trail of heavy wool coat, scarf, gloves, and briefcase as he headed for the coffee machine.

"Damn bitter cold out there," said Lee. "When are we going to start specializing in Hawaiian campaigns, or Puerto Rico? Florida Keys? How about the Keys?"

Ben turned from the window.

"You want hot?" asked Ben. "I've got hot for you."

Good-natured banter was the safe harbor Ben and Lee long ago built as a sanity shelter from their high-intensity business. The partners first met during a campaign for the US Congress. Lee was campaign research director, on leave of absence from his day job as a history professor at the local college. Ben was the campaign's media producer, crafting ads based on Lee's research. Their candidate won, and Lee was offered a legislative research job on the new congressman's staff. Instead, he took Ben's offer to enter the more transient world of campaign politics. Together they were a formidable team. Lee loved pouring over demographic tables, election turnout numbers, census data, the thick research reports that few others seldom read. From Lee's numbers and research, Ben designed artful strategies that would control campaign narratives. Together, the firm flourished, producing far more winners than losers.

Lee wrapped his hands tightly around his coffee mug, his

head so close to the hot liquid he could inhale the steam.

"Aaaah. Needed that," said Lee. "Coming back to life. So, tell me, what do you have that's hot?"

Ben described the conversation with Father Bob and the dilemma it created. Make the next move, or not? And if they did, what move?

"Nasty," said Lee. "I don't see how you can just wish it away and forget you were told anything. You've got to tell somebody. Birch and Kloss were proactive the last time."

National Security Agency director Ken Kloss's surveillance net had captured the incriminating phone calls that led to the last conspiracy's unraveling. Kloss enlisted Attorney General Robin Birch, and together they managed to expose the conspirators and save Tenny's presidency.

"They're the first ones I thought of," said Ben. "After they intercepted voice conversations, they had hard evidence to rely on. But vague stuff comes across their desks all day long, handled downstream and usually under a pile of more urgent cases. This would get lost."

"So it gets lost. Maybe it should be."

"Maybe so. But I couldn't live with it if someone was really out to get Tenny and we knew and ignored it. Imagine how haunted we'd be forever."

Lee took a long sip of his cooling coffee and walked to the plate of morning doughnuts on the conference table. Two half-eaten glazed ones remained.

"Anyone on the staff complaining of germs?" asked Lee. "I'm hungry enough to risk it." He reached for one of the leftovers and began nibbling.

"By the way," said Lee between bites, "I just read a really interesting article about a thing called a 'jeweled wasp.' This wasp injects a cockroach with her venom, and it gets into the cockroach brain through the nervous system. That venom turns the cockroach into a mindless zombie that does whatever the wasp wants it to do, including just sitting there quietly while the wasp and her wasp family chomp away on it for dinner. Think we can come up with something like that wasp juice for Tenny to use on those guys running against her?"

Ben smiled and shook his head in mock exasperation. Lee's strength was his research, and sometimes it led him down bizarre paths. Lee reveled in finding fun facts and often dropped them into conversations with little relationship to whatever else was being discussed.

"Good idea," said Ben. "I'll suggest it next time I'm at the White House."

Unruffled, Lee grabbed the remaining doughnut morsel. Then, he had another thought.

"Say, tonight's that party the Alaskans are throwing for Fish, isn't it?"

"It is. To celebrate her becoming vice president."

"I'd guess all the government wheels will be there, including Kyle Christian. Telling him about it at a party is about as unofficial as it gets. Kyle knows you as a serious guy. If he hears this from you directly, he won't bury it."

Ben let that sink in for a moment. Kyle Christian. Ben's media had gotten him elected to Congress. Before Kyle was appointed CIA director, he and Ben would meet now and then to talk political strategy. Kyle was the most political of all Tenny's appointments, but he was well qualified for the CIA job after spending six years as chairman of the House Intelligence Committee. Ben hadn't seen Kyle for two years, ever since Kyle disappeared into the bowels of CIA headquarters in Langley, Virginia.

Kyle Christian. Perfect. If he came tonight. "Lee, for that idea, it's steaks for lunch. Drop that doughnut—you need to save your appetite. I'm buying."

"Steaks? Great," said Lee. "No sense having salmon. That's for the Alaska party."

10

When you get an invitation from the White House, you go. Tonight's event was particularly irresistible. Both houses of Congress had confirmed Tenny's nomination of Sheila Fishburne as vice president of the United States. Fish was now on the threshold of the presidency, a woman to be strongly courted.

From its picture postcard exterior, the White House is a comforting, unchanging symbol of national stability. Inside, it reflects the tastes and spirit of whoever occupies it at the time. Tenny's tastes reflected her dual background— the open décor of California and the bright and festive colors of Mexico, with just enough traditionalist furniture and portraiture to maintain a sense of history. Tenny's was a festive White House.

And tonight, the East Room of the White House was at its festive best. An airlift of Alaska salmon, king crab, and reindeer sausage fed the invited guests. Alaska Inupiaq dancers, moving to the energetic beat of traditional frame drums, motioned for others to join. In the villages, everyone dances, young and old, in the spirit of village unity and life's continuity. Tonight, that spirit netted members of Congress, lobbyists, cabinet members, and Vice President Sheila Fishburne herself.

Sheila was no stranger to native dancing. At home in Barrow, whether dressed in a fur parka to defend against polar winds or in more simple hand-sewn dresses while she picked crowberries, Sheila was an authentic daughter of the Arctic. But she was equally comfortable campaigning for votes from all strata of Alaskans and a master when it came to navigating the political turbulence of Congress.

Sheila's father, Clyde Fishburne, arrived in Barrow, Alaska's northernmost community, as a young high school math teacher. He had planned it as a yearlong adventurous break from high-pressure academics before moving on to earn a graduate degree. Teaching in the classroom next to his was Kiloonik (Nikky) Etok, recently returned to her Barrow home after graduation from the University of Washington.

Clyde quickly fell in love with Nikky and the Inupiaq culture, people who had survived for eons through a combination of courageous hunting, creative subsistence, and reverence for all life-forms. Sheila was the product of that union—worldly and earthy, compassionate and dauntless.

Through the din of tonight's drums, the merry confusion of the native dancing, and the clusters of A-listers working the room pursuing their own agendas, Ben stalked Kyle Christian. Christian was popular from his days in Congress. In his CIA role, his social appearances were rare, making him a sought-after target for many of the night's guests. Finding an opening proved harder than Ben imagined. Finally, he noticed Christian attempting to thread his way through the crowd toward the bar and a refill. Ben got there first and greeted him with a fresh glass of his favorite Scotch whiskey.

"Mr. Director," said Ben.

"Ben!" said Christian. "My, it's been a while. Great to see you. Going to get our girl reelected?"

"Working on it," said Ben. "Sorry to bring this up at a party, but I need to talk with you about something potentially very serious."

"Not about politics, I hope. That's off-limits in this job."

"Not my kind of politics," said Ben. "Your department's kind of politics."

"Sounds like we shouldn't be talking here, or at my office, either. You remember where I live?"

"Still in McLean?"

"Haven't moved. Stop by tomorrow night, about nine. I'll get word to you if the world falls apart before then and have to reschedule."

"Will they shoot me if I try to knock on your door?"

"Only if I forget to tell them ahead of time that you're coming. I've had a few of these, you know." Christian smiled and raised his glass. Then he gave Ben a friendly wink. "I'll try not to forget."

Ben was only mildly reassured. CIA directors have a lot to remember. This one also had a lot to drink.

11

Kyle Christian still lived in the detached split-level Virginia home he purchased after his first election to Congress. His children were grown and gone. It was just him and his wife now. But they were not alone. A twenty-four-hour security detail and banks of advanced electronic monitoring devices lived in his basement.

From the street, a casual passerby would notice little to distinguish the Christian home from others in the neighborhood. There were differences, though. Ben tripped a silent alarm as he approached. The front door opened before he could knock or ring a bell. The tall, dark-suited security agent who greeted him seemed friendly enough, even as he waved a metal-detecting wand around Ben's body.

"Not packing heat, are you?" the man asked. Ben looked up. The agent was smiling.

"Just my cell phone."

"I'll keep that here for you."

Kyle Christian appeared in the front hall.

"Hey, Ben, come on in. Library's over here. Remember it?"

Ben remembered it well. They had spent many hours here together, planning Kyle's campaigns. Kyle was a political novice when he had first filed for Congress, a long- shot effort to unseat a Republican incumbent. Ben relished such campaigns, ones that challenged expectations and forced him to think outside the box, devising strategies the opposition had never seen nor would expect.

The Republican representing Kyle's congressional district won the seat four years earlier with votes from thousands of registered Democrats. Digging deeper, Ben learned that many of those Democrats were old enough to have family ties to the days when rural electrification first lit their parents' homes, Social Security provided a whole new level of retirement security, and government work programs offered jobs when there were no others to be had. These were people whose families revered President Franklin Roosevelt. Kyle's parents and grandparents shared that tradition. They had lived through the dust bowl days.

Ben introduced Kyle to the district's voters as a Roosevelt Democrat, rooted in the Great Depression. He confirmed that heritage in TV commercials using a simulated family album interwoven with historical newsreel clips of ominous dust bowl black clouds, struggling farmers, and endangered livestock. Kyle identified himself with those hard days, the New Deal programs that made them better, and promises to protect and expand them. Kyle's ninety-year-old grandfather even appeared for a cameo endorsing Kyle. A sprightly, charming figure, his only speaking line was, "Since Kyle was just a child, I've always known him as someone who keeps his word."

When polls showed Kyle within a few points of overtaking the incumbent, opposition attacks began flooding broadcast media, newspapers, and direct mail. It was a relentless assault on Kyle's character. Rather than answer directly, Ben produced television commercials that showed Kyle and his teenage son riding white horses against the golden background of a dawn sun. The message: "In a political campaign, there are many paths to follow. Kyle Christian has chosen the high ground."

The final vote was close, just a three-point difference. But Kyle won. And he kept winning. By four points in his next two reelection campaigns. After that, the opposition basically folded and stopped spending serious money trying to defeat him.

"Bulleit rye, right?" said Kyle.

"Incredible, what a memory."

"It's my job to remember the important stuff."

Kyle poured himself a scotch and settled into an armchair facing Ben.

"Okay, now tell me some important stuff I don't know. What's up with our president?"

"Well, it's not with her, and I'm not even sure it's about her. But I'll let you judge. Better your job to do it than mine."

As best he could remember it, Ben described the conversation with Father Bob Reynolds. "That's about as specific as Bob could be," said Ben. "I guess the first question is how seriously to take intelligence coming out of the Vatican."

Kyle sat quietly for a few seconds, considering how much he could say, a problem for those whose heads were filled with the nation's deepest secrets. Paper can be classified with a rubber stamp. Brains don't work that way.

"Ben. You know that I'm Catholic."

"Sure I know. We had to overcome that with some of your evangelical voters."

"Do you have any idea how many other CIA directors have been Catholic?"

Ben smiled at the question.

"No one's ever asked me that question. I doubt anyone can answer it."

"I can. Almost all."

"Really? Is there a reason for that?"

"It started with the first directors and the close association the CIA had with the church during the fight to keep communism out of Western Europe. After World War II, Italy, Greece, and even France for a while looked like they might go communist. The US didn't want that. Neither did the church. We shared information and worked together to beat the communists in those elections. Ever since then, Vatican intelligence has worked with us, and pretty closely. We've poured a lot of money and training into those guys. They've become very good. And so has the Italian government's intelligence ops. To answer your question, yes, I take them seriously. If they suspect a problem that might interfere with our election, I take it seriously."

"Father Reynolds filled me in on some of this history the other night. I was really struck by what he said about the Knights of Malta."

"Ah, yes," said Kyle. "Knights of Malta. I'll let you in on a little secret. I'm one of the so-called 'Knights.' In fact, many other CIA directors have been Knights. What Bob may not have told you, and he may not even know, is that until the last few years, the Order was the most exclusive club in the world for the richest and most prominent Catholic families. Not just CIA directors but heads of banks and other folks who could influence our government. A number of cardinals were as important in making US foreign and military policy as secretaries of state and defense."

"I didn't read that in my textbooks when I was in school."

"No, but I'm not telling you anything you can't find in history books and magazine articles by journalists who looked into all this."

"It sounds like those times aren't over if the Vatican's still paying attention to our politics."

Kyle didn't answer. He rose from his chair and walked to the table where he stored his liquor.

"Another," he asked.

"No," said Ben. "I have to drive out of here on those dark roads."

"Yeah, we are kind of country here. Horse country it used to be."

Kyle filled his own glass and walked to his fireplace. A dancing gas log flame gave the room a sense of serenity. A welcome oasis from one of the most pressured of government jobs.

"Here's how intelligence works, Ben. To start, you hear something, enough to raise legitimate suspicion. So, you ask yourself, 'What if?' Then you start developing possible scenarios. Like, what if some foreign power wants to intervene to defeat President Tennyson? How would they go about it? Assassination? Disinformation? Vote tampering? Our analysts are good at narrowing down the most likely possibilities. Then it shifts to our field agents. They may not be able to confirm our suspicions, but they pretty quickly eliminate things that aren't happening. If it all amounts to nothing, case closed. If we can't close all the loops, we assign specific intelligence jobs to our operational people and get serious about finding out why.

"We don't like questions we can't answer. So, yes, I'll take the buzz from Rome seriously. We'll get in touch with them through our contacts to nail down what they have. Then we'll go through our regular process of filtering until we either hit on truth or get satisfied that there's nothing to worry about. But since this is political, and I come out of politics, and we're in the middle of a political campaign, you and I both need to handle this carefully. Officially, I'm interested in national security. And if some hostile country or group is planning to take out our president, that's definitely a national security issue. But elections are sensitive. Our role can easily be misunderstood or distorted to make it seem like we're playing favorites. So, you and I shouldn't be in contact again. You can't tell anyone you've been here or talked with me. And if things come up that I can't assign to anyone in the agency because of the politics, you may have to figure out other ways to handle it."

"Wow, that's a lot to chew on. I'm not a spook, pardon the expression."

"But you're here because you are spooked. And if this goes anywhere, you can't turn back. We've got to get our lady reelected, don't we?"

Ben put down his half-finished drink and rose to leave.

"I came here to get this warning off my plate, and I think you just kicked it back to me."

Kyle Christian rose to escort Ben to the door.

"Let's just say we've become partners. And remember, we're silent partners."

12

Since he was old enough to think about his future, Lester Bowles expected to be governor of Ohio. After all, Ohio politics was the family business. Lester's grandfather had been governor. His father had served as one of Ohio's two US senators. Bowles's son

Craig, the ink barely dry on his MBA in finance, was running unopposed to be the Republican candidate for state auditor.

Six years ago, Lester did become governor. Two years ago, he easily won reelection. Now, Lester was midway through his second term, comfortable in the job, enjoying his successes, of which there had been many, and generally popular with voters who appreciated his workmanlike, no- drama style of governing. Growth without glitz, he called it. Growth without glitz prompted this trip to New York and appointments with Wall Street bond brokers. Ohio was about to issue bonds to raise money for state road building and repairs. He could have sent others to discuss amortization tables and other green eyeshade topics with underwriters, but Bowles knew from experience that his personal presence would add an extra level of confidence to the bond issue, and that would result in a lower interest rate. Details, Lester's father had preached. Pay attention to the details. The elder Bowles had drilled the message deeply into young Lester's psyche. Many times each day, like a muezzin calling the faithful to prayer, Lester Bowles could hear his father's voice reminding him to pray at the Altar of Minutia. He responded as a willing disciple.

The minutia of highway bonds was tomorrow's agenda. Tonight was reserved for dinner with one of Lester's closest friends, financier Gil Adonis. Gil, like Lester, had grown up in Columbus, Ohio, the state's capital. Their families belonged to the same country club. Lester and Gil had been partners in club tennis doubles matches and had backpacked through Europe together during their college years.

Gil had become one of the richest people in the US through brilliant management of his hedge fund. He drew on that wealth to travel the world, meeting the rich and powerful. Gil's horizon reached beyond immediate financial interests—science, technology, medicine, education—everything at the frontier of human knowledge. He would read a report on robotics that fascinated him and travel to meet its author. He would attend a conference on astrophysics, knowing nothing of the science, but afterward spend time with those who did. Gil would learn of interesting research grants and visit the universities and laboratories where those studies were underway. At first, he pursued the accumulation of advanced knowledge as a way to inform his investment decisions. As useful as that proved to be, it had long since taken a back seat to obsession. Gil was obsessed with the explosion of knowledge in all of its twenty-first-century forms and in awe of those who worked at its frontiers.

Gil's wealth was his passport to places others might find difficult to enter. His curiosity and genuine interest were welcomed by those who spent their lives in arcane research bubbles. Gil traveled relentlessly. He had his own plane, his own crew, unlimited resources, and unlimited fascination with the world, from its mysterious neutrinos to the expanding edge of the known universe.

Lester found that spending time with Gil always left him energized with creative ideas and a refueled sense of purpose. Gil might think outside the box, but he always remained well between the lines of propriety. Lester could enjoy these meetings with his caution lights off. Never once had Gil attempted to trade on their friendship for personal gain. Tonight would be particularly stimulating. Gil's choice for a dinner venue was New York's exclusive Core Club, where billionaires, artists, and business executives mingled to dine, discuss, transact, and have exotic treatments that pampered mind or body.

"You know," said Gil, "the value of the art in this place is worth about a hundred million dollars."

"Does anyone notice the art?" asked Lester.

Gil smiled. "I guess just first-timers, or people like me bragging about the value of all the art to people like you."

"And answer this for me," said Lester. "What in the hell is light therapy?"

That provoked even a wider smile from Gil. "You don't know about light therapy? Guess you've been living in the dark. It's one of the latest things. Some people get depressed when they spend too much time in artificial light or go through time changes, like jet lag, or don't see much of the sun because they work nights and sleep days. With the club's system, you spend time next to special lighting that affects your body chemistry to correct that. At least, that's the idea."

"Ever tried it?"

"Hell, no."

"I guess these are the kinds of things you go in for when you have so much money you don't know what to do with it all."

"Oh, there are lots of other things you can do," said Gil. "Build yachts five feet longer than the other guy's. Have ten homes scattered around the world that you hardly ever visit. Throw million-dollar birthday parties for yourself or your ten-year-old daughter. You'd be amazed at how some of these people throw money around."

"Better lower your voice," said Lester. "Talk like that can get you thrown out of this club."

There wasn't much chance they would be overheard. Tables were purposely set far enough apart so that private conversations could remain private. Gil and Lester could banter with one another with the casual freedom earned by a lifetime of familiarity and friendship. Intimate talk about families, health, and other unguarded topics, a pleasant relief from the structured conversations that consumed their business hours.

It was not until the main course dishes were swept away, the mango napoleon dessert was devoured, and the Martell cognac was served that Gil introduced the topic of politics.

"Bowman's got the nomination locked up," he said.

"Got a place here I can puke?" said Lester. "I don't understand how that idiot did it. Everyone knows he's an untrustworthy lightweight. Bowman? President of the United States? Good God."

"Well," said Gil, "I helped get him there."

Lester looked at him in disbelief.

"Did I hear you right? You're the money propping up Bowman? Have you lost your mind? Gil? You can't be serious about wanting him to be president."

"I don't. I want you to be president."

Lester shook his head.

"You have lost your mind."

"Hear me out," said Gil. "I want you to be Bowman's vice president."

Lester shook his head again, struggling to process what he was hearing.

"Me? Vice president? To Bowman? You think after four or eight years as his vice president I'd be next in line? After Bowman wrecks things, we'll be lucky to get back to the White House in our lifetimes."

"No, you'd need to wait about a year, maybe a bit longer."

"You think you can get him impeached that fast? After what happened to Tennyson? Congress wouldn't have the stomach for another impeachment."

"I'm not talking impeachment," said Gil. Lester hesitated before responding.

"I hope you're not thinking about the only other alternative."

"Hear me out, Les. We're in trouble. Not just 'we' as in Republicans, but 'we' as in humanity. We have a political system totally inadequate for the age we're in, an age where just about everything important is being driven by science. Look. You've got a bunch of research centers in Ohio. A lot of medical. The Glenn NASA center. All those labs in Columbus around Ohio State. Do you know what's going on in them?"

"I take the tours," said Lester. "They try to explain it to me, and I've seen some great stuff. But you've got to have a head for it. Mine's finance, not science."

"Science isn't my strong suit, either," said Gil. "But I do know that right there in your state, like just around the corner from your office, people are working on things that are probably going to change life the way we've always thought of life. Everything. Our minds. Our bodies. How the hell do we know what's going on when science is reorganizing the atoms and cells that got us here?"

"What's your point?"

"My point is we're living in a political system that says people get the public policy they want by voting. Well, they elected you governor, someone who's smart as shit, and you haven't a clue what's really happening in your labs. And you're no different than every other governor or senator or representative they elect. You don't have a clue, and neither do the people who elect you.

"Think of something as simple as using stem cells from embryos for medical research. A lot of religious people went nuts at the thought we were killing babies for science. People took polls about it. You for it or against it? How the hell does anybody outside the lab know where that kind of research leads? Or this gene-editing thing. You're talking the very basis of life here. The way those genes line up determines who we are and what we are. I've been in labs where guys in white coats have created mice with two heads and frogs with eyes in their bellies. It's so cheap to fool around with that stuff, you can buy it mail order over the internet for a hundred and fifty bucks. Is that a good idea? Science is taking us into places we don't understand. Sure, it may give us a way to create utopia. It's just as likely to kill us all off. Who knows? Who decides? Democracy is a stupid way to make these decisions."

"Are you saying we need a dictator?" asked Lester.

"That's not the only alternative. The obvious way to make decisions about the future in a world where science rules is to give that authority to people who know how to manage it. Some scientists, some great managers. People who have the chops to explain these things to you and me and everyone else so we're comfortable with those decisions. A collection of wise heads."

"That's no Zach Bowman you're talking about."

"No," said Gil, "it's you, Les I can handle Zach for a while. He owes me big. And for a while he'll do what we want. But eventually he'll go off the reservation and I'll lose him."

"Then what?"

"Then the project takes over. You become president. You and other leaders take charge in the few countries in the world that really matter. You manage things so that we're all on the same page, regulating science to minimize the chances for abuse and mistake and making sure we don't use our power against one another."

"Well, I see a few obstacles to that plan, like the Constitution that limits the president's power, and the people elected to Congress who might not appreciate being told they're part of a world order. And then there's the not small matter of coordinating all this with other countries."

"Take a look at that Constitution, Les. It says the person elected president isn't the one with the most votes; it's the one who has the most votes in the Electoral College. When they wrote that they expected the electors would be the most serious and respected people in each state. The guys who wrote the Constitution didn't trust the popular vote, the masses of people, to elect the president, and neither should we. What I'm talking about here is a twenty-first- century version of the Electoral College. Exactly what they had in mind when they wrote the Constitution. Wise heads who understand what's happening in worlds the rest of us don't understand. Particles, quarks, human genes and human cells, nanotechnology doing things that we used to consider magic. We've barely started down this road and look how we're even screwing up the most basic new tech. Social media's warping people's ability to separate fact from fiction. Think of how we're refusing to deal with climate change, even though drought and famine and migration already are happening. Face it, our system of government is unsustainable."

Gil leaned across the table, lowered his voice, and placed his hand on Lester Bowles's arm.

"Les, you're a strong leader. People will follow you. Hell, people are begging for someone like you. They know our system's not working right. They want somebody to fix it. Somebody sensible and honest. You get to the White House and make the tough calls that are fair and don't abuse people. They'd follow you anywhere."

"Gil, I can't disagree about the problem. But this is pretty extreme."

"I thought so, too, when I was first contacted. But follow the logic. If we stay on the road we're on, someone's going to blow up the planet, or kill us all with out-of-control germs or create AI that decides it doesn't need us. You know the old definition of an optimist. An optimist is a scientist who thinks the future of the world is still in doubt. We're not in this for the money. We're not control freaks. We want to save civilization, not see it destroyed. This is a salvation project."

We?" asked Lester, for the first time realizing that his friend Gil was involved with some kind of a group, a movement, a—he hesitated to accept it, but it was unavoidable---a cabal. "Who's we?"

Adonis leaned even closer, his voice lowered to whisper range.

"You know I travel a lot. What I'm talking about isn't my crazy idea. I ran into this movement two years ago. There are people like you and me everywhere, some of them in pretty high places, even the military. Scared about what's happening and willing to go to the wall to change it. You know, guys like Putin and Xi and Erdogan had the right idea, but they're too autocratic, or corrupt, or too nationalistic. But they prove that people will be okay with strong and determined leaders if they think they're getting more out of it than they're giving up. Powerful people in those countries are standing by to replace the bad guys with good guys. Imagine if someone with Putin's power shared that power with a brilliant group who ran Russia without shutting down freedoms, or grabbing the wealth for themselves, or threatening other countries. Now, put the US, Russia, China, Turkey, India, Japan, and Germany together under what I think of as an adult guardianship, run cooperatively, and you'd have the closest thing to utopia the world's ever seen. That's the plan. And if the US is in, if you're in, it can happen."

Lester Bowles stared at his friend, hardly believing that this conversation was real. He came to dinner as a welcome relief from the pressures of his job. Instead, he was being asked by his closest friend to participate in what his detail- oriented mind could only register as unworldly fantasy.

"Gil, you're talking murder."

"No, Les, we're talking self-preservation."

13

The Salvation Project could trace its roots to an agricultural conference. None of the four hundred Southeast Asian agriculture experts who gathered at Singapore's Furama Riverfront Hotel years ago arrived there with a plan for worldwide domination. The agenda was focused narrowly on the crisis in rice harvests caused by global warming. Coastal areas were being flooded. Lives and livelihoods were being lost. Thousands were being forced to migrate. The forecast was for a catastrophic 50 percent drop in rice yields by the end of the century.

Conversations about how to cope inevitably led to discussions of causes and blame. And just as a single spark can ignite a forest, anger at the failure of the United States, China, Russia, India, and European nations--- the world's principal air polluters---to rein in their calamitous emissions swept through the assembled body. While this resentment was not included in the conference's official published proceedings or closing action documents, outside the meeting rooms, over morning kopi, informal dinners, and late-night consumption of Singapore Slings, a separate covert plan was evolving among the more activist conference delegates.

Initially, the plan was to organize an unofficial campaign aimed at galvanizing US public opinion into a higher level of urgency, one that would result in more effective global warming countermeasures. A small operational group was formed, money was raised, and a public awareness campaign was launched. That strategy had limited impact. Frustrated, the campaign's leaders met in Kuala Lumpur to consider more aggressive action, action that would go beyond persuasion into efforts to gain control of the actual decision-making powers. To their surprise, others asked to ally with them—military leaders and intelligence experts with their own concerns, frustrated scientists, some business leaders and government officials who saw the potential for economic and societal collapse. All shared a common fear: the current world order was not effectively responding to existential problems, and not just the consequences of global warming.

It was not a large group at the Kuala Lumpur meeting, but many had impressive credentials. Some had been educated at the great universities in the US, England, and China. Others worked in advanced scientific laboratories. A few of the military attendees had been trained at the US Army War College. The experience and quality of the team forming at Kuala Lumpur raised expectations of the possible.

What emerged was the nucleus of a secret organization whose ultimate goal would be to capture control of as many nations as possible and weld them into a loosely organized world federation. Each nation would be managed by an appointed elite group of experts capable of making informed decisions on the handling of complex scientific and military matters. These decisions would require no other approval, not from Congress or legislatures or voters themselves. A class of issues left to those with the expertise to deal with them.

Overall leadership of the Salvation Project would be vested in a small group, each member with the wooly title of "Project Manager." For security, meetings of the Managers would be rare and always conducted on a virtual private network, never in person. Operations would be segregated into individual country cells. Those responsible for securing control of a country would know nothing of others engaged elsewhere. Everyone involved would take a pledge never to disclose the existence of the Project or the identity of anyone connected with it. The future of humanity was at stake. Neither error nor failure would be tolerated. Security would be enforced, ruthlessly if required.

With missionary zeal and stout discipline, the Project achieved most of its initial goals. Some small nation leaders unofficially agreed to support an effort that promised to protect them from more powerful, unpredictable neighbors. Moving uncooperative leaders aside in some other nations was not particularly difficult. Those nations had histories of leadership instability. But the key to ultimate success was control of the United States.

That opportunity was now at hand. A weakened president was running for reelection against one of their own. Winning that election meant winning the world.

14

During his prime years, Miguel Aragon had visited Manhattan often, lured by Wall Street financial moguls who coveted his business. For his frequent visits, Miguel maintained a 3,500-square-foot apartment on the seventeenth-floor of the elegant Sherry-Netherland Hotel. The view from the apartment was a never-ending kaleidoscope of color and colorful activity. In spring, life burst from Central Park's magnolias, redbuds, and cherry trees. In summer, it was a calming refuge of greenery. Fall brought the warm tones of fading oaks and maples. Winter often dressed those trees in a Hallmark vision of white, framed against a background of rolling hills and Central Park's ubiquitous horse-drawn carriages. All in the center of Manhattan, where eight hundred acres of some of the most valuable land in the U.S. somehow had escaped developers' earthmovers.

When he died, Miguel bequeathed the apartment to Tenny, his favorite granddaughter. A lifetime of memories accompanied Tenny when she walked through these doors. A small girl on vacation with a grandfather she loved, New York adventures with an older brother she adored, countless moments just looking out the window at the magical changing scene. When the apartment became hers, Tenny installed paintings by some of her favorite Latin and French impressionist artists. She lightened the walls' colors and replaced the formal décor with her own preference for California modern. Miguel had used the apartment as his Manhattan business headquarters. For Tenny, it was a coveted oasis, no matter that it existed on iconic Fifth Avenue at one of the most trafficked intersections of the United States.

In a few hours, Tenny would be the featured guest at the Metropolitan Museum's annual fund-raising gala, an event not ordinarily attended by presidents of the United States. Before becoming president, Tenny was a regular patron. Attending as president always added megabucks to the museum's endowment, a role, along with her love for art, she took seriously. The gala's evening schedule was being carefully monitored by Tenny's scheduling staff. Until they summoned her, she was free to enjoy her apartment and to steal some time alone with Carmie. Lifelong friends, shoes off, a few rare shared unofficial moments.

"Stay here with me tonight, Carmie. We won't be at the museum that long. Lord knows you and I have lots to talk about."

"If I stayed, we'd be up way past our bedtimes, gabbing and gossiping. You know how we are when we get together with no time clock."

"That was when we were young and dumb and thought we had to spend all night talking about young and dumb things."

"I loved it."

"Good days, Carmie. Good days. I think about them a lot."

"What I've been thinking," said Carmie, "is that if you lose this election, you should move to New York. You've got this place. I've still got my apartment. We haven't lived in the same city with lots of free time since we were in college. And this is my town. I know it. This would be a good life for us."

After graduating from the University of Southern California, Carmie had won an internship on Wall Street. Over the years she rose from entry level to the executive suite, building a résumé so strong, and a reputation so respected, that she faced little opposition when Tenny appointed her secretary of commerce.

"Tempting," said Tenny. "I do love Southern California, but there isn't much for me to go back to."

The room fell silent. Words lagged behind thoughts. Finally, Carmie broke the spell. She took Tenny's empty wine glass from her hand. "Refill?"

"Better not. I can't be slurring my words in front of a thousand of New York's richest people."

Carmie poured chardonnay into both glasses anyway.

"Hell, that crowd never listens to anyone. You could say 'all together now, take down your pants' and they'd never notice."

She handed Tenny a refilled glass, then settled in beside her on the red leather chesterfield sofa.

"Okay, lady. Let's really talk. It would be so much more comfortable for you to bail out, move here, and live a good life. You've made your mark, done great things already. No one would blame you. You could spend your last year as president in the warm glow of applause. Great show. Well done. Instead, you're heading to a meat grinder of abuse. Why are you really running for reelection? To get a pound of flesh from Carmona?"

Tenny turned to her friend. "I don't want a pound of his flesh; I want his head on a spike, the way the Mayan warriors used to deal with their blood enemies. Why wouldn't I? I'm sure he had my brother killed. First, I want to torture him knowing that I'm coming after him. I don't want him to take a piss without looking over his shoulder to see if I've sent someone to castrate him while his pants are down. Yes, Carmona's a part of it, but I can get Carmona this year, without running for reelection."

Tenny rose from the sofa and walked to the table where the wine bottle was resting in its silver ice chiller. She swallowed the remains of her half-empty glass and refilled it.

"I've got a historic opportunity, Carmie. *We* have a historic opportunity. You know, when I talked you into coming with me to Washington, my mind mostly was on reforming the economic system. Making it painful for all the big players abusing it. Throwing some in jail. Evening the playing field. Rebuilding the middle class. Finally doing the right things to end poverty cycles. All of that. My thinking was that if we could pull off even half of what I tried, we could make a world of difference."

"You still think that. I know," said Carmie. "And don't sell yourself short. You've done a lot already."

"Yes, I still do think that. And yes, we have done some good things. But Carmie, if that's all we expect to do in the next four years, we're shooting way too low. My mind's really been opened to a world hardly anyone in politics is paying attention to. It's not just that we're into a new type of industrial revolution; we've got at least half a dozen revolutions going on at once. A revolution in energy and how we use it. A revolution in materials that's going to let us build amazing new homes and everything else. A medical revolution where we know every cell in everyone's body and how to manipulate them. A knowledge revolution with quantum computing. A genetic agriculture revolution. And who knows where we're going with artificial intelligence and robots. I've seen so many amazing things, talked with so many brilliant people. Everything familiar to us, everything we think we know, about work, about education, about life itself, it's all about to be transformed."

The spacious living room suddenly became too small for Tenny to fully express what she was feeling. She stood and began pacing, arms synchronizing with her words. Words that began to fly like verbal bullets, in bursts, with pauses only to reload.

This was a long-ago Tenny, reemerging for an appearance in the here and now.

"Tenny!" said Carmie. "Slow down. I'm just an audience of one."

But it was difficult for Tenny to brake her thoughts. "Sorry," said Tenny. "But I honestly haven't felt this excited since my early days in the White House when we came in with a mission to save the world. Now I understand just how small that mission was compared with what's possible over the next five to ten years when we'll need to figure out how to manage all of the life-changing things pouring out of labs and think tanks."

Carmie threw her legs onto the sofa space Tenny had vacated and with her eyes followed Tenny as she paced.

"If you're still president, you won't be the only one dealing with all this."

"Exactly," said Tenny. "We not only have to deal with it, we have to get it right, and then sell those ideas. Congress needs to understand. The public needs to understand. And we're not even talking about just the US. Amazing things are coming out of China, Japan, and Europe. We have to have a tighter relationship with all of them. None of it can be contained."

"You think you can do this in four years, if you get four more years?"

Tenny returned to the sofa and moved Carmie's legs to make space.

"I can make one hell of a dent in it. And then I pass it on to Fish. Fish and I have talked about it. She takes it on for the next four, maybe eight years. By then the course will be set. We'll get the right mix of public and private. We'll put in place the right incentives and controls. We'll get international cooperation so that we work together, not destructive rivalries. This is what's driving me, Carmie.

"This is what I have to do. I know my body's not in great shape and that it's risky to add the pressures of the campaign and another term. But I also know this. It would kill me to lose."

15

"I watched the president's speech last night, you know, the one at that big New York party. Did you?" Marion asked her sister, Cathy Lincoln. The sisters were drinking coffee in Cathy's kitchen, preparing to go to their church where they volunteered to serve at the weekly lunch for the homeless.

"Just the start," said Cathy. "Lyle wanted to watch something else. He hasn't much use for our president."

"What did you think of it?"

"You know, I used to like her a lot. Being a woman and all. And she was so enthusiastic. But the poor thing looks so tired now."

"I noticed that, too. That seems to happen with every president. Their hair turns gray pretty fast."

"And, of course, the explosion. I just don't think she's been the same since."

Cathy poured Marion more coffee. Marion scooped some sugar and added cream to the steaming cup.

"Thanks, Cathy. Delicious coffee. Do you still use Folgers?"

"Wouldn't think of using anything else," said Cathy.

Marion stirred her coffee, eyeing it contemplatively.

"I wish she wasn't running at all. She's done her part."

"That's what I'm thinking."

"Earlier on the news they had that young man who's running against her, that Mack Bowman," said Marion.

"Zach. It's Zach Bowman, the one who did the impeachment."

"Yes, that's the one. Very nice young man. Speaks well. He was respectful of all she's been through, but I thought he made some very good points about why it's time to change."

"Lyle and I like him, too. I could vote for him. I like him better than the others. Our girls think he's cute."

"Well he is!" said Marion emphatically. "Cute never hurts when you're on TV."

"Young and smart, too," said Cathy. "But enough politics. We don't want our homeless folks to go hungry. Time to go."

And so it went. Intimate talk between sisters, the way sisters do. Except they weren't really sisters. They were actresses, cast members of a TV family known as "the Lincolns."

For two hours each morning and two more at dinnertime, *The Lincoln Family* lit up screens across America. Cathy and Lyle Lincoln, their teenage daughters, Gerry and Kelly, and their preteen son, Scott, were touted by the network as "America's family." The extraordinary thing about their popularity was that the family gained a large and faithful audience by doing nothing extraordinary, nothing except live what their media promos termed "traditional American lives, with traditional American values."

In the mornings the family had breakfast and readied for the day. During evening hours, they shared the day's events, dined together, often entertained guests, visited with neighbors, and watched television. Sometimes, the TV screen would display faux video of newscasts or commercial ads, or the scenes would shift from the family home to follow an outing—shopping, church, an office situation, a school event, a ball game. The scripting was so artful that millions of viewers became intimately attached to the family members, their successes, and whatever drama that was present in their lives. Births, deaths, injuries, scandals—often affecting other family and friends. Viewers never knew what to expect and were seldom disappointed.

The Lincoln Family was a faux-reality twist of what was once the popular daytime soap opera, with two new defining features: commercial product placements and politics.

When Marion and Cathy Lincoln swooned over the satisfying flavor of Folgers coffee, they were ringing the network's cash register. Each product the Lincolns used—clothes, athletic gear, lawn seeds, paper for the home printer, all the food they ate and drank, all of their furniture and electronics—each and every product and service was paid for. It replaced traditional commercial advertising, allowing each episode to continue without interruption. Integrating the ads into the programming prevented electronic zapping of defined-time commercials. As the credibility of the Lincolns increased, so did the value of their endorsements. *The Lincoln Family* became a hugely profitable brand for the network.

The other feature defining *The Lincoln Family* was politics. More precisely, the politics of Cadance Earl, the show's creator and the network's CEO.

For years, Earl had watched with admiration the way Rupert Murdoch had assembled his faithful cohort of viewers through unwavering devotion to right-wing politics. It was an audience she coveted. Occasionally Earl would game out strategies for building her own stable of talking political heads. Chances for success in a direct battle with Fox News seemed marginal. Searching for an alternative, Earl's market analysis detected that Fox's unrelenting diet of anger was wearing thin. Each rant sounded like the one before it. Each new call to arms fit predictably into an all-too-familiar template. How long could you ask your followers, however devout they may be, to maintain extraordinary levels of outrage? Rather than reproduce Murdoch's formula, Earl opted to deliver messages equally satisfying to the political right, but with a lighter touch. The messengers were not angry commentators but the reasonable Lincolns.

Along with the Folgers coffee Cathy Lincoln served to her sister Marion was the concept that President Tennyson looked tired and spent. When Marion replied that Tenny shouldn't run at all, "poor thing," she confirmed what countless *Lincoln Family* program viewers were thinking. And when the sisters looked favorably on Zach Bowman, that gave viewers permission to pay attention to him.

Behind the scripts, Cadance Earl hid an experienced and savvy news operation that often integrated real and exclusive news into the Lincolns' conversations. Mainstream media outlets were forced to monitor the show for such nuggets to protect their own credibility.

The Lincolns began hitting full stride as a commercial and political success during Tenny's first term as president. Her reelection campaign offered Earl the opportunity to use the elevated interest in politics to increase audience share, while at the same time mobilizing the Lincolns' faithful audience to influence the outcome of the campaign. For those managing the campaign to deny Tenny a second term, *The Lincoln Family* was an ideal media mother ship.

16

Political strategist Crystal Kranz was always in demand by high-profile Republican candidates. For most of the previous year, however, she had dropped off the political map to care for her terminally ill mother. That made her available when, days after her mother's funeral, she was recruited to manage the late-starting Zach Bowman for President campaign. She had never met Bowman and considered the odds of winning to be low. But the pay was good, the campaign seemed well financed, and the job kept her in the game rather than on the sidelines during the presidential election.

Dozens of tough campaigns had hardened Crystal's management skills. She made quick decisions and had little tolerance for distractions. Crystal was working out of the campaign's Chicago headquarters, her home base, when the first call came from Buddy Rufus.

Buddy Rufus fell into the distraction category. Worse, he was a potentially dangerous distraction. The long reign of powerful Chicago machine politics left a legacy of hangers-on, men and women, mostly men, who fixed things. Time and the loss of city hall patronage were thinning their ranks, but some, like Buddy, remained. Operatives like Buddy once were positioned at the tail end of a long political organization chart. But now, even Chicago politics had been transformed by the new "gig" economy. One-time handlers became self-employed contractors, needing to find their own things to handle.

Buddy's first attempt to reach Crystal was a phone call, taken by her assistant, threatening to blow up the Bowman campaign if she refused to see him. Her first reply was simply, "Go to hell." Buddy responded with a voice-mail message: "You're going there with me." Next, she sent her deputy campaign manager to meet with Buddy. Her deputy returned, shaken by the experience, and handed Crystal a handwritten note that said, simply, "Think again. You don't want anyone else to see what I've got." Finally, to end the nonsense, Crystal hopped in a taxi and met Buddy at a Starbucks.

"Nice of you to make it, Crystal," he greeted her.

"Cut the crap, Buddy," said Crystal. "I told the cabbie to wait for me with the meter running. Why are you acting like a political terrorist?"

"Look at these," he said. He handed her three photos.

The most prominent feature of the first photo was Zach Bowman's bare ass, pants at his knees, straddled over a woman whose face was partially covered by the red blouse pulled high to reveal her ample breasts. The second photo was from the same vantage, only now Zach was easily recognized. The woman's red hair popped out, nicely framing her closed eyes and her hand on Zach's bare crotch. The third photo was the two of them fully clothed exiting a Cessna Citation that Crystal had chartered for a quick, unexpected downstate campaign stop three days earlier.

Crystal eyed the photos without visible reaction, turning them left and right, back to front, as if going through a forensic inspection. Stalling for time, she pulled her cell phone from her purse, turned on the phone's flashlight, and carefully studied all three photos again.

Buddy Rufus broke the silence.

"I thought you'd like to see these before they turn up in the newspaper or TV or somewhere," he said. "Zach's my guy. I'd hate to see him go down in flames over something like this."

Crystal, repressing two competing urges—flee or punch out Buddy, which she could because the table separation was narrow—counted quietly to herself, to ten, a trick she had taught herself earlier in her career when faced with a difficult decision. Finally, Crystal returned her cell phone to her purse and stood as if to leave. In a low voice, almost a whisper, seething with disdain, she leaned into Buddy's face, mere inches away. "You drag me over here for this penny ante shit. Even an amateur can see these were photoshopped. You think Zach Bowman would be waving his nuts around like this when he's six inches from being elected president? No one would believe it!"

Buddy wasn't easily deterred. He, too, was a professional at this game, and he expected a paycheck.

"Calm down, Crystal. I don't want to hurt Zach. I'm trying to help. You can count on me. But the pilot and Zach's back-seat friend don't know from politics. I don't want anything for myself. They just want to be paid for their troubles."

Crystal put both of her arms on the table, still hovering over a seated Buddy Rufus.

"Bullshit, Buddy. This is a pretty lame excuse for a shakedown. It might have worked with somebody running for alderman, but this is the big leagues. Huge money and powerful people. They'll find a judge to put this red-haired honey in jail and yank the pilot's license. You. They'll break your legs or worse. Don't mess with it."

Then, her expression transformed from rage to motherly kindness. She sat down next to Buddy, on his side of the booth, and looked intently into his eyes. Very intently.

"Buddy, let me give you a preview of coming attractions. These show up anywhere other than this table and first thing that happens is that Zach and a few others sue your asses off—all of you. Got a million dollars and five years to spend in court fighting people with deep pockets?

"Good luck with that. While that's going on, you get slapped with criminal charges. Maybe transporting whores across state lines. Maybe kidnapping. I don't know. She looks like she'll sell out cheap to testify against you. You do have a rap sheet, don't you? You'll be so hot you wouldn't be able to raise a quarter in a tin cup on the best corner of Michigan Avenue. You'd be done, Buddy. Finished.

"Now, let me draw another picture for you. You really are Zach's friend. You really did want me to know that some awful people, probably working for the Democrats, had rigged these pictures to crash his campaign because they knew he'd be the toughest one to beat. Zach would owe you, really owe you. And because Zach is really kindhearted and forgiving, he wouldn't go after the pilot's license. And this babe, she wouldn't go to jail as a drug-pushing hooker. Isn't that a nicer picture?"

Buddy's eyes were held tight by Crystal's. He wanted to look away, down, up, whatever. But he couldn't. Such was the intensity of her stare and the element of possibilities embedded in her message. A message that increased his heart rate and caused sweat to collect in his armpits. Seconds passed.

"I'd need to give them something."

"You mean, besides this warning?"

"Gas money for the pilot. Maybe round-trip fare for the lady to take a nice vacation."

Crystal reached into her purse, pulled out a notebook, and

turned to a blank page.

She handed it to Buddy with a pen and no comment. None needed.

He wrote down some numbers and handed the notebook back.

17

"You asshole!" she screamed at Zach Bowman. "You goddam idiot! Leave you alone for five minutes and you're in somebody's pants."

Crystal Kranz was alone with Zach in his room at Chicago's Palmer House hotel. But he wasn't in her pants. Far from it. She was in his face. Zach had just returned from one of the most exciting rallies of his young campaign. More than ten thousand people packed into Chicago's Wintrust Arena. Democratic-voting Chicago. With lots of media, especially TV. Zach was now the hot political property for the legions of media that follow the presidential scent. An unexpected entry into the race, joining long after others already had staked their claims to veteran organizers and contributors. Even with the late entry, Zach had run a surprisingly close second in Iowa and had actually won the New Hampshire primary. Now the field had thinned to just three serious candidates. Could Zach be the Republican who would challenge President Tennyson for the White House in November?

Zach fed on the adulation. He was handsome, articulate, father of two beautiful young daughters and husband to a made-for-Sunday-supplements wife. The Republican Party seemed to be falling in love with Zach Bowman.

But there was no love from Crystal Kranz.

"That little joy ride you took to Springfield the other day. Did you know the pilot? No. Did you know that piece of ass posing as a campaign volunteer? No. Did you stop to think the pilot might get interested if you dropped your pants right in the airplane? No, you dumb fuck. Most people want selfies with your face in it. The pilot wanted a picture of your bare ass fucking in his fucking airplane so he could blackmail you."

Zach, still riding the high from his rally, wasn't easily let down. He found Crystal's tirade amusing, more curious than alarming.

"Really, he took pictures?" said Zach.

"Yes, he took pictures. And I've let the pilot know that if anybody but me sees them he's going to wind up at ten thousand feet with sugar in his gas tank. And that whore who was with him knows she'll be dropped from that plane without a parachute."

Zach laughed out loud. Being untouchable was the story of his life and his political career. He had been born into a moderately wealthy banker's family. He grew to be tall and handsome. A high school football hero. A fraternity president, followed by a seamless job glide into his father's bank, local popularity, and a seat in Congress. Things always broke his way. He could do whatever he wanted, and people like Crystal would be there either to cheer him on or repair the damage.

"Sorry," he said. "Didn't mean to put you into that kind of trouble. I'll behave."

"The hell you will. You don't get it, do you? A hundred people I know personally would die to be in your shoes. Being nobody. Coming from nowhere. Most likely becoming president, the most powerful person in the goddamn world. And you acting like you're still a frat boy thinking with your prick. Well, I'm hired to get you elected, and by God, I'm going to do it."

"Okay, okay, I said I'll be good. Don't worry about me."

"Oh, I'm not going to worry. I'm going to put you in a straitjacket. From here out, my guy Eddie Young will be like glue to you. Glue. Where you go, even to the shit house, he goes. He sleeps where you sleep, eats where you eat. If you so much as shake a woman's hand too long, Eddie will call me."

"You don't need to do that."

"I don't. You do. You can't stop yourself. If sex was a high cliff, you'd go headfirst off it."

Zach shrugged his shoulders, lifted his arms as if he was about to protest, then thought better of it.

"What about the pictures?"

"You better pray that I've fixed it. If I haven't, those pictures will be gold for the media and a horror show for both me and you."

Zach had removed his jacket and rolled up his shirtsleeves when he'd arrived back in his hotel room. Now he grabbed his jacket and started for the door.

"Can I go now? Next stop on the schedule's coming up."

"No, you can't go. Wait a minute."

Crystal pulled her cell phone from her jeans pocket and punched her speed dial. Gil Adonis answered.

"Ready," she said simply. And then disconnected.

"You've got to talk to Gil."

"Gil's here?" said Zach, surprised.

"Room 1219. Don't keep him waiting."

"You mean you and I don't have time for a quickie first?"

She wheeled toward him like a category five hurricane.

He grabbed the door handle. "Just kidding," he said.

She wasn't so sure about that.

18

In the weeks after Gil Adonis summoned Zach to New York, the money tap opened, influential people endorsed Zach, and seasoned professionals, like Crystal Kranz, arrived to design strategy and manage an organization that would quickly grow into hundreds of paid staff and thousands of volunteers. Zach's job, his only job, was to be the candidate. A role he played well. What hadn't happened since Zach became a presidential candidate was a second visit with Gil Adonis. Until now.

Gil ushered Zach into his hotel suite with a handshake and an arm around his shoulder. The suite was impressive, a high floor overlooking the iconic Chicago skyline. It was a brilliant April day. Adonis suggested they enjoy it on the suite's balcony.

"I know you're on a tight schedule," said Adonis. "This won't take long."

"Thanks," said Zach. "And thanks for all you're doing to help me."

"You can see," said Adonis, "my word's good."

"Absolutely."

"So, when I tell you that I'm about to pull the plug on your campaign, my word's good for that, too," said Adonis.

Startled, Zach turned to him, mouth open, words that wouldn't form since he didn't know what they should say.

"You know, Zach, there's no free lunch. You've been feasting on me and never asked to see the bill. It's time we discussed it. Crystal told me about that damn fool thing you did on the airplane. That tells me that you're more than just a foolish and horny bastard. It tells me you don't understand our relationship. Let me spell it out for you: The money in this campaign is mine. The people running it are mine. It's because of me you're getting so many endorsements. I'm behind a lot of the shit that's being thrown at the president, bringing her down. That's all mine. And if you get elected, you're mine, too."

The euphoria that had traveled with Zach from his last rally was now gone. He was bewildered, off balance. He still couldn't say anything, unable to mentally compute what was happening, afraid to say anything that would make it worse.

"I like you, Zach. That's why I'm doing what I'm doing. You've got it in you to win this whole damn thing. You've also got it in you to lose it. I don't do losers. And I don't do people who don't get the big picture. Let me draw it out for you. If you win, you win a lot of glory. You become powerful. You become historic. Eventually you become rich. Fewer than fifty people among everyone who's lived in this country since the American Revolution can say they've been president. There's George Washington, and Lincoln, and Kennedy, and now maybe Zach Bowman. That's what I call a big win. What do I get? I get what I want. It's as simple as that."

"Yeah," said Zach, finding his voice, "I'd be really grateful."

"Look at me," ordered Adonis, grabbing Zach by the arm and turning his body so they faced one another directly. "Gratitude isn't this game. Power is. You're president; I'm power. And what do you think I want to do with that power? To help you be the best president you can be. To use everything I've got and every contact I have to help you succeed. I play hard and tough, but I play straight, and anybody around me who doesn't takes a walk. Nothing illegal. Nothing even close. Why would I go to all this trouble electing you and then risk it all on stuff that means nothing to me? For what? Money? I'll never be able to spend what I already have. Fame? Guys like you eat that shit up. Guys like me don't. The less said about me the better. I can make you great, Zach. That's the game. But I'm not going over the edge with somebody who doesn't understand all of this."

"I understand," said Zach.

"I'm not sure you do," said Gil. "Jake Larson would understand. I'm not convinced he could win in November, but if he did, he'd understand." Larson was the former Wyoming governor who had run against Tenny four years earlier and lost to her in a close race. "Some of my people have been talking with Jake. I like to keep my options open. And after hearing about your little airplane ride, I'm glad I did."

Zach was now fully aware of his danger. His political survival instincts were on full alert.

"I made one mistake, Gil. One mistake. Thank God Crystal was there to clean it up. I couldn't have got anywhere close to where I'm at now without her, without you, without everything you're throwing in here. You want me to say, 'I'm yours'? Here it is: I'm yours. And I'm not just saying it to be saying it. I mean it. Whatever you want when I win you get. Whenever you talk, I listen. If you were in the Oval Office yourself, you couldn't want more or do more than when I'm there."

Gil nodded his head, disengaged from Zach, and looked out over the Chicago skyline from his hotel window.

"Then quit acting like some dumb fuck and go out and win this sucker."

19

"This Sanchez woman, tell us what you know about her. She seems to have an extraordinary hold on President Tennyson. Are they lovers?"

Imam Musa Kartal was rocking back and forth in an ancient rocking chair, one of the few seats available in a room that appeared to be suitable only for storing old used furniture. The day was warm. The windowless room warmer. Kartal, Javier Carmona, and Turkish industrialist Tahir Badem were sipping iced mint tea as a cooling antidote. They had chosen this meeting place at Cairo's Al-Aqmar mosque for privacy, not comfort.

"Lovers?" answered Carmona, smiling at the prospect. "Doubtful. Tennyson has bedded so many men her sexual bona fides are not in doubt."

"One never knows," said the imam. "Those easily aroused sexually often do not discriminate."

"Well, I don't claim expertise about the president's sexual preferences," said Carmona. "But from reading my files you see that she's been married, to a man. They divorced long ago. He became a prominent surgeon. After the divorce, her grandfather, Miguel Aragon, gave her a job selling wealth management services for Groupo Aragon. She spent many years traveling the Americas, with great success in that role. Many of us believed at the time that much of her success resulted from selling her body as part of the account. The file has many lovers' names, situations we've verified."

The imam pursued this prospect. "But the files also say she and this Carmen Sanchez have been together since they were young girls, schooled together, traveled together, and now Sanchez is in Tennyson's cabinet as secretary of commerce. Such a long and close history is most unusual. And I see Sanchez never married."

"No, Sanchez is the daughter of one of our employees in Los Angeles, now retired. She's the same age as Tennyson. They've been friends since Tennyson's family moved to California from Mexico City. As for being part of government, Sanchez had a very successful banking career on Wall Street, so she was qualified for her appointment."

"Interesting," mused the imam.

"See, Carmona, this is why we asked you to come to Cairo, said Tahir Badem."Your files on Tennyson are very valuable, very helpful. But some things are best explained in person."

Javier Carmona was reluctant to be anywhere near Imam Musa Kartal or Tahir Badem. They were killers. He could not assume polite conversation ruled out deadly intent. Carmona complied with their "invitation" to meet with them in Cairo only because he had no other choice.

"Now about this fellow, Sage. Ben Sage. Is he one of her lovers?" Kartal asked. "I don't see that in the files."

"I don't know," said Carmona. "Possibly. He's what they call in the United States her 'political strategist' and has been since her first election to Congress from Los Angeles. He has other clients, but of course she is the most prominent. They do spend much time together. None of our people who followed them reported dalliances. It could be that Sage is homosexual. He has a business partner, a man named Lee Searer, who also is unmarried."

"That's worth knowing," said Kartal. He wrote a note to himself.

"What makes me think it's just business is that Sage was married once," Carmona added. "His wife was killed in an automobile accident. Sage has a second home, at a beach resort in the state of Delaware, not far from Washington. During our investigation last year one of our people entered his home and found a diary, a diary of letters he writes to his dead wife. Copies were photographed. They are in the files."

"Old letters?"

"No. New. He writes to her often. News of what he's doing. Love letters. As if she never died."

"Extraordinary. We saw them and didn't know their significance. How long ago did she die?"

"I'm not sure. At least ten years ago, I believe."

"Is he deranged?"

"I doubt it. He's very successful. Someone who writes love letters to one's wife years after her death is not likely having affairs with anyone else, even the president. But, of course, anything is possible."

Kartal looked at his notes and ran his finger down the page until he found what he was looking for. "There's a third person who interests us, Carmona. Perhaps you can provide insight.

This Harold Thompson, who once was governor of California."

"As you can see, the files have many notes about Thompson," said Carmona. "Before either of them ran for political office, Tennyson and Thompson worked together to help the poor in Southern California. They became lovers. Then Tennyson was elected to Congress and Thompson married someone else and was elected governor of California. One of California's senators resigned while Thompson was governor, and Thompson appointed Tennyson to fill that vacancy. We used the old sexual affair between Thompson and Tennyson to try to defeat her. Unfortunately, we were not successful. You can find much of the story of that campaign in the files, and it was also a topic in her impeachment trial."

"I see," said Kartal. "This might prove useful. Especially now that she's appointed him ambassador to France."

Carmona seemed startled. "I wasn't aware she had made Thompson ambassador to France."

"It happened just a few weeks ago," said Badem. "He's only recently moved into the ambassador's residence in Paris with his family."

This was not pleasant news for Carmona. His Groupo Aragon had a large and expanding business relationship with French agricultural interests. Thompson was well aware that Carmona had been behind the scurrilous advertising that tied him and Tenny together in the "strange bedfellows" advertising attacks. He also knew that Carmona was one of the impeachment conspirators. Thompson as the US ambassador to France posed a threat of retaliation that could affect Carmona's business in France and perhaps elsewhere.

Imam Kartal and Tahir Badem understood Carmona's dilemma.

"Don't be alarmed," said Badem. "We will find ways to help you manage any obstacles Thompson presents."

Carmona was not reassured. Badem's Fertile Crescent Industries was both a competitor and a customer. Carmona's loss could be Badem's gain. The Thompson news disturbed him, and he did not trust Badem to be helpful. In fact, he distrusted everything about this new, involuntary relationship with Badem, Kartal, and whoever else was now pulling his strings. For more than an hour, Carmona had been quizzed about details in the Tennyson files he had assembled. For most of that hour, Carmona waged a losing battle with sweat glands pouring forth from both the heat and his anxieties. Finally, relief.

"Musa, I've reached my limit of tolerance in this oven of yours," said Badem. "I've reserved a private meeting room at the Palace Hotel where we can continue our talk in better air, with food and drink, and with a casino where later I intend to try my luck at baccarat. That is, if you have no more questions about our friend's files."

"Oh, I believe we're finished for now," said Imam Kartal. "It's been very helpful and given us thoughts to pass along to our contact in the United States to help our objective."

"Who's the contact?" asked Carmona.

Imam Kartal rose from his rocker.

"You will learn with time, my friend, that there are things you best not learn."

Carmona's brow wrinkled. "I don't understand."

"Best that you don't," said the imam. "Best that you don't. Our enterprise will survive and succeed because those who do not need to know are not told. I know our contact, but there are many things I do not know and do not ask to learn. For now, consider unanswered questions important to your security, as I do to mine."

20

The presidential primary season moved on. Each week another state, another result, another key date crossed off the election calendar. Tenny's Democratic Party nomination was assured, even though Kevin Egert, a tech billionaire self-financing his own campaign, remained on the ballot, questioning her competence and policies. On the Republican side, three finalists continued to trash-talk one another, desperation increasing as the pool of remaining delegate votes shrank. No need to get in the way of that, counseled Ben. Let them tear one another down. Tenny was in Tokyo, meeting with other heads of state at an economic summit, being presidential. No need to get in the way of that, either. Being presidential was much better for her image than being political.

For those involved in the turbulent world of high- stakes politics, intensity has its limits. Bodies and brains tire. Strategists lose their horizons. The risk of unforced errors increases. Before committing to a strategy for the remainder of the primary election phase of the campaign, Ben decided that now was time to take a few days away from it.

Ben's refuge from politics was his beach home at Lewes, Delaware, about 120 air miles from Washington, DC. Occasionally he would drive the distance, a pleasant three- hour trip. But more often he would pilot his own Piper Cherokee to get there, guaranteeing travel time not much longer than an hour and avoiding summer beach traffic that clogged the Chesapeake

Bay Bridge and the few roads available to reach Delaware's beaches and Maryland's Eastern Shore. Ben long ago had earned his pilot's license. That license, and this plane, had allowed him to quickly move from one client to another when remaining campaign days were short, surprise developments were frequent, and the unexpected required immediate attention.

The plane also was Almie. Almie. Each time he settled into the pilot's seat. Each time he felt the lift under the wings. Each time he was alone in the clouds with his thoughts. God, he missed Almie. They were married for so short a time before the accident. She had been so reluctant to fly with him. So dangerous, she would say. Until one day he coaxed her into the passenger seat with words from Walt Whitman.

> *O to realize space!*
> *The plenteousness of all—that there are no bounds;*
> *To emerge, and be of the sky—of the sun and moon, and the*
> *flying clouds, as one with them*

They hadn't known one another long enough for Ben to have earned Almie's complete trust. But she loved and trusted Walt Whitman. At ten thousand feet, Almie also gave her heart to Ben.

Where Delaware Bay feeds the Atlantic Ocean, that's Lewes. Population around 2,700 year-round. Tens of thousands more during summer months, drawn by the colonial-era quaintness of the shingle-sided homes, gambrel roofs, and other reminders of the town's Dutch settler heritage. Even though the Dutch had control of the area for only a few decades, their presence remained prominent, four centuries later.

Ben's Lewes home was everything campaigns are not: quiet, peaceful, serene. Stepping into the sand from his kitchen door, Ben could walk the beach undisturbed for miles. From his porch he could watch large ships from exotic ports make their way north on Delaware Bay to unload their cargoes in Wilmington and Philadelphia. When the breeze was full and the sun high, the bay was alive with colorful sails. During fishing season, day boats joined them, transporting fishermen to and from nearby sunken wrecks. Others left the docks of Lewes in hopes of intersecting humpback whales and dolphins as they plied their traditional coastal routes to feed.

Early April days on the bay could be chilly, but today the sun was high, and Ben needed only a windbreaker for comfort on his outdoor porch. Lee Searer, Ben's partner in the Sage, Searer Political Consulting Agency, suffered cold with less tolerance. He wore a full winter jacket, gloves, and wool cap. Both were inhaling the aroma of hot cider from their mugs and the pervasive salt air wafting in from the southeast.

"I'll light a fire when we go inside," said Ben. "But really, it's not that cold."

"Mind over matter," said Lee. "You own this place and have to like it."

"You don't?"

"Oh, I do. June to August."

Ben sipped his cider, still too warm for gulping but pleasant in the light chill from the breeze sweeping off the bay.

"You have sharks here?" Lee asked.

"Now and then," said Ben. "Not so much in the bay. A lot more off the coast. Some run hundreds of pounds."

"I just read that sharks in Greenland live to be 500 years old and that they don't get sexually active until they're 150."

"Hey," said Ben, "maybe we can use that in one of our TV ads attacking the bankers. Besides the shark news, have you run across any research that actually might be useful?"

"Yes, I have, as a matter of fact. Bowman's going to get the nomination."

"Bowman?"

"Bowman," Lee replied.

"Sure about that?" said Ben. "He's such a jackass. "

"Doesn't matter. Bowman. Just reading the polls tells you all you need to know."

"He doesn't have the delegates yet, and where's he going to get the money for the big state primaries coming up?"

"I don't know about the money," said Lee, "but according to all our research, the Republican base loves Bowman for trying to impeach Tenny. They're coming out big in those rallies. And every time Jake Larson attacks Bowman, Jake's negatives go up with Republicans most likely to vote in primary elections."

"Well, if it's Bowman I think things get easier for us," said Ben. "No matter who it is, we've got to get Tenny's poll numbers up."

"Ideas?"

"Lots of them. We've got a chance to make a strong contrast between Tenny's positive character and Republican negativity. I see us getting on the air before the conventions with really high-road stuff. Not just Tenny with cute kids and puppies, but beautiful ads, the kind of ads you can see over and over and never get tired of."

"Like?"

"Waving wheat fields. The Grand Canyon. The Saint Louis Arch. Soaring bald eagles. Guaranteed positive symbols."

"And what issues?" Lee asked.

"Doesn't matter. Associate her with places and people that make people feel good about America. Beautiful images. Tenny looking strong, healthy, and visually appealing. We write a minimum of words for the scripts and let the pictures do the talking, maybe even add a signature at the end like a fine painting. It would be like America itself endorsing her. Maybe we could run them right into the fall if polls show they're working against the shit-kicker ads the Republicans will be running against her. I like the idea of the extreme positive, extreme negative contrast."

"And how do we handle the actual issues?"

"News. She's the world's leading newsmaker. We ramp up the workload of the White House communications team and coordinate it with her travels and our paid media. The issues campaign is the daily news."

Two fishing charters slid past with their day's striped bass bounty. Beyond them, the car and passenger ferry *Twin Capes*, half-full, headed north from Lewes to New Jersey's Cape May.

Quiet filled the space while they absorbed the moment. Ben broke the silence.

"How's my idea for media fit with your thoughts about the ground game?"

Lee reluctantly unlocked from the water scene and turned to Ben.

"Oh yeah, ground game," said Lee. "Back to reality."

"No, this is reality," said Ben. "That's why we're here, to get real. Clear our heads of the small stuff and think big picture. The main thing is to rebuild the trust Tenny once had."

"Interesting that you mention trust," said Lee. "That's exactly what needs to drive our voter contact strategy. People get so many nuisance calls, even on their cell phones these days. I'm sure our usual phone contact systems won't work as well this year. You get a call from someone you don't know reading a script about Tenny like a robot and right away you associate that with the last call you got from someone hawking time shares in Florida. It all comes across as spam. What do you do? You do what you're conditioned to do—hang up and curse the fact that these damn people keep bothering you. That's no way to build trust."

"True enough," said Ben. "But people on our call list aren't exactly strangers. We know a lot about them before we call."

"Yes, we do," said Lee. "We know party affiliation, whether they're likely to vote, whether they have school-age kids, usually what they do for a living, maybe even what magazines they read. In fact, with enough money and time we can design individual campaigns for every likely voter in America. It's all in the database. But even with that information, we're still making a stranger-to-stranger call. If they're Democrats and we're calling to ask for money or time to volunteer or to remind them to vote, that's okay. But the people we need to persuade are more like you and me getting nuisance calls."

"What's the alternative?"

"I've been studying a lot of results from past elections. What I'm seeing is tribe voting."

"Tribe voting?"

"Yeah. More and more people are voting not so much as individuals but as members of a tribe. They vote the way most people around them vote. Race, or sex, or occupation, or whether they're urban or rural. Education. Age. Huge gaps. Whole precincts, even towns that vote 60–40 or even 70–30. Same goes for old and young, men and women. You don't see many 51–49 divisions on exit polls. It didn't used to be this way. And here's why I think that is. It's all become too damn confusing for individual voters. The issues are more complicated. They don't know who to believe or what to believe. So, they default back to people they trust to tell them."

"Like I might buy a Florida vacation package from you because I know you but hang up on that robot trying to do the same thing?"

"Exactly. So here's my campaign idea. We do a full- court press to win the support of as many opinion leaders and as many trusted groups as we can. We make it a peer group campaign. We pick the states where we're most likely to win 270 electoral votes and add a few more targets just to be safe. Then we have our state coordinators list all the interest groups they can get lists for. And instead of putting most of our people and money into cold-calling or even going door-to-door, we campaign for the opinion makers in those groups. We communicate with them the way they communicate among themselves—in their newsletters, websites, Facebook groups, Listservs, email loops, and all—mostly to win over the leadership. If we win over the leaders, in this political environment we have a chance to bag most of the followers."

"Actually, that sounds easier and cheaper than what we've been doing."

"It would be. We don't give up on door-to-door. It just gets lower priority."

"Interesting. We'll need local messages."

"In a lot of ways, just showing the flag, giving them attention, is the message. We get the research. What's important to each group. Maybe it's school bus schedules for PTAs, or the fact that Tenny plays a mean game of bridge for bridge clubs."

"Sounds like you're suggesting that Tenny run for president like she's running for the city council."

"City council, school board, class president, chief tail twister of the local Lions Club. She does what she personally has time for, and we promote those events with media. The rest we do with volunteers and surrogates. Virtual Tennys."

"You got an artificial intelligence program to keep all this straight?"

"I do. And the best part is that the program is so good it doesn't seem artificial at all."

21

Dear Almie:

Even when the moon is shrouded by clouds, we know the moon is there. Even though it's been a while since I've written, my love for you has been there, too. It's a love that ages as fine wine ages, maturing, becoming more complex, more mysterious, more precious. Just as with wine, there is alchemy. Few can fully explain why water and acid and alcohol break down, only to reemerge in time as flavors we covet. Neither can I explain, or want to explain, how my love for you deepens with your absence.

I find it especially strange that I can be so consumed by our romance at the same time I spend most days doing what I do, entering other people's minds to tell them what to say and how to say it so they can have power over other people's lives. I often think that I'm part of a tradition that's as old as the pyramids. The pharaohs left images of themselves bigger than life. Not just bigger, but with stronger bodies, handsome faces, courageous poses. Not much different than what I try to create for my candidates with political television commercials.

The statues and tablets survived, but the culture that created them didn't. Why is that, Almie? Shouldn't civilizations that had thousands of years head start, like the Egyptians, the Greeks, the Romans, be far ahead of the rest of us in development now? Why isn't cultural advancement linear? The Greeks developed a body of thought so advanced that it's the foundation of much we say and do today. Their language, their concepts of governing, a military that under Alexander conquered much of their known world. So why isn't Greece a richer and more powerful nation now? The Arabs gave us algebra and so much more while Western civilization was still struggling to feed itself. Why aren't today's Arabs space and medical pioneers?

Oh, how I wish you were here so we could talk about these things the way we used to. Not just the progress of civilizations, but the essence of language, the psychology of change, all those mysterious and wonderful and unanswerable questions we once asked each other. Most of all, why our love was so rich and enduring.

It still is, Almie. It still is.

Love forever,

Ben

22

"I don't see how you can eat the same thing, morning after morning. Don't you ever think about say, just once, having something besides unflavored yogurt, dried dates, almonds, and unbuttered rye toast?"

Lyle Lincoln looked up from his morning newspaper to rib his wife, Cathy, about her morning breakfast routine.

"You get that Chobani, mix it with Blue Diamond brand almonds and Hadley—only Hadley—dates, and slices of rye from Arnold. No variety at all."

"Why not?" retorted Cathy. "It's healthy. And besides, it stays with me all morning. I used to snack about ten, but no more. It gives me most of my daily vitamins and keeps my blood pressure low."

The Lincolns had a comfortable relationship. They seldom argued. Now and then they showed affection for one another. Nothing sexy. Hugs and kisses. Mostly, they engaged in bouts of good-natured banter. That's what made them so personally attractive to the millions of TV viewers who checked in on them daily.

With every product reference, Lyle either held up the packaging so the TV camera could zoom on it, or the camera panned to the product on the table. The Lincolns were so nice, so believable, so much a model for their growing audience that any product they endorsed seemed worthy of trying. Earl Media's cash drawer was ringing up record ad sales from these endorsements and other product placement advertising.

That same credibility applied to political views. The Lincolns were not in-your-face Republicans, but they had political opinions, almost always conservative Republican opinions. They came at you with the innocence of casual conversation rather than rants or lectures.

"Now, Geraldine here," said Lyle Lincoln, gesturing to his daughter, "I never know what she'll turn up with at breakfast, except she always has her Microsoft Surface. Isn't that right, Geraldine?"

Gerry Lincoln was unpredictable in the ways of most fifteen-year-olds. But connected. Always connected.

"Yes, I've been meaning to mention that," said Cathy. "Geraldine, can't you just once come to breakfast without that computer?"

"Well, Dad's got his newspaper. This is what I read in the morning."

"Your father is reading the news."

"So am I. It's just different news. Like, here, this story I'm reading now is about how two doctors made an emergency call to the White House to check on the president when she had some dizzy spells the other day. They thought it might be a stroke or something."

"I hadn't heard about that," said Cathy.

"Well, it's right here on this website."

Lyle put down his newspaper, his full attention captured by Gerry's news.

"What was wrong with her? Is she okay?"

"I guess. It says they gave her some pills."

"I don't understand why it wasn't on the news," said Cathy.

"It is in the news," insisted Gerry, defending her tablet and her news site. "See, it's right here."

"I mean TV, the newspapers," said Cathy.

"Well, they cover things up," said Lyle. "You know how the media defend her. They don't want us to know. But I'm not surprised. From what I've read, no one goes through the shock of an explosion like she did and comes out normal. Your body's never the same."

Mainstream editors everywhere had learned to keep the Lincolns on their newsroom screens. The Lincolns often broke news no other outlet yet had, in ways you might not expect. Sometimes news broke while the Lincolns were pretending to watch TV. Now and then actors playing the role of journalists friendly with the Lincolns dropped by with hints of news not yet published. Or it could be like this morning's breakfast episode, with one of the actors discovering a news item somewhere else. Almost always the pretend news discussed on the show had enough credence for other media to check the stories out for themselves. Competitive news directors never knew when a scoop was coming, so they felt pressured to watch the show—just in case. Behind the scenes, Cadance Earl had a formidable staff of journalists and private investigators. Entertainment celebrities were constant targets. Breaking scandals about them always bumped up ratings. To feed Earl Media's right- wing-biased audience, politics also had a place in each day's show.

The basis of this morning's conversation about Tenny's medical condition was a report filed by one of Cadance's young reporters who had spotted two men carrying what looked like medical bags entering the White House through a seldom-used gate. Inquiries at the White House press office confirmed that the doctors were there to see the president. No other details needed.

In Earl Media's playbook, that was enough to run with and speculate about. Following up on what seemed like a tip from the morning edition of *The Lincoln Family*, other news outlets took the bait. Finally, the White House elaborated. Tenny had not been feeling well, and, playing it safe, the White House physician had been called for consultation. The doctors all agreed that it was nothing more serious than a mild virus. They prescribed Tamiflu.

Because of Earl Media's speculation, though, most of the US read stories like the one that ran on the AP wire.

A morning alarm that the president may have suffered a stroke turned out just to be a case of the flu. A White House spokesman said that specialists were called to the White House by the president's personal physician when President Tennyson reported feeling ill. White House physician Marcelle Leary said the matter was a routine precaution, given the president's injuries from last year's assassination attempt. Earlier reports had indicated a more serious medical problem. Those reports proved unfounded.

The day's news cycles included stories about Tenny's health. Right-wing media promoted the incident with Martians-invade-Earth enthusiasm. Conspiracy-inclined websites suggested the official White House announcement omitted details of a serious brain condition. One commentator said he had it from a source inside the White House that the specialists were neurologists. Another said the subject of her failing health was so sensitive that they kept her real health records in black boxes as secure as the one that held the nuclear codes.

The White House explanation seemed credible to the mainstream press corps and there was no follow-up. But the story did remind them that this was a physically damaged president and to be alert to any sign of change in her appearance or behavior. Did she look tired? Did she just slur a word? Was she searching for names or places she couldn't momentarily remember?

With a brief scripted scene on a well-watched morning cable television show, the Lincolns had ensured that Tenny's health would get attention, even if she coughed twice at a public reception.

23

In retrospect, Jake Larson never had a chance to win the California Republican primary. Yes, he had an admirable record as governor of Wyoming. And, yes again, he was as steady and reliable as a Lexus sedan. But voters who live among the stars and drive a disproportionate share of Corvette convertibles can easily have their heads turned. Zach Bowman was exciting to watch and thrilling to be near, even on TV. He had youth. He had energy. He had bare-knuckle attacks on a Democratic Party president many California Republicans had turned against years earlier, when she served as their US senator.

When it came time to choose a nominee to deny Tenny four more years in the White House, California's Republican voters punched Zach Bowman's ticket. It was the last of the big state primaries, the final delegates he needed to claim the nomination.

Jake Larson had spent four years organizing his California primary campaign. Nearly every important California Republican officeholder and party official had endorsed him. As the votes were counted and Jake's loss and the need to salvage their reputations became obvious, the party heavyweights quickly suggested a "dream ticket." Zach and Jake. Bowman and Larson. Flashy and solid. Bowman from Pennsylvania, Larson from Wyoming. East and West. Many of the night's TV pundits promoted it. Now, in this victory moment, in the glow of certainty that he would he would head the Republican ticket and be within touching distance of the White House, Zach Bowman was swept up in the Bowman-Larson enthusiasm. Zach took Larson's concession call while being interviewed live on CNN. After listening for a moment, Zach nodded in agreement at something Jake said and replied, for the media and public to hear, "We'd make a great team, Jake."

Among those viewing what amounted to the sealing of a deal for the vice-presidential nomination was Gil Adonis, alone in his suite at San Francisco's Ritz-Carlton hotel, purposely distant from the celebration party at the Hyatt Embarcadero. Adonis quietly mouthed just two words in reaction: "Stupid shit." For a few minutes Adonis sat quietly watching the remainder of Zach's interview, watching, but not hearing. Nothing else Zach would say mattered. Finally, he came to a decision. He punched Crystal Kranz's numbers into his cell phone. After five rings she answered, barely audible against the victory party's background noise.

"Gil?" she answered.

"Congratulations, Crystal. You did a great job. Put Zach on."

"Zach? Oh, he's in the can. Had to piss for an hour. I thought his bladder would pop while he was on CNN. He couldn't even wait to get back to the campaign hotel suite. He's still in the ballroom. Did you see him?"

"I saw him. Go into the shit house and find him."

"Find him? Can't it wait 'til he comes out?"

"Find him," Adonis insisted.

Crystal hesitated a few seconds. "Okay, guess I won't see anything I haven't seen before. Hang on."

She elbowed her way through the mass of revelers in the ballroom, pushed open the doors marked "MEN," and stepped into an equally crowded bathroom. Zach was relieving himself—just in time, he felt, before he peed into his best silk suit pants. A line of supporters, startled at seeing the potential next president among them, had moved aside to give Zach urinal priority. Now, here was Crystal marching assertively to the head of the line, ignoring everyone else in the room, including Zach's Secret Service detail.

"You need to take his," she said, handing him her cell phone.

Zach, startled, but conditioned now to do whatever Crystal told him to do, took the phone with his left hand, continuing to aim his still-streaming penis into the urinal with his right hand.

"Shit! Crystal!" he said. "Can't this wait until I finish pissing? Who is it?"

"Take it," she ordered.

He put the phone to his ear. "This is Zach."

"Adonis," said the voice on the other end. "Knock off the Jake Larson crap. It's not going to be Larson. Walk it back, fast."

"Well, who?" asked Zach.

"I'll let you know in the morning." Adonis disconnected.

That left Zach Bowman, newly anointed Republican presidential nominee, with a cell phone in one hand, an open fly he was unable to zip closed with the other, and dozens of curious male admirers focused on the peculiar show in which Zach had just starred.

"My phone," Crystal reminded him. She took it and exited the men's room as matter-of-factly as she had entered.

24

At exactly 6:30 a.m. eastern time the next morning, Gil Adonis made another phone call. This time to Lester Bowles. He knew that Bowles would answer, and he did, on the second ring. After a lifetime of friendship, Adonis knew Bowles's morning routine, a routine that had not changed except for an occasional bout of the flu or travel. Awake at 5:00 a.m. An hour run or gym time. Shower. Dress. 6:30 breakfast. 7:00 a.m. arrive at the office.

"Les, it's time."

Bowles needed no explanation. Since that dinner with Gil Adonis, months ago when Gil first insisted that he run for vice president, they had had other conversations about it. In deference to his friend, Lester had remained neutral as the battle for the presidential nomination unfolded. He even had remained neutral during Ohio's primary election but cheered privately when Larson won the bulk of the state's delegates. Bowles viewed the prospect of a Bowman White House with horror, an image made worse when he pictured himself in it as vice president. Last night, watching California's results, his heart sank at what that meant for the Republican Party and, because of Gil's role, what it might mean for him personally. Then, the moment of reprieve, when Zach Bowman all but offered the vice-presidential nomination to Jake Larson. This morning's newspaper headline seemed to confirm it: "Republican Unity Marks End of Primary

Trail: It's Zach and Jake."

"Les, it's time" were not words he expected to hear from Gil this morning. They were not words he ever wanted to hear from Gil.

"What about Jake?" Lester asked.

"Zach made a mistake."

"Zach makes lots of mistakes. He's an idiot."

"I'm going to call him next and tell him it's you."

"Think about it, Gil," said Lester. "Jake Larson's popular with everyone who matters. All our people in Congress. Most of the governors, even a lot of Democrats. He had the nomination last time, and a lot of people think he deserves another chance. He's got his organization in place. And they all woke up this morning expecting him to be on the ticket. That's a lot for you to try to buck. And to all of them I'm going to look like a real asshole."

"Only one vote matters on this, Les. Mine. Zach knows it. He doesn't really give a shit who's vice president. He just wants to win. I'll tell him he can't win with Larson. Too dull. From a small state he's going to win in November anyway. Too many things he and Jake said to trash each other during the primary that the other side will use against them. You on the ticket gives him Ohio and probably Michigan. You can waltz into Wall Street, and they'll throw money at you for the campaign. They love you there. And hell, name one governor or senator who doesn't like and respect you. You're an easy case for me to make."

"Gil, you know what I think of all this. I don't like it. I haven't liked it since you first laid it out for me. If we weren't close as brothers, I wouldn't even consider it."

"But we are close as brothers. And sometimes, Les,

patriotism and love of country means more than waving the flag and singing 'The Star Spangled Banner' at a baseball game. Lots of people have had to go kill other people. Lots of people have had to spy on other people. You and I are going to war to save America, Les. You're not enlisting; you're being drafted."

"What if Zach doesn't see it that way?"

"He doesn't have a choice. Zach and I have an understanding."

"Does he really understand, Gil?" Lester asked quietly. "Does he really understand everything you have planned for him?"

25

Ben Sage and Carmen Sanchez arrived in Cleveland together on an early wave of what would soon crest as a human tsunami. Thousands of delegates and elected alternates to the Democratic National Convention, fifteen thousand reporters, writers, editors, photographers, broadcasters, podcasters, bloggers, their technical staffs and equipment, high-priced agents of influence, low-priced sellers of buttons, bumper stickers, and bobbleheads, those plotting serious protests, others into made-for-TV street theater, spouses, spectators, the curious and the deranged. National political conventions nominate candidates for president and vice president. They also tightly focus hopes, fears, and follies.

President Tennyson would be nominated by the Democratic Party for a second term. No doubt about that. Vice President Sheila Fishburne, her longtime friend and political partner, would share the Democratic presidential ticket. No doubt about that, either. One potentially disruptive crimp remained in planning for what the Tennyson campaign hoped would smoothly unfold as a display of partisan unity. His name was Kevin Egert, or Eager Egert, as insiders called him, the wealthy tech company founder who, among many others, became a candidate for the Democratic Party presidential nomination at a time when it appeared Tenny would not. Then Tenny survived impeachment, once again becoming politically formidable and prompting all other contenders to exit the campaign on the first available off-ramp. But not Egert. Now he was here, in Cleveland, with 22 percent of the delegates and a well-coordinated campaign of party platform disruption.

Egert's challenges prompted Carmie's early arrival in Cleveland. Party platforms seldom sway votes, unless, that is, embarrassing promises slip into the fine print. Carmie's job was to see that they didn't. As commerce secretary she was an unlikely policy enforcer, but as Tenny's longtime best friend and constant companion, no one knew the president's mind on policy better.

Ben Sage's mission had nothing to do with policy and everything to do with image. Four nights of TV shows, each worthy of network prime-time real estate. Drama! Glamor! Enough creative edginess to keep ratings high and sufficiently persuasive to build compelling narratives for undecided voters. Many decades ago, national political conventions were rapped to order with no one candidate having enough delegates to secure the nomination. The tension created by the uncertainty of outcome, like a closely fought Super Bowl or deciding World Series game, was intense enough to glue most Americans to their TV sets. Now, those conventions competed with endless other forms of entertainment, where the script is written in advance and the best writing and production wins the highest viewer ratings. Like those scripted shows, conventions occur at fixed times and dates. Last-minute cramming is inevitable, and last-minute loose ends hung like unraveled balls of yarn around both Carmie and Ben.

For Carmie, one of the most compelling problems related not to policy but to the convention role Ben had cast her for, a prime-time speech where she would be expected to rouse thousands of delegates to foot-stomping frenzy. As commerce secretary, her audiences had been exclusively interested in business policy. Numbers. Statistics. Forecasts. She could handle all that. But she had never been on the political circuit, where emotion counted for more than data. That was beyond anything Carmie had ever attempted, and its prospect made her anxious and uncertain.

"No one can do this like you can, Carmie," Ben said. "You've known her since childhood. You can be personal and even emotional. She needs that. With the baggage left over from impeachment, she has too many hard edges. We need to soften them."

"Yeah, emotional. That's exactly what worries me. I do numbers, not touchy-feely. And once I get going about Tenny, I'm sure I'll get teary. That could happen, you know. I'm a real softie when it comes to Tenny."

"Teary? No, that's no good. It's what you do at funerals. Look, neither of us has time, but let's have a proper lunch together and talk this through. It's important that you get comfortable with this speech and that it comes off well."

Neither Carmie or Ben had eaten more than grab-and- go food in days. Too many must-dos packed into too small a remaining time window. The lobby bar of the Renaissance Cleveland Hotel, where both Ben and Carmie were staying, seemed the most reasonable place to refuel.

Carmie was at a table scooping the last lobster morsels from her bowl of bisque when Ben arrived.

"Should have been here a few minutes ago," she greeted him. "While I was waiting for you, I reread the outline of the speech you sent over. I choked up just skimming it."

"Hey, look, it'll be okay. I promise." He waved to a server and without looking at the menu ordered a hamburger and fries. Ben turned his attention back to Carmie.

"On my way over I thought of how we can handle this. After lunch we'll go somewhere and you can read the speech out loud to me, over and over. So many times your problem will be getting too bored with it, not too emotional. You're good at this, Carmie. I know you. Rehearsal does wonders."

"Maybe so," she said. "But then there's this other problem. I'm in an arena with twenty thousand people. I'm supposed to project my voice so they react and scream their straw hats off, right?"

"Right."

"But I'm also on television with maybe twenty million people watching me. For them I'm going to sound like a raving maniac if I'm shouting to stir up the twenty thousand in the arena. What do I do about that?"

Delivery of Carmie's tuna sandwich interrupted their conversation. Ben's day already overflowed with scheduling conflicts. But Carmie's speech would be one of the prime- time highlights of the show he was about to produce. He needed her to perform with confidence and feeling.

"You know, here's what we'll do," said Ben. Let's take an hour after lunch, go over to the arena, and we'll do the run-through right on the stage. The sound system's set up. I'll make sure there's a camera and monitor. No one else will be there except technicians and carpenters. If you cry or do anything embarrassing, I'll be the only one to know. We'll rehearse until you feel confident."

"I can't spare an hour. I can't even take time to finish my sandwich."

"So would you rather do it for the first time when the red lights are on and your audience reaches from New York to LA?"

"I'd rather not do it at all."

"Not an option."

Carmie took another bite of her sandwich and drained the remaining coffee from her cup.

"Okay. Look. Petra Galen, my chief of staff, is waiting for me in the lobby. While you're finishing your lunch, I'll run up to the room, freshen up a bit, grab my speech, and then we'll go over to the convention center."

Carmie rushed off just as Ben's hamburger arrived. He devoured it hungrily and rapidly, paid the check, and walked to the lobby, expecting to find Carmie waiting for him. Instead Petra was alone, pacing.

"Call her cell, will you, Petra," said Ben. "She's probably changing her whole wardrobe."

"No answer," said Petra. "That's strange. Didn't go right into voice mail like it does when she's talking with someone else."

"Try again."

Petra did. Twice more. "I'd better go up," she said.

"I'll wait here just in case she passes you in the elevator."

Ben remained in the lobby, scanning email on his cell phone.

He dialed his partner, Lee.

"Lee. I need to postpone that two o'clock. Going with Carmie to the...."

Ben was distracted in midsentence by three hotel security men racing for the elevators and the stairs, ordering people already in the elevators to get out. Two EMTs wheeling a gurney rushed through the hotel's doors to an elevator being held open by a guard. Ben watched the elevator indicator light stop on the twenty-sixth floor—the floor where both he and Carmie had rooms. His cell phone began buzzing.

"Gotta go," Ben said to Lee and abruptly ended the call.

He picked up the incoming call. Petra.

"It's Carmie," said Petra. "Something's happened to her. Can't talk."

A third elevator door opened in the lobby. Ben rushed for it.

"Out," called a security guard. "Emergency." "I know," said Ben. "My friend."

"Out," the guard repeated.

Not heeding the guard, Ben punched the button for the twenty-sixth floor and the doors closed to launch a ride that seemed to last an eternity. Finally, the twenty-sixth floor and into hallway bedlam. EMTs. Hotel security. Housekeeping staff.

"What is it?" yelled Ben.

"I don't know," said a frantic Petra. "I knocked and knocked. Didn't get an answer. I got one of the maids to let me in and she was on the floor, facedown, looking terrible. I called 911 right away. Then the desk. Then you."

EMTs hovered over Carmie. An oxygen mask covered her

face. A bottle of fluid was being fed intravenously into one of her arms. Carmie's skin was a ghastly montage of pink and red. Her eyes were tightly closed. She clearly was unconscious. Working quickly, the emergency crew lifted her onto the gurney and rolled her to a waiting elevator. The doors closed. She was gone.

A hotel security woman approached Petra. "You found her?"

"Yes," said Petra. "We were waiting for her in the lobby and became concerned when she didn't come down to meet us. She's the secretary of commerce, here for the convention. How is she?"

"I don't know," said the security woman. "I'm not a medical person. When the EMT people got here, they took her signs and called them into the ER; then they tore open that box and started an intravenous injection."

"What do they think happened to her?"

The security woman walked into the room and picked up the box.

"It says this is for treatment of cyanide poisoning."

26

"Tell me again, as far as you can remember, what she ate," asked FBI agent Durazzo.

"I think it was the lobster bisque," said Ben.

"Did you eat any of it?"

"No. She offered me a taste. But to tell you the truth, I don't drink milk or eat milky things. My digestive system punishes me if I do."

"How about drinks? What did she order?"

Ben thought for a moment. Coffee? Was it coffee? Tea? None of this was real. None of it made any sense. This wasn't a discussion about food. It was an investigation of an attempted murder. Commerce Secretary Carmen Sanchez lay unconscious in an intensive care room at the Cleveland Clinic, watched over by a team of doctors and Secret Service and FBI agents.

She had been stricken four hours earlier. Four blurred hours earlier. Four hours of waiting in the hospital ward lobby for answers. Is she still alive? Will she recover? Any brain damage? Was it really poison? How could it be poison? Why would anyone poison Carmie? Ben's phone calls with the president and the convention team. The insistent media questions, media that flooded the hospital lobby and grounds monitoring, it seemed, Carmie's every breath.

Cyanide doesn't get consumed at a first-class hotel restaurant by accident. Somehow, it found a path into Carmie's body. Once in the body, cyanide attacks quickly. She might have ingested it in her hotel room. More likely it was at lunch. A lunch where the only other person at the table was Ben.

"Water. Did she drink much water?" pressed Agent Durazzo.

Ben searched his memory. His mind was full of detail. Press releases. The order of speakers at the convention. Too many details, not enough time, and now, all of it seeming so frivolous compared with the question of how much water Carmie drank at lunch.

"I can't say for sure. We were both in such a powerful hurry. She got there before I did. She might have eaten some bread with her soup. I drank the water; maybe she did, too. Coffee. I think coffee's what she ordered."

"You said bread? Bread and butter?"

"Bread. I don't know. Bread's my weakness. I know I had a few pieces."

"Did she salt and pepper her soup?"

"I wasn't there when it was served. I came late. She mentioned how much she liked it."

"And she had a tuna salad sandwich."

"Yes, but she only finished half. I ate the rest after she left the table."

"What else did you eat?"

"Hamburger. French fries. Oh, it came with a pickle. I ate that."

Agent Durazzo looked at the white pad in front of him and made a notation. Not that it was needed. He already had told Ben that his statement would be recorded. Ben assumed that others somewhere were watching through a camera he couldn't detect.

Durazzo put down his pen, leaned back in his chair, and looked at Ben wordlessly for a few seconds. He wasn't smiling. FBI agents seldom show emotion when they're on the job.

"Mr. Sage, we know of your long relationship with the president and why you're here in Cleveland. We won't keep you longer than necessary."

"I appreciate that. It's an extraordinarily busy time. But if there's anything I can do to help figure out what happened, I want to do it."

"You were the only person with her just before she collapsed, and so your recollection of the details is important to us. For example, her state of mind."

"Frantic," said Ben. "Just frantic with an impossible schedule."

"You were observed arguing with her. Was she agitated?"

"Yes. That was the whole reason for the lunch. She was feeling really uncomfortable about having to make a speech in front of millions of people. She asked if it was necessary."

"And what did you tell her?"

"I told her it was. And I offered to go with her to the arena right after lunch to rehearse it with her. She wanted to go to her room first."

"For what reason?"

"She said to freshen up. I suppose she also wanted to use the toilet and put on lipstick or makeup or change clothes or anything else people do when they know they're about to have their pictures taken, even if it's just practice."

"When she left you, did she seem ill? Any signs of distress?"

"Sorry, I wasn't even thinking in those terms. If she felt sick, she didn't say. Maybe that's why she wanted to go to her room. My mind was on so many other things."

Ben mentally scolded himself for not being more aware, more observant. These were all legitimate questions, and he felt he was letting Carmie down by not having answers.

Agent Durazzo silently checked his notepad again, an extended silence, a silence whose every second increased Ben's level of anxiety.

Finally, Durazzo looked up. "I know how busy you are," he said. "I have no other questions for you now, but we're likely to want to interview you again once other members of our investigating team arrive from Washington."

"Maybe when I'm not quite as rattled by this I can fill in a few of the blanks," said Ben.

Durazzo stood up.

"Certainly. We've got your contact numbers. Here's my card. If anything comes to mind, no matter how small a detail, call me."

Ben felt Agent Durazzo's eyes on his back as he walked the long corridor from the FBI interrogation room to the front door. The interview had not been hostile; the questions were reasonable given the situation. Nevertheless, there were unaccustomed sweat stains on Ben's shirt. Never in his life had he been at odds with the law, save for a few red traffic lights ignored or unnoticed. Ben left the building mildly nauseous and struggling to restore mental balance.

Lee Searer was waiting for Ben in his rental car outside the FBI offices.

"How'd it go?"

"Okay. Lots of questions."

"Any suspects, other than you?"

It took a moment for Lee's comment to register.

"Me? You think they suspect me of poisoning Carmie?"

"Certainly. You're on the short list. The cyanide was likely dissolved into her food or drink, and you ate and drank with her."

"That's nuts. Carmie's one of my closest friends. What possible reason would I have?"

"Just saying. The public poisoning of the president's closest friend and an important cabinet member isn't something the FBI can leave unsolved. They need a suspect, a person of interest. If that hadn't occurred to when you went in, they likely had you off guard while you were there. Think hard about what you told them."

Ben was stunned. His mind raced back to the interview. Durazzo had raised the question of an argument between Ben and Carmie. Ben had admitted there was one. He had opportunity.

Suddenly, his own situation vaulted to the top of his long checklist.

27

Gerry Lincoln abruptly stopped scrolling through her computer screens. Her brown eyes opened wide as one of the production set's cameras slowly zoomed in to exaggerate her display of amazement.

"Oh my God! Oh my God!"

"What's wrong?" asked Lyle Lincoln. A second camera locked in on her father, a newspaper spread next to his plate of bacon and eggs, open to the sports section.

A third camera revealed a wide-angle shot of a routine Lincoln family morning. Coffee, toast, scrambled eggs, and Cathy, Lyle's TV wife, with her morning yogurt.

"Tenny's got a secret lover!" said Gerry.

Cathy looked amused. "You're not on the *National Enquirer*

site, are you?"

"Mom!"

"Well, what are you reading?"

"I'm reading the news that Sandy sent me."

"Really?" said Lyle. "And who is this 'lover'? What's his name?"

"Not him, Dad, her. It's a woman."

Lyle and Cathy exchanged glances.

"The president's a lesbian?"

"Dad, that's the first thing you think about, isn't it? Lesbian. I think this is really romantic."

"Lesbian. That's the proper way to talk about two women lovers," said Lyle. "Even lesbians call themselves lesbians."

"Well, I know you don't approve, but I don't see anything wrong with it. Anyway, it looks like this has been going on for a long time. It's a woman by the name of Carmen Sanchez, and it says she's the secretary of commerce."

Lyle closed his paper as the camera slowly zoomed in on his look of surprise.

"You mean you've got a story there that says the president and this Sanchez woman have been sex partners?"

Cathy interrupted, turning to Lyle. "Do you think we should be discussing this now? Here?"

"Oh, Mom," said Gerry. "I know about sex."

"Even so...." said Cathy, her voice trailing.

"Let me see your story," said Lyle.

Gerry got up, walked over to her father, and handed him her electronic tablet, with a close-up of the Microsoft Surface label.

Lyle scanned the screen, then, aloud, read from it with faux romantic inflections.

"Carmie, it's so lonely here without you. I long for the nights we would be together. Oh, Carmie, I often think about our trip together to Capri. The blue water and sky, how we laughed and enjoyed the freedom of being together."

The camera cut to Cathy Lincoln, listening intently. "Well, I can see best friends talking to each other that way."

"Gerry and Sandy might," said Lyle. "That's girly talk."

"We don't talk that way. That's stupid. I don't know anybody who talks like that."

"See," said Lyle. "They're lesbos. Disgusting."

"Daddy!" Gerry exclaimed. "That's awful. I'm going to get ready for school."

Lyle continued to scan the screen.

"Wasn't it that Carmen Sanchez who was poisoned the other day?" asked Cathy.

"Sure was," said Lyle. "I've never paid much attention to her, but it says here they grew up together in Los Angeles."

"Tenny and Sanchez?"

"Yes. They've been lifelong friends."

"That doesn't mean they've been lovers."

"No. But this does."

Lyle again read aloud in a pseudo-romantic voice.

"I'm so tired of being in this hospital bed. When you visited, I almost asked you to curl up here beside me, but.... what would people say?"

Cathy listened with what appeared mild embarrassment bordering on distress.

"What are you reading from?"

"It says here that these come from a private email server. You know, like the one Clinton had. Someone hacked into it."

"Well, the poor woman, her injuries from that explosion were so bad. I can understand."

"Okay, then understand this. An email from Sanchez back to our president: *Never forget that I love you, dear Tenny. And I always will.*"

Cathy got up from the table to remove the breakfast dishes.

"It's the times we live in. Women with women. Men with men. I guess we need to get used to it."

"This isn't just women with women, Cathy. This is the president of the United States in a lesbian affair with her secretary of commerce. How would you feel if it was two men? In fact, the president having a love affair with anyone in her cabinet, man or woman, is just not right or normal."

Cathy continued the breakfast cleanup.

"If it hadn't been for the fact that the Sanchez woman was poisoned, I doubt any of this would have come out."

In that, Cathy was right. Until she was poisoned, Carmen Sanchez was a low-key figure in an administration otherwise populated by economic, political, and foreign policy stars. The poisoning had landed Carmie at the top of news cycles for days.

And now this.

Beneath the last few scenes of the exchange between Cathy and Lyle Lincoln, an on-screen message appeared:

To read the actual emails, visit letters.TheLincolnTVFamily.com.

And when you clicked on that link, there they were. Email exchanges between Carmie and Tenny, some going back to the start of Tenny's White House administration, carefully selected and edited to reinforce the idea that there was a romantic relationship between them.

No other media had the letters, but once they showed up on *The Lincoln Family*, reporters wasted no time following the scent. Within minutes, phones were ringing in the White House, in Carmie's Washington office, in the Cleveland hospital, and in Los Angeles, where reporters searched for those who knew Tenny and Carmie during their school years together. The email exchanges between Tenny and Carmie would have been news whenever *The Lincoln Family* posted them on the website. Coming just days after Carmie's poisoning, the emails were a feast for thousands of story-hungry reporters assembled for what until then had been a routine Democratic Party convention in Cleveland. Few journalists remarked on the perfection of the timing, linking the poisoning, and the emails. Was it coincidence? Or exquisite planning by Tenny's political enemies? Few cared.

28

Ben's political life had been spent behind the cameras, not in front of them. He saw no value in promoting himself to the world. His candidates were the stars. Calling attention to how the sausage of their campaigns was made only undercut the images he was hired to create.

But now it seemed that every camera in Cleveland was aimed at him. Ben Sage. They were waiting, right next to the elevator, bright lights and mics as soon as the doors opened.

"Have you slept with the president?"

"How long have you two been lovers?"

"What about Sanchez? Are you rivals?"

"Do you confirm it's your diary?"

What diary? His private diary? No one, not even Lee, his best friend and business partner, knew about the diary. It was his secret bond with Almie. It was where they remained close to one another, even years after the ghastly car wreck that took her away. He lived not just for himself but for the life they no longer physically shared. With the diary he continued to feel her touch, delight in the natural perfume of her body, share his every thought with her. Almie carried his heart to her grave. He would carry hers to his. How did this pack of journalists know about his diary?

CNN's live camera showed him at first startled at the questions, then quizzical, then horrified. His words a jumble of "What?" "I don't understand." "I'm sorry." Then a quick exit out the hotel's front doors to the safety of Lee's waiting car. The cameras followed him, Ben's head ducked to his chin, reminiscent of so many scenes of the accused hurrying with their lawyers toward courthouse steps.

"What the hell's going on?" babbled Ben.

"I didn't know myself until I turned on the car radio coming over here. I tried calling to warn you."

"My phone was off."

"Unfortunate," said Lee. "I would've picked you up out back if we'd connected."

"Why didn't you come to the room?"

"I didn't want to pass you in the elevators and leave you stranded."

Ben folded back into the passenger seat, processing the last few minutes.

"They got my diary?"

"Story broke just a little while ago."

"My diary was locked in a bottom desk drawer at the beach house."

"Somebody found it. Your place isn't very hard to break into."

"What else did they take?"

"I don't know. These reporters don't care if somebody took your TV set. That's not part of the story."

"And they think what I wrote in my diary was about Tenny?" Ben was incredulous at the prospect.

"Someone leaked some things from your diary to Drudge. Things that make it sound like you were writing to Tenny. That's the way Drudge played it. Headline: 'Love Triangle Linked to

Poisoning.' You were jealous of Carmie."

"Jesus Christ, Lee. We've been had. Set up. It's insanely brilliant. One stroke gets Carmie and us out of the picture, Tenny looking like an equal opportunity whore, and all of it while ten thousand reporters are collected in this beehive for maximum impact."

"It's a trap."

"Of course. None of us have convincing answers to this. I can't say I wrote to a dead wife. They'd think I was nuts, and I'd lose all political credibility. Tenny and Carmie do love each other, the way lifelong friends do. Father Bob's right. Getting past impeachment didn't end the conspiracy. It just made them smarter. Where are we going?"

"Can't go to the convention center," said Lee. "They'll be waiting for you there. I've got a friend with an apartment just out of town. He offered his spare room. I'll arrange to get your bags and stuff delivered over to you."

"I can't hide forever, and we can't cancel the convention. You know how much work we have to do."

"I do. And I know we've got a lot of people on board to help do it. You haven't any good options right now. Do you know what to say to the press?"

"Not a clue."

"So, take your own advice. In spots like this we tell our clients if you don't know what to say, don't say anything until you figure it out. We need some time to figure it out."

"So I hide like I'm guilty?"

"I'll let Durazzo know where you are so the FBI doesn't think you're hiding from them."

"Tenny will think this is a disaster. Have you talked to the White House?"

"No. You should."

Ben pushed the speed-dial number for Henry Deacon, Tenny's chief of staff.

"Deacon? Ben. She's heard?"

"Oh yeah, she's heard. And she's wild that you didn't warn her first."

"I didn't know. They just blindsided me this morning."

"What did you say to the media?"

"Nothing. I just ran out like my hair was on fire. Watch CNN. It's not pretty. I did everything I tell my candidates not to do. Look, I'm with Lee. We're talking about how to handle this. I'm avoiding the media until we know more."

"Fine. What's your suggestion on our end?"

"Treat it lightly, not seriously. Just have our press people smile like it's a joke and wave off questions. We'll think of something and get back to you."

"Think fast. She shows up in Cleveland at ten tomorrow morning. And Ben, a bit of advice."

"What?"

"Don't be alone with her in your new hideaway. People might talk."

29

Air Force One landed at Cleveland's Hopkins International Airport reasonably close to schedule. No arrival ceremony had been arranged. Tenny had no interest in attracting media. Not today. Reporters traveling with her on Air Force One were held on the plane until she disappeared into her waiting limousine. No others were allowed close to her on the tarmac.

But her destination was no secret. Reporters and TV trucks had set up camp at the Cleveland Clinic shortly after Carmie arrived at the emergency entrance and had been there since. The media's vigil now was rewarded. Platoons of state and local police arrived, along with a reinforced Secret Service detail. The hospital grounds immediately turned into a cone of tight security. Editorial desks were alerted. Cable news cameras went live. By the time the presidential caravan wheeled into the main entrance driveway, police barricades and White House staff could barely contain the media scrum. Tenny ignored it all. Her rush to Carmie's hospital room was delayed only by a detour to the hospital administrator's office, where Dr. Brenda Ballard and two other members of her medical team were waiting. As anxious as Tenny was to see Carmie, she was grateful for the chance to sit for a moment. It helped mask the weakness she felt in her own body, the anxiety that had absorbed her for every waking moment since she'd heard the news.

"She's recovering," Dr. Ballard assured Tenny. "We've confirmed that she ingested potassium cyanide. Fortunately, the emergency crew arrived quickly enough to administer the antidote, and that quick action should mitigate any long-term complications."

"Thank you, Doctor, for all you and everyone here is doing for her," said Tenny. "Do you have any idea how the cyanide got into her body?"

"Not yet," said Dr. Ballard. "We're hoping micropathology can tell us. It was either in liquid form, something she drank, or in a powder. Apparently an amount large enough to disable her but not enough to cause complete oxygen deprivation."

"And you're confident there won't be long-term damage?"

"As confident as we can be. Cyanide molecules are tiny, allowing them to spread through the body very rapidly and cut off oxygen to the heart, lungs, and other organs. In sufficient dose, the heart stops, or the patient quickly suffocates. It's very dangerous. When our emergency response team arrived at the hotel and reported that Ms. Sanchez's face had discolored to pink and red, that was a clear indication of oxygen obstruction. It's very unusual that we see a case like this. When we see cyanide poisoning, it's usually the result of an encounter with fire and smoke. We couldn't be certain what had caused the distress, but because cyanide is so fast acting, we instructed them to administer hydroxocobalamin, which dilutes the poison's effects. That had immediate palliative results. When she arrived in our emergency room, she was still in a mild coma and her heart rate and blood pressure were elevated, but she was breathing and stabilized."

"And now?"

"Oh, now she's awake, fairly alert, and regaining her strength after such a shock to her system."

"I can't thank all of you enough," said Tenny. "Now, I would like to see her."

"Of course," said Dr. Ballard. "She knows you're here."

Surrounded by her Secret Service escort and hospital personnel, Tenny navigated the hospital's corridors to Carmie's room. She waved away everyone and entered alone. Carmie, her hair carefully brushed, fresh lipstick applied, was sitting up, smiling.

"You didn't have to come, you know," Carmie greeted her. "I know you care. I know you probably called the hospital every five minutes to make sure they babied me. They have!"

Without a word, Tenny walked to the side of her lifelong friend and instinctively reached down with both hands and kissed her on the lips.

"If you had died, I would have died inside," said Tenny. "I know what the doctors tell me, but how are you? Really?"

"A little weak. Getting stronger. All the effects should be gone by the time I speak for you at the convention."

"Don't be ridiculous. I won't hear of it. Get well enough to leave the hospital and go home. Politics isn't worth it."

"Politics isn't, but you are. Unless what happened was just a fluky accident, the people who want you out aren't just playing politics. This isn't how normal politics works. Whatever they want, we can't let them have it. You know that, or you wouldn't even be running."

Tenny seated herself on the bed, brushed a few stray hairs from Carmie's face, and looked closely into her friend's eyes, searching for confirmation of recovery. Carmie took Tenny's hand and held it.

"Ironic, isn't it?" Carmie said. "A few months ago, after they tried to kill you, you were in a hospital bed and I was on the outside, sick with worry."

"Life's all we have, Carmie. Yours and mine. I don't want to lose, either."

"Give me a hug."

Tears, long delayed, now found outlets. Once flowing, the well proved deep.

Tenny finally eased away. Still grasping Carmie's hand.

"When I first heard about this, I almost fainted, Carmie. I'd never had a feeling quite like it. It was a sudden rush of cold. A loss of vision. A loss of balance. I was in my office, alone with Deacon, who gave me the news. Thank God he was there when my knees turned to rubber. He held me up until I could catch my balance and my breath. All I've wanted to do since then is be here and watch over you."

Tears continued to stream down Carmie's cheeks. Tenny dabbed at them with a tissue.

"*Las hermanas*, remember," said Carmie. "*Las hermanas.*"

"Not just *las hermanas*, but *salvages!*" exclaimed Tenny, straightening up and gathering herself.

"Sisters, and wild ones, that's us," chimed in Carmie. "We fight together, lady. We always have."

"Oh, Carmie." With both hands, the president of the United States cupped Carmie's shoulders.

"Those awful stories about us the last few days. They're right. I do love you."

30

Dr. Ballard was waiting for Tenny in the corridor outside Carmie's room along with three Secret Service agents and two nurses assigned to the ward.

"She looks better than I hoped to find her. Thank you again for all you and your staff have done for her," said Tenny.

"We have excellent medical staff here," said Dr. Ballard. "It's fortunate the dose of poison she consumed wasn't higher and that we had an emergency team so close by. Minutes matter in poisoning situations. Is there anything else we can do for you?"

Tenny hesitated for a moment, stopping just steps away from the elevator that would return her to the ground floor and her presidential limousine.

Dr. Ballard looked at her quizzically, wondering if she had said something to disturb the president.

After a brief silence, Tenny said, "Yes, yes there is something I'd like to discuss with you, privately. Is your office nearby?"

"On this floor," said Dr. Ballard.

"Please take me there and let's talk for a moment," said Tenny.

Reaching Dr. Ballard's office, Tenny motioned for her security team to remain in the corridor. Inside, Tenny immediately found a chair and collapsed into it.

"Is something wrong, Madam President? Should I call for assistance?"

"No. Please don't. And I must trust you to keep what I'm

about to tell you in complete confidence. Can you promise me that?"

"Of course."

"The attempt on my life, that explosion at the hotel, left me with acute respiratory syndrome. For the most part the symptoms are manageable. But the attack on Secretary Sanchez and anxiety about the convention apparently triggered something. I'm finding it harder to breathe, and I feel weaker than usual. Can you provide me with some oxygen in a way no one else will notice?"

"Should I call your personal physician?"

"No. She's waiting in the motorcade out front, and if she left the car and came into the hospital, a hundred reporters would write stories about it. That's why I'm talking to you now. It wouldn't be unusual for us to consult in private about my friend's medical condition. No one would suspect I was having any kind of treatment."

"May I draw some blood to take your oxygen level, Madam President? I can have it analyzed in ten minutes."

"No. Too risky. The lab would need a patient name, or someone there would figure out who it was for. Just stick that oximeter on my finger."

"You know the procedure, apparently."

"I live with it nearly every day," said Tenny.

Dr. Ballard reached into her nearby medical kit and attached a device much like a clothespin onto one of Tenny's fingers. The reading appeared in seconds.

"Sixty-two," she said. "Yes. That's low. Do we have a half hour?"

"Twenty minutes tops before the outside world begins to ask questions about what I'm doing here."

Twenty minutes later, the president of the United States returned to her motorcade with a sprightlier step than when she left it and, and, with a packet of medication in her jacket pocket.

31

"Carmona! All this rain. Heat I expected. I heard Mexico City was like a desert. Desert? It's like a flood out there."

"I find it refreshing," said Javier Carmona. "July is our month for rain. If you were here after many days of sunshine, I'm sure you would find our smoky air more disagreeable."

Carmona could be relaxed, meeting with Tahir Badem in Mexico City. Today they were on Carmona's turf, under the watchful eye of his security team, not in Istanbul or Cairo or other places where they had met, places Carmona feared. Also, this was an actual business meeting, an agricultural arrangement between two large agribusiness behemoths. The purpose was profit, not political conspiracy. Firmer ground for Carmona, much easier to understand and control. So, with little concern for his own safety, he welcomed Tahir to the boardroom of Groupo Aragon. Their staffs would soon join them. Tahir had asked to come early, for some private time with Carmona.

"Quite a palace you have here," said Badem, seating himself at the room's conference table, a table artisans fashioned from rare Bolivian rosewood.

"It's Miguel Aragon," said Carmona. "This room was his

special project. All the marble, the silver serving pitchers, the paintings. He made it a museum."

"Intimidating for those who come to negotiate," said Badem.

"Yes. That was the idea. Are you intimidated?"

Badem laughed. "Sorry, I mean no disrespect. But we already have our deal, and you, I must say, did very well. Groupo Aragon will profit handsomely."

"I have no complaints. I hope that when our staffs work out all the details, things will continue to go as smoothly."

"Yes," said Badem. "I'm certain they will. But before they arrive, there's something I want to discuss with you. You've been following the election in the United States, I presume."

"Of course."

"Then you have been reading the shocking news about the president's sex life, perhaps with both her secretary of commerce and her political assistant."

"I have."

"Speaking for myself and other mutual friends, I want to convey our appreciation for the valuable information that has now become public."

Carmona hesitated. Was he being secretly recorded? Would admitting his role in delivering images of the incriminating diary someday be used against him? Would it become a form of blackmail?

Carmona nodded acceptance, without speaking.

"Oh, Carmona, don't worry," said Badem. "Unless you are taping the conversation, it is just you and me. We thank you, but we also want you to recognize how cleverly your material was used. We want you to have confidence that our organization is quite creative and professional. You are a valuable member of our team. We all want you to know that. And your value will increase as we deploy other information from your files."

The words would have been more welcome and assuring if Carmona had not been frightened out of his mind by the "team's" assassin and the chilling way they made his security chief Soto disappear from the earth without a trace. Now they had managed to poison the president's best friend, secure the president's private email correspondence, release pages from her aide's diary, and turn all of it into a media sensation, apparently without anyone suspecting how it all was arranged. Yes. These people were true professionals. Professionals at news manipulation, wiretapping, burglary, blackmail, and murder. Badem expected Carmona to be comforted by knowing all of that? On the contrary, Badem's words only resurfaced his now near permanent state of personal terror.

32

The man in a six-foot-tall ostrich suit walked in circles to attract attention. Now and then he stuck his head into a mound of sand, strategically placed in front of a sign reading, "You can't hide from the debt. Fix it!" Nearby, a bearded, white-robed man shouldered a "vote for Jesus" cross. Another carried a sign that simply read, "I'm afraid." Street musicians and jugglers. Pop-up T-shirt malls selling whatever candidate and message that prompted you to be a walking advertisement. For anyone with a candidate or a product to sell, this was the place, the pathways around Cleveland's convention center, where the intensity of noise and action grew as one moved closer to the crowded and tightly secured entrance gates. National political conventions create their own ecosystem.

Inside the convention center, a different type of political theater. The platform committee's work was completed. Had Carmie been there to guide things, more concessions could have been made, more tender egos soothed, more historical memory applied to negotiations. Without her, Tenny's committee members spiraled into an adversarial relationship with those representing Kevin Egert. More than 20 percent of the convention delegates were pledged to Egert, far fewer than he needed to mount a credible challenge for the Democratic nomination but enough to have a robust presence. Egert was a tech billionaire, imbued with that culture's libertarian values, at odds with Tenny's vision for a more active role for government, particularly in reining in the power of corporate and individual wealth. Egert's acolytes on the platform committee had battled Tenny's fiercely. The wounds from that fight would reopen in full view of millions as the convention moved to its close. In a dramatic attention-getting spectacle, dozens of Egert supporters marched into the closing ceremony together, their mouths taped shut, symbolic of being muted by Tenny's convention managers.

A night earlier, it was Vice President Sheila Fishburne's moment in the national spotlight. A popular choice. Irreverent, quick witted, intensely likable. Her background as the granddaughter of an Inupiaq whaling captain added an exotic dash to her solid résumé of experience in the US House. For the first time, a major national political party would have two women leading their presidential ticket, one the product of an American native culture, the other, a woman whose family's roots could be traced to the first Spaniard colonists. Historically, both lineages could claim to be the first Americans.

When Tenny spoke to this convention four years earlier, she was the gift everyone coveted for Christmas, the head-turning window display that made the purchase irresistible. Her name was Tenny, but that hardly described the object of energy that paced the stage, her words a whitewater rapids rush transforming you from observer to willing co-adventurer on whatever course she steered. Suddenly, you were there, part of it, wind in your face, your body a frenzy of sweat and hot blood, on a journey to somewhere you had never been. From her first days in politics, campaigning for a congressional seat in Los Angeles, Tenny had a gift for converting a speech into an indelible memory. She was her own reality show— unscripted, unpredictable, passionate.

Now, despite significant legislative success during her nearly four years in the White House and all the ancillary drama connected with it, the thrill of the new had given way to a general fatigue. No matter how exciting a high-wire act could be, four years of it was draining. Occasional slips spoiled invincibility. Familiarity dulled expectation. Oh, she's actually human? Not a goddess? How disappointing.

Tenny was well aware that even in the eyes of her most avid supporters, she had returned to earth. Where the sight of her once automatically ignited sparks, now she had to work harder to generate heat. She heard it in the diminished hum of excitement when she entered a room. Her success in business and in politics had flowed from a fine-tuned sensitivity to such signals. Most everywhere she went now, she detected static on the circuit that connected her with others. Public opinion polls confirmed that she could never recover the magic of her first presidential campaign and her early White House years.

But magic would not be a factor in her campaign this year. This would be a reality-based campaign, not one woven on impossible dreams. She felt she could win on such turf by being more open than ever, more emotionally honest than ever. Tonight likely would be her best opportunity of the entire campaign to reengage trust, if not high expectations. The terrible events of the past few days created an environment where authenticity would be required. She intended to deliver it.

Before Tenny would take the stage, those in the arena, and tens of millions watching on TV, would hear from Carmie. Having her make the introduction was Ben's idea, and she quickly agreed. The exchange of emails between Carmie and Tenny had become one of the defining stories to emerge from this convention. Were they lesbian lovers? Was there a Carmie-Ben-Tenny love triangle? Was Tenny bisexual? Promiscuous? The opposition saw Tenny's morality as a heavy anchor. Polls suggested it was, indeed, threatening to drag her down.

That's why, Ben argued, tonight's spotlight, the brightest light they would have for the entire campaign, had to be directed toward healing Tenny's character wounds. That could best be done by Carmie and Tenny together, telling the story of their lifetime of friendship. Carmie had been scheduled to speak two nights earlier. That was before the poisoning. Now she would speak on the convention's closing night, the night with the maximum viewing audience and just twenty-four hours after being discharged from the hospital. Ben scrapped the speech he had written for her, the speech she feared would be too emotional for her to deliver. Instead, he encouraged Carmie to speak from an outline, not a written speech, not from someone's else's talking points but from her heart, and to be as emotional as she felt. Ben, like Tenny, knew that tonight demanded emotional honesty. Don't hold back, Ben counseled Carmie.

She didn't.

The poisoning and the seemingly romantic email exchanges

with Tenny made Carmie's moment the most anticipated of the four-day convention. Carmie needed an escort and a cane to help her reach center stage. Though still a shade pale, she compensated for her visible body weakness by entering with confidence. Her light-brown Latin skin was a striking offset to the high-necked ruffled lavender blouse she wore under a plum-colored linen suit. The cheers and applause were enthusiastic and prolonged. She gripped the podium hard, praying to herself that her strength would not drain before her time in the spotlight was over.

When she was able to make herself heard as the cheers and applause faded, Carmie lifted the microphone from its stand and moved to a straight-backed cushioned chair that had been placed next to the podium.

"Thank you, thank you all," she said. "I hope you don't mind if I speak while sitting down. I've had an unusually trying few days."

(more cheers and applause)

"And I hope you don't mind if I begin by telling you a story. A story that starts with the meeting of two ten-year- old girls. One of them fresh off the airplane from Mexico City, where she had lived her early years. The other, born and raised in Los Angeles, and sharing a Mexican heritage. That girl would be me."

(cheers and applause)

"Take this new girl under your wing, I'm told. Help her with the language. Help her understand the world of girls your age, I was told. That girl who became my project, as you may also have guessed by now, was named Isabel. We all know her as 'Tenny.'"

(extended cheers and applause)

"You know her as Tenny because I gave her that name. I was

afraid that the girls at our school would tease her if we introduced her as Isabel. After all, we couldn't call her Izzy."

(extended laughter)

For the next twenty minutes, Carmie described their school years together, their boyfriends, mutual adventures, their support for one another as life raised hurdles and presented opportunities. With the audience clearly enthralled by her story, Carmie turned to what had become known as the "love mails."

"I've been asked many times about the letters and emails that we've exchanged. They seem to prove that Tenny and I have a relationship. That we love one another. Yes, we do love one another—we love as family loves, as lifetime friends love, as those who have shared life's joys and survived life's tragedies together love. In school they would call us *las hermanas*, the sisters. I am so proud of my sister. She is so wise, so good, so accomplished, so decent, and so great a president for this country of ours."

(prolonged applause)

She said no more about the emails. She didn't have to. Her description of the lives she and Tenny had shared required no more explanation.

Carmie rose from her chair.

"Please, join me in standing for the president of the United States, our party's nominee, and my loving sister, Isabel Tennyson. Tenny!"

As one, the twenty thousand delegates and guests in the arena stood and cheered. Tenny, dressed in colors that closely matched Carmie's, walked onto the stage, waving and blowing two-handed kisses to the crowd. When she reached Carmie, they embraced and held one another. Lip readers could clearly see Tenny saying, "I love you."

Tenny walked to the microphone and shouted the words that her lips had just formed in private. "Carmie, I love you!"

The weariness Tenny felt from events of past months dissolved, giving way to renewed enthusiasm for the reform agenda that had long enflamed her passions. She read her acceptance speech with the zeal of a religious convert, turning the huge convention hall into a temple of belief. The spirit of missionary zeal consumed the delegates, swept through the rows of spectators, and, for the moment, even brought amens from much of the media.

The sex and love triangle was still out there, open to exploitation. The mystery of Carmie's poisoning was unsolved, promising more drama ahead. But for now, the Tennyson team was happy to get out of town, having survived a week in political hell, newly energized for the combat ahead.

33

Air Force One had been airborne for two hours. Breakfast had been served to those in the media pool who roused themselves for the 6:00 a.m. departure from Cleveland. The destination: Sea-Tac Airport, midway between Seattle and Tacoma, Washington. The day ahead: two campaign rallies, a photo op at the renowned Fred Hutchinson Cancer Research Center, then an evening flight to Anchorage and the campaign's only planned Alaska visit.

Ben hadn't expected to be on this flight. Since the public release of his diary, he had kept his distance from Tenny and from the media, handling things as best he could through staff and other convention intermediaries. With the convention behind him, he planned to take a few days with Lee Searer and others to review and update the campaign plan, adjusting for the new realities. Tenny and Fish would begin their post-convention tour together in the West. Then the campaign would reduce its visibility while media attention turned to the Republican convention in Houston. Ben had plans for disruption there. Weeks earlier, another of his teams, armed with opposition research, checked into Houston hotel rooms and set up workspaces. They would be ready to drop a few surprises on the media pool, forcing Republicans to deal with unexpected developments, just as he had to do in Cleveland. That was his plan.

Then the summons. Tenny wanted him aboard the campaign plane to Seattle in the morning.

"Can't do," said Ben. "Too booked,"

A few minutes letter, a reply obviously dictated by Tenny herself.

"Yes, you can. Be on the plane."

That was unlike Tenny. They had a his-and-hers arrangement. Policy was hers. Politics was his. She rarely questioned Ben's judgment when it came to campaign planning. He made his own schedule. She was the obedient client. That was the arrangement.

Ben spent the overnight hours shutting down convention operations and adjusting his schedule for the next few days. Lee remained in Cleveland to tie up loose ends. Too late to get any serious sleep, Ben headed for the airport. Just as well to board early to avoid the media. He settled into the staff quarters in one of the plane's forward compartments, bolted down a tray of pancakes and bacon, and allowed himself the luxury of reclining his seat, momentarily emptying his mind of the convention past and the campaign ahead.

Ben had traveled on Air Force One before, always marveling at the facilities available while cruising at thirty thousand feet. The onboard telephones, fax machines, and TV sets. The quality and variety of food that emerged from two fully equipped galleys. The president's private suite, with beds, bathroom, shower, a situation room, and an office so spacious a portable treadmill could be rolled in when she had moments to exercise.

Only when Fish, emerging from Tenny's suite, nudged him on the shoulder did Ben realize he had slept through the first two hours of flight.

"You're on," she said.

"On?" He was groggy and disoriented.

"Tenny. She's ready for you, guru."

Ben caught Fish's hand.

"Wait. Here. Sit next to me for a minute."

Fish tasseled Ben's hair and sat down.

"Come on, sleepy guy. Can't keep her waiting."

"What does she want? Why am I here?" asked Ben, finally taking charge of his brain.

"Didn't tell me. You two have a lot of secrets. I don't ask. Now I'm going to pull some media guys' chains. They're as groggy as you are. It'll be fun to catch them off guard. By the way, after how you managed that closing convention bit between Carmie and Tenny, I sort of feel like I should be bowing before you, not just sitting here."

"Just carry Alaska for us, that'll be enough," said Ben.

"You got it. Alaska and our mighty three electoral votes."

She gave Ben a friendly punch on his shoulder and headed aft.

Ben went forward, flushed with Fish's compliments, inwardly agreeing that the decision to have Carmie introduce Tenny the night before, and to allow Carmie to be freewheeling with her words, was one of the best political decisions he had ever made. A decision he was confident would pay off in strong post-convention poll numbers.

Tenny greeted Ben warmly in her office where two staffers were at work, one on the telephone, the other sorting papers. She motioned for Ben to follow her into her private suite, closed the door, and then turned and embraced him with a bear hug unlike any he could remember in all their long years of working together.

"It was a beautiful evening, and I love you for it, Ben," she said. "I love you for so many things, but last night, politics aside, for Carmie and me it was incredibly special."

Taken aback, Ben said, "I love you, too."

Tenny let go of Ben, "I know, I know, and that's good. Remember that after what I'm about to say."

A moment of silence passed as she seated herself behind her desk, a moment when she transformed from emotional and grateful friend to decisive authority, said:

"I want you off the campaign."

He stared at her, disbelieving. "You're firing me?"

"That's not what I said. I want you off the campaign," she repeated, even more firmly. "When we get to Seattle, a ticket will be there for you on the one o'clock Alaska Airlines flight back to Washington. Be on it. And don't contact me again in person, by phone, text, or any other way until after the election."

Ben shook his head. Dreaming? Awake? Disoriented, he dropped into a chair in front of Tenny's desk. Long seconds passed. He could not hold back from saying the first thing that came to mind.

"You think I tried to murder Carmie?"

Tenny smiled. "Don't be ridiculous. You love her as much as I do. I know that."

"Then you must think this ménage à trois crap they've been throwing at us is sticking."

"You know it is. It's too juicy a story not to. It's selling lots of *National Enquirer*s and loading up visits to lots of websites. The Lincolns don't have room for all the ads they're selling. You know all that. But that's going to happen whether you're on the campaign or not."

Ben was seldom at a loss for words. Now he reached to find them, any words that would explain why Tenny wanted him out of her campaign.

"Tenny, I'm the nerve center of your campaign. There's no guarantee you're going to win. Even less if you're breaking in a new team now. Why would you do this?"

"To save your life."

"Save my life!"

"Don't you understand, Ben? Federico was murdered. Carmie was pushed to the edge. Why? Most likely to do just what happened—create a political hole we have to dig out from. You and Carmie are the most important people left in my life. Whoever's after me knows that. You're next. They know where you live. They've already been there. They could come again, and not after your diary but after you. They know how much I depend on you. You're a marked man. I would die if they harmed you to hurt me. I won't risk it. So, go home. Save your life. Take the rest of the year off, and we'll see each other again after the election, win or lose."

Ben had not even considered his own safety. He was focused on the embarrassment of the diary, the explanation for its existence, appalled that his home had been violated by intruders who rifled through his possessions, finding and exposing his most personal thoughts. Not for a moment had he considered that his death or injury might be useful to Tenny's conspiratorial opponents.

"Look," he said. "I'll get bodyguards. I'll install alarm systems. I'll be more careful crossing streets. Firing me is too extreme."

"No, it's not. It makes all the sense in the world."

"Well, who would replace me?"

"Susan Cipriani," she said, without hesitation. "I've spoken with her. She'll do it. And she'll be in Washington when you get there to spend a day with you to get the torch passed."

Susan Cipriani was one of Ben's competitors in the political management world. A tough competitor who Ben greatly respected. In fact, he had enlisted Susan's help in Tenny's first campaign for president.

Ben shook his head. He realized now this was not an emotional, spur-of-the-moment decision. Tenny had been considering this and acting on it for days.

"So the news will be you fired me," he said in resignation.

"No," said Tenny. "The news will be that you're resigning

from the campaign because your presence would be a distraction. I urged you to stay on, but you were too good a friend to do it."

"The media won't buy that."

"I'll sell it as hard as I can. Besides, your reputation's too good for this to hurt you. If I win, I'll make it up to you. If I lose, it will be because I made the mistake of letting you leave the campaign. Either way you'll be okay."

"So, the bad guys are going to win this round."

"By this round you mean that they'll get away with turning our convention into a crime scene?"

Ben nodded.

"Yes," said Tenny. "But I'm doing this so there won't be a next crime. My sanity couldn't survive knowing that I was the instrument of another death in our family."

34

"Ironic, isn't it," said Susan Cipriani. "Four years ago, I was here, right here in your office, pleading with you to talk Tenny into running for president. Now I'm here again, and I'm taking over Tenny's campaign."

Her words hit Ben's gut like well-aimed rubber bullets. Each word more painful than the last.

Susan didn't seem to notice. "I watched all the dirty tricks they pulled on you in Cleveland. Brutal. But I never dreamed it would split you and Tenny."

"Dirty tricks? I wouldn't call attempted murder a dirty trick," said Ben, bitterness accenting his words. "Breaking into my home? Stealing my personal stuff? Dirty tricks?"

Ben liked and respected Susan. They had gone head-to- head in more primary campaigns than he could remember. The campaigns she managed always were tightly disciplined and creative. Four years earlier, Susan had assembled what appeared would be a winning White House campaign for US Senate Democratic leader Reed Guess. Before the first primaries, Guess was diagnosed with an aggressive malignant pituitary tumor and withdrew from the campaign. Guess and Tenny were political allies, and he urged Tenny to pick up his banner. Susan bridged the gap, transferring the organization she had built for Guess to Tenny and then stayed on to help that campaign succeed.

"Look, I know how tough this is on you guys," said Susan. "Don't take all this personally. I didn't lobby her to move you out. I wouldn't do that, and it would have been stupid to even try, not with your history together."

"Sorry, Susan. Didn't mean to suggest that you did. I'm still trying to ditch the disbelief stage. I hate it that I'm leaving the campaign. The fact that she wants you makes it more tolerable. If I sound bitter, I am. But not at you."

"So, then," she said, "let's leave the psychology stuff for beers after Election Day. Clock's ticking. Tell me what I need to know."

"Right," said Ben. "Well, we've always known this would be hard. Too many scars on her. Impeachment ended only in December; we lost a year of organization building."

"I'm glad I didn't inherit that problem."

"We've taken a few shortcuts. First, we can't hope to make up the lost year in just a few months. Not enough time. We've zeroed in on states that could add up to 350 electoral votes and hope like hell we can carry 270 of them, even if we lose the popular vote."

"That's a switch. Democrats usually win the popular vote and scramble for 270."

Ben reached for two manila folders on his desk and handed them to her.

"Here's the list of what we see as sure-thing states and battleground states. And here's the list of target peer groups. Lee explained our peer group strategy to you? The strategy of prioritizing opinion leaders?"

"He did."

"Do you agree with it?"

"I do, and it wouldn't make any difference if I didn't. We're too far down the road to switch. It's your strategy. I'll make it work."

"We've got a coordinating center in Mountain View, California. Major control room for real-time information and response, electronic tally sheets, cross-state peer pressure lines, round-the-clock polling, the works. That's the first stop you need to make. Go there today. Lee's there already. He'll let all our people know you're coming, and why. Transition shouldn't be a problem. We've got regional satellite headquarters in Detroit, Boston, Jacksonville, and Saint Louis. All electronically connected for data and visual coordination. The technology is leading edge, top of the line. Great people installing it and running it. You'll be impressed."

"You're not going to Mountain View?"

"Me? I'm toxic, remember?"

"Hard to wrap my head around. Sorry. How about her travel

schedule?"

"Got an algorithm for that. Dynamic priorities developed by field reports. Except for a few key events, we're scheduling no more than one week ahead. For the last month only twenty-four hours ahead. Total flexibility. But she's still president, and we can't be confident of anything on her schedule. We lose her every time the White House rings the official fire alarm."

"Fish?"

"Fish is great. A ball of energy. Don't burn her out. She'd go 24/7 if we let her. Wherever you need her, send her."

"Media?"

"Up to you. We've got the media plan mapped out. See what you think. Use our media people or yours, or both. You choose. You worked with most of that team four years ago."

"Good. Money?"

"No problem. All covered by separate groups. Lee will fill you in. Let them know how much you need and when, and the money will be there."

"Well, that's different from any other campaign I've been in."

"It helps that she's a billionaire."

"I keep forgetting that. Now, how about Zach Bowman?"

"Big surprise to us. Never expected him to have enough money to go the distance."

"Who's put up that money?"

"Very mysterious. The usual deep pockets backed his competitors. The heaviest hitter he has is Gil Adonis."

"Yeah, I've read that somewhere. It's not like him to be

taking such a gamble."

"Surprises us, too. He's always played it more conventional."

"Well, considering how much Bowman's spending, Adonis must have squeezed his network pretty hard. What's the opposition research show?"

"Can't really say yet. We honestly hadn't focused on Bowman until lately."

"Better hurry up. The Republican convention's just two weeks away, and we can't let him get a big bump from it."

"Our team's in place in Houston, cramming on Bowman's background. We've got some nails ready to throw in the road at the Republican convention. I expect our team to come up with more. Shouldn't be too hard since he's such a lightweight."

"A handsome, articulate lightweight without principles and scruples."

"You've noticed?"

"Yes, and I've also noticed he's been doing pretty well in the polls."

"Well, here's something you don't know. Our internal polls show we got a good bump from our own convention. And we really needed it. That sex thing definitely hurt us. Before the closing night of the convention we actually were underwater in poll numbers."

"So where are you now?"

"Tenny 46, Bowman 41."

"Ouch. Not comfortable numbers for an incumbent everyone knows. Bowman's got a better chance to pick up undecideds than we do."

"That's the way Lee and I see it."

Susan stood and grabbed her shoulder bag.

"Sounds like I need to get to work."

Ben walked her to the door.

"You're kind of heroic for taking this on with so little prep time, Susan. Thank you."

"What's the real reason, Ben? I don't buy what she's putting out, that with what happened in Cleveland you quit because you thought you were an unnecessary distraction."

"What's wrong with that story?"

"What's wrong is that you're not a quitter, and nothing in our conversation just now convinces me you left the campaign voluntarily. You're really hurting. That's not hard to figure out. And I also know that when the bombs are falling in a campaign and decisions have to get made on the fly, the tighter the team, the more they trust one another, the more experience they've had together, all that's key to winning the close ones. For her you're irreplaceable. That's worth a lot of distraction. There's more to it, isn't there?"

"She doesn't want me killed."

Susan's hand dropped from the office door handle.

"Pardon me?"

"She doesn't want me killed. She thinks that if I stay on the campaign, the same people who poisoned Carmie will come after me."

"What do you think?"

"Hell, I don't know what to think. If they want to kill me, they know where to find me wherever I am. I might as well be working on the campaign."

"She really thinks you're in danger?"

"Her brother was murdered. Her best friend was poisoned. She was blown off a hotel stage by a bomb that killed dozens of her friends. So, yeah, the idea of one more killing, why not? You don't have to be paranoid to consider it."

"You think that goes for me, too?"

"Doubtful. Carmie and I are pretty high profile. They got huge press for attacking her and involving me. You coming in now, with only marginal connection to her before, I don't see how hurting you helps them that much."

"Hmm. You mean I'm not worth the trouble. You really know how to hurt a girl's feelings."

"Okay," said Ben, "let me put it another way. Watch your back. Lock your doors. Don't hit the streets alone at night. Does that make you feel better, or does it want you to change your mind about doing this?"

"Actually, I find all this cloak-and-dagger stuff exciting; you know, like perverse foreplay leading up to a big climax."

"Gee, that's kinky. Never considered that reaction."

"In that case, let's agree to have telephone sex."

"Phone sex?"

"Yeah, when things are hot and I need advice, I'll make secret calls to you in the middle of the night."

"That's what you consider phone sex."

"Hell, Ben, in this business that's all there's ever time for."

35

Was his life really in danger? Problematic. What did anyone have to gain by knocking off a political consultant? The damage already was done. Carmie's poisoning took him out of the campaign. The theft and disclosure of his diary was another form of poison, deadly for his further personal contact with Tenny. Love triangle? That belonged in the dirty tricks hall of fame. As a political professional, he was in awe of the brilliance of whoever conceived the plan, the skill required for its execution.

That made him even more cognizant of his own failures. His failure to anticipate the threat of the Zach Bowman campaign; his reluctance to accept as very serious Father Bob Reynolds's warning of a high-level conspiracy organized to defeat Tenny. Voters often get incumbent fatigue when leaders they elect remain in office too long. Maybe consultants get campaign fatigue. Until now he had been free of the burden self-doubt can impose. Each new campaign added to his experience, widened his sense of campaign possibilities, increased his feelings of invincibility. For two decades he had journeyed through the campaign thicket like a resident guide, instinctively aware of winning paths. Now for the first time, he felt himself at a dead end. Maybe he had been doing this too long. Less creative. Careless.

And maybe he did need time off, time away from it all. Not just a few stolen days at the beach. Time to reflect on whether he still wanted to do this. It had been a profitable business. But increasingly, he wondered whether it should be a business at all. Perpetual campaigns? Ten million dollars to run for Congress? Fifty million to run for the Senate? Messages stuffed into thirty seconds, like soap ads, encouraging quick-hit salacious attacks?

How was a voter to know who to vote for and why? Broadcasters make millions, and truth and reason get starved. Was this really the way it was supposed to work? How could all those originalists who revered every written word of the Constitution as gospel defend a system that turned the fundamentals of democracy inside out?

When Tenny fired him—yes, fired him; what else would you call it—much of the reason for his daily existence evaporated. Too late in the season to work in other campaigns, even if he had the stomach for it. Besides, all the publicity about the letters and the FBI's interest in him had made him as professionally toxic as the poison that almost killed Carmie.

Ben's thoughts churned as he sat, eyes closed, leaning as far back as his swivel office chair would allow, reflecting on what next. Not just what next for the moment, but for the rest of his life. He was so deep in thought that he almost missed the vibration from his muted cell phone. He didn't want to face anyone or anything in the world outside his own thoughts. He looked at his phone screen and saw an exception.

"Carmie?"

"Yes, it's me. I'm outside the locked door of your office. Let me in."

Ben found her standing alone, in gray sweatshirt and denim jeans. She could have been mistaken for an inconspicuous weekend gardener, if not for the two Secret Service guardians standing a discreet few steps behind her.

"What's going on?" said Carmie. "Door locked. No one here?"

"Lee's in California. I gave the staff a few days off while we figure things out. What are you doing here?"

"I'm a message bearer."

She turned to her two security overseers. "Wait here, guys."

Ben led her into his private office. "I hardly ever see you in jeans. This some sort of disguise so people won't associate you with my leper colony?"

"I'm trying to be inconspicuous. We're supposed to be part of a ménage à trois, aren't we? I didn't want to give them more to talk about. And by the way, quit feeling sorry for yourself. Your candidates get beat up in public all the time. Learn to take a few punches yourself."

"Maybe I'm too old to change my ways."

"Nonsense. You're a sex bomb. Love letters. Two women. Me included. Some guys would kill for that kind of advertising. Anyway, we can talk sex and pity some other time. I'm here to deliver a message from Tenny."

"Different from the one she delivered in person?"

"Much different. She told me about your talk on the plane, and I reminded her that the reason she's running for reelection is to save civilization."

"Save civilization?"

"Skip the details for now, just know this: if she's reelected, she intends to bring you aboard full-time to run a permanent campaign for her while she's in office. Tenny's got some really exciting ideas and is amped up as hell. She knows now she can't separate the policy from the politics. Trying to do that the first few years was her biggest mistake. She knows that."

"But I'm not sure she's going to get another chance. Are you?"

"No. And neither is she. So here's the message. Forget what she said about keeping hands off the campaign. Susan will manage it day to day and see to it that you and Lee are kept in the loop on everything. We're already on track to run the campaign with the strategy you have in place. No disruptions to that. But as things change and you want to make adjustments, contact me and I'll be your delivery channel."

"Why not directly?"

"Because she meant what she said about worrying about your safety. She doesn't want to give whoever's after us any excuse to hurt you."

"So why the change of heart, having me do it from behind the curtain?"

"The truth is that I put her head back on straight. I said if the future of civilization depends on your election, your election depends on having Ben involved. It's that simple."

36

Tenny was certain to win California's vote in November. California was her home state, Los Angeles her home city. She was Tenny, voice of Latinos in a state where the Latino vote was large enough to be decisive. She was a political progressive in the most politically progressive state in the US. For years she had been a member of California's delegation to the US House of Representatives. Twice California voters had elected her to the US Senate. No, she would not lose California this year.

So why was she in San Diego when there were so few

undecided votes to mine there? Because as president, Tenny also was commander in chief of all military forces. Hundreds of thousands of uniformed marines and sailors and their families lived in the San Diego area, along with equal numbers of retired military. She would spend two days inspecting military facilities, studying maps with commanders, holding open sessions with active-duty enlisted men and women, and relating to veterans. These images would dominate front pages and newscasts throughout the US, just as the Republicans were convening their political convention. She would wrap the flag tightly around her shoulders, show who was boss, and accept the admiration of the nation's fighting forces. All designed to make it harder for Republicans to portray her as too soft on the nation's military defense. Powerful visuals. The president at work keeping America safe, contrasted with carping GOP politicians.

After the turmoil of the Democratic convention and nonstop campaign rallies in Alaska, Washington state, and Oregon, Tenny was looking forward to the relative ease of her San Diego schedule. Her base of operations would be San Diego's Hotel del Coronado. From a distance, the del Coronado presented itself as a large Victorian castle, surrounded by a storybook landscaped moat. In reality, it was acres of hotel buildings and grounds, considered a modern technological marvel when it first opened its doors in 1888. Nearly every president since Taft had stayed at The Del Coronado. Tenny looked forward to adding her name to that list.

An extra hour of sleep. Breakfast alone on the veranda imagining the whales breaching beyond the horizon. A mild July day. Brilliant blue sky. Sunlight that caressed cabana rooftops. Bathers testing early-morning waves. She viewed all of this from her suite in the hotel's iconic Victorian tower. Oh, how she would love to board one of those charter boats and bob around on the waves looking for humpback whales. She had seen them often in younger days, as a wealth management officer for Groupo Aragon, the family business. Lazy days when she could steal time with friends off the west coast of Mexico, a prolific birthing region for whales. Family business. How quaint that sounded now. Once so central to her life. Her grandfather, Miguel, her hero. Miguel Aragon, one of the most important businessmen in all Latin America. She was so proud.

Papa Miguel. Oh, Papa, how was I to know how corrupt you were?

Her reverie was interrupted by a young traveling appointments aide. "Madam President, there's a Mr. Navarro in the hotel lobby asking to see you and refusing to talk to a staff person."

She smiled at the aide indulgently. "Many people say they simply have to see me," she said. "What's different about this one?"

"Well, Janet in scheduling thought maybe we should ask. This Mr. Navarro claims he's your husband. I know you're not married, but—"

"Andres Navarro?" she asked.

"Yes, that's the name. And the Secret Service—"

"Andres is here? Andres Navarro?"

"That's who he says he is," said the aide. "You do know him, then?"

Tenny looked longingly at the sea before her, recalling a name that she thought had long since sailed beyond her emotional horizon.

"Yes. I once knew someone by the name of Andres Navarro,"

said Tenny.

"The Secret Service has that twenty-four-hour rule about checking out your visitors, Madam President. We told him it wouldn't be possible for him to see you. At least today."

"Well, we don't want to upset the Secret Service, do we?"

"No, Madam President."

"Is this Andres Navarro still here?"

"He is. I wanted to check with you before we had him removed from the lobby."

"Take me to him."

The aide looked at her blankly.

"Yes, take me to him. I don't want to upset the Secret Service by breaking their rules and inviting him here. I'll go to him."

"But what if he's an imposter?"

"Then I'll make the rounds of the hotel lobby, shake a few hands, lift a few babies, pose for selfies, and distract everyone while our boys down there quietly hustle him out the door."

Tenny headed for the door, opened it, and said to her aide, "After you."

They walked down the short corridor to the elevator. Presidents seldom move from place to place without giving their security staff time to build protective space ahead. This was a trip no one had planned. Two surprised agents scurried to the elevator.

"You're leaving?" asked Agent Simmons.

"Not the hotel," she said. "Please escort me to the lobby."

"But we don't have it cleared."

"If no one's expecting me, it's not likely a stalker's there, is there? But just call the lobby team and hotel security and let them know I'm on the way down."

"But Madam President. ..."

"Now, please."

Into his lapel microphone, Agent Simmons reported the abrupt change in schedule: "Regent moving your way." Then, replying to an obviously surprised recipient of that message, "Yes, now, entering elevator now."

A president and her Secret Service escort are not hard to identify. The moment Tenny stepped out of the elevator, all other lobby activity stopped. Front desk admissions and checkouts. Bellmen with luggage carts. Conversation by the dozens of guests milling about. Cameras and cell phones were raised, as in rehearsed unison. Parents quickly directed children's attention. Younger ones were lifted on shoulders for better views. All eyes turned to Tenny. Someone applauded. Others joined in.

Tenny methodically scanned faces. She would know if this person claiming to be Andres Navarro was the knight to whom she had pledged her heart and soul decades earlier, when both were young and the future was a blank slate on which they would create their own fairy tale. She would know. How could she not know?

Sunlight streaming through the lobby's front windows made it difficult to see detail, but one form seemed familiar. Tenny locked her gaze there, and slowly he emerged in clear profile, as if posing for a portrait. Such a handsome face. She had melted the first time she saw it. A *god*, she thought to herself. A living god. They had sex in his car the night they met. They were engaged soon after. Then married. Too soon divorced. His handsome face little changed by the decades of separation.

The buzz around them intensified, but Tenny was oblivious to the applause, the photos, the commotion her presence had detonated. Her world compressed into the sight line that connected her to Andres. Twenty feet apart. Tenny took purposeful strides to close that distance. He cautiously turned to face her, not wanting to make a move that would cause him to be a blocking dummy for the muscular and well-armed Secret Service agents moving with her. She took both of his hands in hers and stared into his blue eyes, eyes that once had drowned her so that she could hardly breathe. Then she enveloped him with emotion she thought she had packed away forever.

Cameras recorded the scene in a moving circle that surrounded them. So many cameras. This was, after all, a tourist hotel. Equipment to memorialize vacations transformed into a news photo pool. The actual traveling media pool, caught off guard after being assured there would be nothing newsworthy this morning, raced into the lobby to catch up.

Tenny finally broke the clinch, turned, and waved to the excited crowd.

"I don't do this with everyone," she said. "This is my former husband."

And the crowd once again broke into applause.

Andres, bewildered by the scene, smiled gamely, still unsure what to do that would not provoke Tenny's security. He knew the odds of seeing her were long. Would she even want to see him? He had been such a scoundrel. There was much to apologize for. So much had happened since. He hardly expected this.

Tenny took his hand and steered him to the elevator. The doors closed behind them. The scene, and her words, migrated to every network TV newscast, and popular web site. The moment of her passionate greeting appeared on most newspaper front pages, the video of it watched millions of times on mobile devices, laptops, and desktops. Few reunions between divorced couples had ever received such public attention.

37

So much to say to one another, but not for the ears of the two stone-faced security agents ascending the elevator with them to the presidential suite. In place of words, memories filled the silence. Memories of a young Isabel, nurtured in the protective isolation of her wealthy family's Mexico City compound, imagining herself a princess. A radiant twenty- two-year-old Isabel, returning to Mexico City for her wedding, strikingly beautiful in her hand-sewn wedding gown of silk and lace, bejeweled with graduated diamonds that encircled her neck, sharing the altar with the prince of her dreams, Andres Navarro.

Few invited to Mexico's City's four-hundred-year old San Lorenzo del Campo mission that night would ever forget the opulence. The courtyard fully covered by soft white nylon tenting that rippled cloudlike above guest tables. On each of those tables, a centerpiece of three-dozen white roses, stems two feet tall, topped with blossoms the size of tennis balls, the product of the rich volcanic soil and long hours of sunshine in Ecuador's Cayambe Valley. Those seated at the tables shared the illusion of drifting in a floral sea.

The evening began with angelic strings from three harps while tuxedoed waiters served beluga caviar, freshly arrived from the Caspian Sea. Then the eight-course dinner, the twelve-piece orchestra for hours of dancing, late-night dessert and French cognac. At 1:00 a.m., older guests said their goodbyes as the rockiest of bands took the stage for those with the energy to dance until dawn. Mexico City had seldom seen such a wedding. Miguel had promised his granddaughter a wedding fit for a princess. He spared no expense delivering on that promise.

So long ago.

So much had happened since. What had not happened, Tenny realized now, was a loss of her love for Andres, a love burrowed deeply, wherever consciousness hid unattainable desire for its own protection.

"I had hoped to see you," said Andres when they were finally alone together in her suite. "I never expected this."

"Why did you come now?"

"I felt you needed me."

"I've needed you since our first dance at that fraternity party, that night we almost obliterated the back seat of your car, that night I lost all sense and all reason and fell in love with you."

"And now that you actually are a queen," said Andres, "you could probably say 'off with his head.' I'd have little defense."

"I've never even thought it, Andres. I've always wondered where I went wrong, why you stopped needing me."

"I was young and stupid. I wanted children, and after we realized that couldn't happen for us, something just changed in me. And all those nights away in surgical residency didn't help. I cheated on you. You did nothing wrong. It was me. All me. But I never stopped loving you."

"You never stopped loving me? Even when you married Catherine?"

"I loved Catherine. We had many wonderful years together. I matured with her. But she's gone. Breast cancer. Terribly aggressive form. Our girls are married and have their own families."

"Oh, I am sorry about Catherine. It's possible to have more than one love in life. I understand that."

"You have someone?"

"Andres, I've had many lovers but little love. And the love I've had, it's frightening. My first real love was grandfather Miguel, and he turned out to be a criminal. I loved Federico, but he was murdered trying to save me. Carmie and I are inseparable, and someone tried to kill her."

"What about Hal Thompson? I followed that story when it was in the papers."

"Hal's very important to me. He introduced me to the world of social need, a world I never knew existed. When he was mayor of LA, he encouraged me to run for Congress. When he was governor, he appointed me to the Senate. He helped convince me to run for president. And for a while, yes, we were lovers. But he's always been an affair of the head, not my heart."

"Miguel, Federico, Carmie. That's a short list."

"Now you might understand why I greeted you the way I did. You're in an exclusive club."

Tenny led Andres to the balcony. They stood for a moment, watching the sunlight kindle endless blue diamonds on the gentle waves, uncertain of what would, or could, come next.

"Can I get you anything? Food, coffee, something stronger?"

"Not a thing, Tenny."

Andres hesitated.

"Oh, I'm sorry. Is it okay to call you Tenny?"

"It's required," she smiled. "So, now, tell me about your life."

"Well, after residency I never left San Diego. Catherine and I had a good, comfortable life together. The girls have moved on. Amy's a tech whiz, neck deep in a cyberware start-up. Beth's a linguist. Spent time in Japan teaching and married a very nice guy there. They live in Osaka. Each of the girls has a small child, so I'm Grandpa Andres now."

"How do you spend your days?"

"I do a bit of teaching and consulting. I read a lot. Travel some. I have a nice circle of friends. And you know I had a very large inheritance. I set up a foundation for medical research and keep my hand in there, board meetings and all. Now and then they call me in to consult on a particularly unusual case requiring thoracic surgery. It's a good life. It suits me."

"I appreciated the notes you sent during impeachment and when I was recovering from the explosion."

"I just wanted you to know I was here for you."

"And now you're really here. Why?"

"Because after the brutal beating you and Carmie took in Cleveland, I thought a friendly face would be welcome. I hoped I'd still be a friendly face but wouldn't have blamed you otherwise."

The suite's front door opened, and two staff assistants entered, a signal that it was time for Tenny to leave the hotel for her late-morning schedule.

She unlocked from the moment, took Andres's hand, and led

him inside.

"Look," she said, "after my trip here I'm flying to Denver for an event. I know this is very impetuous of me, but why don't you come with me on Air Force One? I'll make the arrangements."

"Really?" said Andres. "They'd let me do that?"

"I'm the president and it's my plane, at least for a few more months."

"Think about it, Tenny. The novelty may wear off sooner than you think, and then you'd be stuck with me."

"Novelty? I've carried you with me for decades. There's a lot of catching up to do."

"Don't you have to run the country or something?"

"Piece of cake," she said, feeling her strength and emotional resolve increasing with each moment they remained together. "All I have to do is manage the economy, keep us out of war, get along with Congress, and fend off everyone trying to run me out of the White House or maybe even kill me in the process."

Andres couldn't help smiling.

"You know," he said, "we haven't flown anywhere together since the wedding express."

"Oh my God," she said. "The wedding express."

Tenny's family had moved from Mexico City to Los Angeles when she was ten years old. Returning for her wedding ten years later, her friends were American high school and college classmates, all living in Los Angeles. Andres had been born and raised in Los Angeles. Miguel had sent the company plane to transport the his-and-hers wedding party. No sooner had the seat belt sign blinked off than Carmie, Tenny's maid of honor, popped champagne corks, signaling the start of a three-hour airborne party. The drinking. The singing. The dancing in the aisles. The pairing up of his friends and hers. Even the male and female flight attendants joined the infectious bacchanal. For a half hour, until the hammering on the door grew too persistent, Tenny and Andres had locked themselves in one of the plane's two toilets, practicing for their honeymoon.

"The wedding express!" she repeated. "I'll serve you champagne on Air Force One, Andres, but when you need to use the toilet, this time you go alone."

38

Lester Bowles waited for the call with dread. In a few moments, he would be summoned to the hotel lobby. A scrum of aides and security would escort him to a limousine. He would be driven a few blocks to the Republican convention. He would wait in the wings while Janine Larkins, one of Ohio's two US senators, completed her introduction. Then, thousands of screaming delegates would be on their feet, chanting "Les is More, Les is More." Twenty million others would be watching on TV as he accepted the nomination as the Republican Party's candidate for vice president. His speech already was loaded into the teleprompter, a speech he had carefully rehearsed so many times he probably could deliver it from memory. A speech that would praise the GOP's candidate for president, Zach Bowman. A speech that would glorify Bowman's background and exaggerate his leadership qualities. On cue, Bowman would bound onto the stage. They would embrace, raise their arms in unity, and produce images that would drive up the poll numbers for the

Bowman-Bowles ticket, perhaps high enough just from this convention to grab the lead and keep it.

Bowles dreaded the thought of making that speech and others like it that would be required in coming months. If they lost in November, he would be considered an idiot in his political world for accepting the vice-presidential nomination. If they won, it could even be worse. He would have to endorse every damn fool thing Bowman wanted to do and become his policy lackey. That very morning, he had spilled his frustration all over Gil Adonis's breakfast plate. They were alone in Bowles's hotel suite.

"God, this sticks in my throat like a bad chicken bone. I woke up this morning wanting to pull the covers over my head, like I have every day since you talked me into this. I can't tell you how many times I almost called you and said I want out."

"But you didn't call, because you know I'm right," said Adonis. "President Bowles. President Bowles. Just keep telling yourself that. It sure sounds good to me."

"Vice president. It's vice president. Vice president to one of the world's biggest horse's asses. That's if we win. If we lose, I'm the horse's ass."

"You're not going to lose. You've seen the polls. She's a wounded lion, nowhere near the fifty percent she needs, and that's with everybody knowing her and having an opinion of her. And we've got more spears to throw her way to bring her down."

"Like the ones you hit her with in Cleveland? That was brilliant. Raunchy, but brilliant."

"You know me, Les. You know I never get into anything to lose. I wouldn't have steered you here if I wasn't dead sure we'd pull it off."

Gil poured himself a second cup of coffee from the room service cart. He hesitated for a moment, unsure whether he should continue. But Bowles needed reinforcement.

"You saw what happened over the weekend in Greece."

"The coup?"

"Yes, the coup. Our guys."

"The papers said it was a military thing."

"It was. Our guys in the military. The Greeks are so upset over their economy and living so long in austerity, hardly anyone pushed back. The military will give them security. Some serious new trade deals with Turkey will help revive the economy. It will happen pretty fast."

"I didn't think the Turks and Greeks got along."

"They don't. But they will. It's part of our plan. Without realizing it, Erdogan did all the hard work of getting rid of the most high-ranking Turks who would object to our plan. Soon, our guys will grab power."

Les shoved back from the breakfast table and walked to the hotel window. Before him spread the diversity of Texas. Rich neighborhoods and poorer ones. Oil tanks and shipping channels. One of the world's great medical centers. All divided by an endless stream of cars and trucks on a confusing tangle of four- and six- and eight-lane highways. In the distance, NASA. Farther south, fishing fleets.

"That's what most people want, isn't it, Gil? Just the chance to do what they want, earn what they can, have a sense of security. That they won't die poor. They won't be gunned down in the street or bombed into vapor. If everybody in the world voted, it'd be ninety-nine to one for peace, not war. Never war. I don't understand why we're always at each other's throats. Maybe hundreds of years ago they were too dumb to know better. But there's no excuse now, not when we've got all we need to feed the world and pull everybody up."

Gil walked to the window to share the view.

"That's why you're our guy, Les. That's the world we want to build and keep."

"Can we build it on a foundation of deceit and murder?"

"It's preferable to war and destruction."

"We might have been able to do it if I ran at the top of the ticket and got elected president the old-fashioned way."

"Trust me, Les. You couldn't get elected. Don't think I didn't take plenty of polls trying to figure that out. It takes a pretty boy with a golden tongue to become a star these days."

"That's a helluva indictment of democracy."

"Exactly. Democracy doesn't work anymore, Les. People have pretty much given up on democracy anyway. They're ready to try something new that works. Believe me, once we're locked in, people will love the new system."

Memory of the morning's conversation kept forcing its way into Lester Bowles's consciousness. Through meetings and interviews and rehearsals. All day. Gil made sense, but was he right?

The call came as Lester was deep into uncertainty. Right or wrong, he had made his choice. The limo was waiting to drive him into an entirely different world from the one he knew.

39

One hundred and twenty men are on their knees. Shoulder to shoulder. Foreheads pressed tightly to prayer rugs. A ritual performed five times daily for more than a thousand years. Prayers little changed, even in this age of planetary travel and genetic editing.

As in past centuries, an imam, their spiritual leader, stands on a balcony prepared to speak to the faithful. His topics—life, personal behavior, salvation, as prescribed by Allah and entrusted to God's messenger, Muhammad.

Imam Musa Kartal waits passively while the men rearrange themselves into seated positions. It is Friday, the most sacred day of each week. A day when the Prophet was born. A day, as sacred texts teach, when sins are absolved and when salvation is assured to those whose fortune it is to die, as the Prophet died, on a Friday.

"When man spreads disorder on earth, there is no peace for any of us," begins the imam. "Neither is there security for any of us, or for our families and loved ones. Allah revealed his teachings to the Holy Prophet, peace and blessings of Allah be upon him, in order to remove disorder from the world. In his final sermon, his final teachings, Allah declared that it is the responsibility of all who believe in him to propagate Islam's message of peace, and love, and compassion."

There is power in Imam Kartal's voice, cultivated power. The authority of station. His words resonate as serum for the soul, restoring strayed thoughts to a proper path, injecting energy into long-held faith. On many other balconies this day, other imams are similarly at work, though few with the same riveting ability to reach deep inside the hearts of the faithful and touch emotions beyond duty and fear. Even as he pauses, as he is pausing now, the silence has meaning.

Imam Kartal scans his flock, assuring himself of their silence and attention.

"A non-Arab possesses no superiority over the Arab. Neither do we Arabs possess superiority over those who bow to other gods. All men, whatever nation they inhabit, no matter their station in life, are equal. The Koran permits self-defense against those who make war first but does not permit the war some extremists among Muslims are flagrantly abusing. A Muslim invites insult to Allah when he or she takes up arms on account of religion. Security is replaced with selfishness, conflict, and death. Love and harmony are replaced with jealousy and malice."

For nearly fifteen minutes, Imam Kartal delivers a message of peace, tolerance, and harmony. Then, his work done for this moment, the imam retires to his office. Tahir Badem, rises from among the faithful, folds his prayer rug beneath his arm, and follows him.

"I was quite surprised to see you," says the imam. "That prayer rug appears to be new. Not much in use, I take it."

Badem smiled. He seldom attended Friday prayers. This was his first at Imam Kartal's mosque.

"Not new, Musa," said Badem. "Just preserved for special occasions. That was a most interesting message you just delivered. Do your regular patrons accept your moderation even as from other balconies other imams are talking jihad?"

"You see the attendance," said Kartal. "Peace has charms for most who fear disruption. And by preaching moderation, I do not attract attention from authorities who might not agree with disruption of the current order. But now, what brings you here? It is a risk, as I'm sure you realize."

Badem settled into a chair before the imam's desk and removed a check from his pocket.

"If anyone asks, I'm here to help support your work and this mosque," said Badem. "Very deserving."

"And the actual reason?"

"I am to be in touch with Singapore later today, and they want a report on the American project. What do you know?"

Kartal reached into his briefcase and removed a piece of paper. He handed it to Badem. "This email arrived this morning."

Badem silently read the words: As-salamu alaykum. We have twins! – Abia.

"Who is Abia?" asked Badem. "And what is this with twins?"

"Abia is my former assistant who has transferred to a mosque in Houston, Texas."

"And twins?"

"Our American contact has succeeded. Twins means we now have placed both of our candidates in a position to assume power over the United States government."

Imam Kartal bowed his head in simulated prayer.

"God is good."

40

A thousand miles from Houston, detached for the first time ever from a Tennyson campaign, Ben Sage and Lee Searer watched the newly anointed Republican ticket of Bowman and Bowles take its first bows. Zach Bowman, his custom- made powder-blue suit perfectly matching his light-blue eyes, Lester Bowles, a full head of graying hair, both of equal height, both model trim, both practiced at finding the live camera and posturing for maximum positive effect.

They stood frame-close to one another, arms outstretched, as welcoming friends. Behind them, ever so subtle, waving gently in a full-stage dramatic graphic, an American flag, topped by a golden eagle ferrule. Balloons, red, white, and blue, floated from the arena's ceiling, along with a snowstorm of confetti. The roar of the crowd was underscored by a full orchestra's edited version of Aaron Copland's inspirational "Fanfare for the Common Man," its lean trumpet call to action cutting through the bedlam of the moment.

Compelling television. Ben took a long swallow from a beer bottle, his fourth beer since they tuned into the final night of the Republican convention. He was now officially buzzy, a state where he intended to travel tonight. He needed an antidote to his withdrawal pains. A presidential campaign. His campaign. And instead of being in the thick of the action, against his will and every professional instinct, he was at his beach house with Lee, eating crab cakes and swigging beer.

"What do you see?" Ben asked Lee.

Lee also was deep into an alcohol rush. He didn't hesitate.

"Two assholes."

Lee seldom swore.

"No," said Ben, "what do you really see?"

"I see two good-looking dudes. One handsome as hell. The other looking as wise as a Tibetan guru, both really good at mugging the camera. I see danger."

"That's what I see. Two guys running against two women. One of them shallow and flashy, the other, an excuse to vote for the prick anyway, both of them looking farm fresh compared with a beat-up Tenny."

"Well, they've got them packaged right. All the Republicans in Houston will leave the convention jacked. I don't see them losing many of their own people. We've got to hope we guessed right with our peer strategy and that Susan executes."

Ben pushed up from his lounge chair. He needed air, and the mild August night was accommodating. He slid open the screen separating his living room from the porch. The sky was clear. A full moon was rising as an orange flame, spreading beams brightly over Delaware Bay's waters. Small waves in the moonlight reminded him of wrinkled tinfoil. Too few nights were spent here, like this, with Almie. *Oh, Almie*, he thought, *now, because of those bastards, I can't even write to you anymore.*

Someone uninvited, unwanted, had been here. They hadn't wrecked the place. That's the only good thing he could say about it. They probably had copied his hard drives, inventoried his recent web page visits, checked his bureau drawers and closets. Who knew what else? The home was isolated on the beach, no neighbors to get suspicious. How long were they here? Did they leave bugs to listen in on whatever else he might say, like now, tonight? Would they be back? Was he really in danger?

Damn, a beautiful night, and all I can think of is ugly.

Ben's cell phone lit up, breaking his chain of thought. Charlene Pine, their Washington office manager.

"Getting numbers," she said.

"Let me put you on speaker."

Lee punched the TV remote to mute and joined Ben on the porch.

"Looks like they're hitting home runs," said Charlene. Needle's moving into the sixties, seventies, peaking about eighty. Bouncing around, but all positive."

Charlene was tapped into Brit Kelly's audience reaction meter, measuring how fifty independent voters watching the Republican convention were judging Bowman and Bowles in real time. The meter allowed those on the polling panel to turn a knob as they saw things they liked or didn't like. The score ranged from zero to one hundred. Britany Kelly had done volumes of research for Sage and Searer. She was doing it now for Tenny's campaign. Ben and Lee were getting a real-time bootleg report.

"I'd guess this will translate into a ten-point bump for them," said Ben.

"What's the latest tracking?" asked Lee.

"Let me check," said Charlene. "I'm putting down the phone for a few seconds."

"There's the family," said Lee, watching the TV show with the sound still muted.

"Geez," said Ben. "Did they hire those people?" Perfect.

Picture perfect."

On the screen, two beautiful women, the wives, and six children, two Bowmans, four Bowles, aged two to adult, boys and girls, men and women, appealing in their modesty.

"I'm back," said Charlene. "Latest overnight poll, before tonight, 47–42. Tenny up by 5."

"That means the next published poll will show her down," said Ben.

"That's national," said Lee. "What matters are our target states."

"We're hanging in there on those," said Charlene through the speakerphone. "Not much room to slip, but all the target state work's showing up in the numbers."

"Thanks, Charlene. Might as well call it a night. We're getting sloshed here, anyway."

"Hey, you guys. You get a few days off. Enjoy it. She needs you. You'll be back."

"Don't leave the light on for us," said Ben.

"Now what," said Lee.

"Let me put it another way," replied Ben. "What now? Just once with Tenny I'd like to run a normal campaign. You know, the kind where people don't get murdered. There's no need for the FBI. Where we're not spending a month talking about her sex life."

"You want to talk issues? You must be drunk."

"No. My wish list is modest. I just don't want to have to wonder about conspiracies."

Ben's cell rang again.

"Charlene?" Ben answered. "Got more?"

"Charlene?" said a man's voice. "Do I sound like Charlene? This is Bob."

Alcohol dulling his mind, Ben couldn't focus right away. "Bob? Bob who?"

"Your guardian angel. Bob Reynolds." Ben and Father Bob Reynolds hadn't spoken since the night they'd met for pizza and Ben walked away with a mission to warn authorities about a vague conspiracy.

"Oh God, Bob. Sorry. Lee and I are in Lewes just watching Tenny's poll numbers being flushed down the toilet and holding a wake."

"Wakes are for the dead," said Bob. "Find another excuse to get drunk. Did you fly or drive to the beach?"

"Took the Piper."

"What's that, about an hour flight?"

"Yeah, about an hour and a half from the office with the drive from the airport."

"Which airport?"

"Why do you want to know? You coming here to join us? Got an extra cot you can use."

"No, you're coming here. Which airport?"

"Freeway Aviation, right off Route 50, Bowie, Maryland."

"I'll pick you up at seven thirty tomorrow morning, and we'll go somewhere and talk. Lee can take your car downtown. I'll be your chauffeur."

"What's up?"

Before Bob could reply, Ben realized why Bob must have

called with such urgency. Even after four beers, it was sobering.

41

Despite mild hangovers, Ben and Lee roused themselves at 5:00 a.m. for the half-hour drive to the Coastal Airport in Georgetown, Delaware, stopping only at an all-night diner for coffee to jar open eyes that seemed intent on remaining closed. Light rain pelted the windshield of their rented car.

"Think you can fly this morning?"

"Hard to say," said Ben. "Depends on the ceiling between here and there. Radar on my cell phone app says it's pretty local."

Ben had called ahead to operations, alerting the overnight crew that he would be taking off at first light. The weather forecast was for improved visibility. Ben was a cautious pilot, never flying when conditions seemed marginal. Neither did he take shortcuts with his preflight checklist. By the time Ben completed it and filed his flight plan, the overcast ceiling was well within tolerance for safe travel.

The path for the eighty nautical miles of air travel between Georgetown, Delaware, and Bowie, Maryland, crossed Chesapeake Bay, the marine channel connecting the Port of Baltimore with the rest of the world. On days when the seas and wind aligned properly, the bay was filled with white sails and powerboats. But frequently the elements conspired against both water and air travel. With deadly suddenness the bay could become treacherous for small boats, the sky challenging to light aircraft. Even auto traffic over the four-mile bridge connecting Maryland's Eastern and Western Shores could be whipsawed with gusts and squalls.

This morning the earth was blanketed in cloud shadow, but the winds were calm, the ride was smooth, and except for a few small downdrafts while crossing the bay, Ben and Lee's arrival met Father Bob's seven-thirty deadline. Bob was waiting for them when they emerged from Freeway's Aviation's small office. They greeted one another with nods and little conversation. Lee wheeled Ben's Jaguar out of the parking lot toward Washington. Ben climbed into Bob's sedan.

"You've picked up something?" asked Ben.

"Yes. Our people are absolutely convinced that there's some sort of international cabal at work to deny Tenny reelection."

"Like the conspiracy that almost took us down last year? That Carmona guy out of Mexico? The oil and bank people?"

"This sounds more serious. Some national intelligence agencies involved. Some military, too."

"Wait a minute. We blew up their plan just a few months ago. All the guys they caught in those calls the NSA taped, they've been fired, or downgraded, or humiliated, or, for all we know, are in hiding. How can they be doing this again so soon?"

"Different guys. Hard as it is to believe, there were three simultaneous conspiracies, apparently not connected to each other. The militia guys who blew up the hotel were locals. The one we exposed, financial and business guys who wanted to get rid of her before she changed their money game. And now, from what our people tell me, a group far more organized and more dangerous."

"What do they want? And how in the hell can a dumb bastard like Bowman help them?"

"I don't pretend to know the players or the strategy. But something's in motion, and we've confirmed it."

"Confirmed it? How?"

"The Chinese. They pay close attention to the cyberworld, and they're onto it."

"Really? The Chinese? If they've tipped off your people to it, they must not be part of it."

"Well, they're either playing a double game here, or they must consider it a threat to them, too. Think about it. Their people went to ours with the information."

"What information?"

"I don't have the details. But I know where to get them, and that's where you come in."

"My game's politics, not espionage."

"We'll talk over breakfast."

Bob steered his car out of Freeway Aviation's parking lot and headed for a nearby diner. As they entered, Bob carefully surveyed available seating options. The restaurant was half-full of early risers, none of whom showed the slightest interest in the new arrivals. Bob chose a corner booth, two tables removed from any other customers.

"The place doesn't look suspicious," said Ben. "Why the cloak-and-dagger stuff?"

"They know me now as your contact," said Bob. "I'm never sure of anything."

"Sounds like you're getting as paranoid as I am. Wouldn't blame you after all that's happened."

"It's not paranoia," said Bob. "Too many signals on our

grapevine for this not to be real. My contacts say I always should check for signs I'm being watched."

"Bob, where do I come in? And isn't there something hard here we can hang on to? Names, places, things we can check into? Last time we talked, all you had were rumors."

"Getting to that. You say your game is politics. Your game right now is to save President Tennyson. You're closer to her than just about anyone on earth. If what the Chinese have gets passed on to you, it will get to her and she can mobilize US agencies. Otherwise the agencies may be reluctant to act while there's an election going on. You know, they don't want to seem partisan."

"Last time we talked, I went to Kyle Christian; you know, head of the CIA. He's an old and trusted client and friend. He said he'd get his people on it."

"Have you heard from him since?"

"No. Why don't I get back to him and put his people in touch with yours."

"We can't risk it. They tell me our intelligence agencies have been infiltrated."

"Even the CIA?"

"Possible. Want to bet the election on it? Maybe the future of the country?"

Ben emptied his coffee cup and signaled a waiter for a refill. Bob said nothing to interrupt Ben's thoughts.

"So where is this information?" asked Ben, breaking the silence.

"It's in Paris, with someone you know well: Ambassador

Harold Thompson."

"Hal! We're old high school friends. I got him into politics, got him elected governor of California."

"Yes. And from what they tell me, he and Tenny were more than friends for a while."

"Way back. Way back. Plenty of history there."

"He knows you and trusts you. He'll give you everything he has. You pass it on to Tenny. Then she mobilizes US agencies, and whatever and whoever is out to get you gets exposed. The scandal probably would be enough of a story to ensure her reelection."

"Whew. Wait a minute. You want me to go to Paris. Why can't Hal come here? She'd trust him if he delivered it directly."

"Too obvious. Remember what happened to the last messenger, Federico."

"But doesn't that go for me, too? What makes anyone think I can go to Paris, collect the information, and connect with Tenny without getting my head blown off?"

"Because it won't be you. It will be Brother Ben, traveling as a member of a group of priests to Paris for a conference. Your group will pay an obligatory visit to the American Embassy, where you pick up the files. Then you and your group return to the US and travel to wherever Tenny might be at the time. If we think you're at risk after that, we'll hide you in one of our protected monasteries."

A waiter delivered their breakfast orders, momentarily shutting down the conversation. They became aware of four newcomers sliding into the booth next to theirs. All middle-aged men engrossed in rehashing last night's baseball game. With closer company, Ben lowered his voice to a near whisper.

"This is what you've got planned for me? This is why you called me here?"

"This is what I've been instructed to tell you."

"Instructed? By who? I'm a political hack, Bob. I run campaigns. I elect candidates. I don't do spy stuff. I don't ski because I don't want broken bones. I don't scuba because I don't want to drown. I don't drive fast or bike on steep hills. I've never liked roller coasters. I'm the wrong guy for this."

"You're the only guy for this. No one else can be trusted with information Hal Thompson possesses since we don't know who in the intelligence community to trust. Whatever this conspiracy is has infiltrated into a lot of key government agencies, right here in the US and other countries. That's why no one else can present the information to the president directly and in a way where she won't question the source. If you want to save Tenny, if you want to see her reelected, you have no choice. It won't be done with the usual political strategies. It won't be done with a TV commercial, no matter how brilliant. To get her reelected, we need to break up this conspiracy."

Ben turned away from Bob's piercing eyes and looked longingly at the yolks of his two sunny-side-up eggs, the rasher of bacon, and the hash browns he had ordered. How he wished this could be a friendly breakfast, filled with mindless chatter and gossip. How he wished he could dive into his breakfast with appetite. But now he had none, nor did he have an appetite for what Bob had planned for him.

"One more thing," said Bob. "If Tenny loses, the bad guys win, big. My people in Rome don't scare easily, Ben. Our club has survived for two thousand years. But for them, this threat is scary. I'm in the business of saving individual souls. I've got the impression that my mission with you is to save what we value most here on earth."

42

A quick trip to the mall to buy underwear, a pair of pajamas, a few toiletries. An afternoon secluded at a Ramada Inn adjacent to Baltimore-Washington's Thurgood Marshall Airport, awaiting the delivery of priestly clothes and a black travel satchel. The departure lounge where he blended with nine men similarly dressed in black shirts, white collars, and black jackets. All boarded coach seats together for the nonstop Air France flight to Paris. Ben was assigned a middle seat. A muscular priest occupied the aisle seat next to him, a man who introduced himself as Brother Foster. Was he placed there for Ben's protection? Was he really a priest or, like Ben, playing the role in whatever game this was?

Father Bob's extraordinary phone call summoning him from Lewes and Bob's obvious unease with every new customer who entered the diner that morning stamped "warning" on Ben's alert system. He thought this must be the way cops and other security professionals see the world, measuring every passerby on a mental danger meter, hesitating a moment more than usual before turning corners when the view ahead is obstructed.

His senses now on trip wire, Ben observed on arrival at Charles de Gaulle Airport that none of his traveling companions entered France through the "Euro Residents Only" customs gates. One member of the group, introduced to Ben only as Brother Clement, appeared to be the leader. Brother Clement wore his priestly habit like a tuxedo. Smart, tailored, formal, the gray of his close-cropped hair seemed premature given his unblemished facial features and eyes that scanned surroundings like a radar beacon searching for unexpected blips. Brother Clement was tall and obviously muscular, like one who spends countless hours bodybuilding as well as soul saving. Was he also playing the role of priest? Were any of his companions who they seemed? Or was this a Vatican version of a special forces detail? Whoever they were, Ben was comforted by their presence.

It was late morning when they checked into the Ephrem hotel, a guesthouse adjacent to the Sacré-Cœur Basilica, one of the most visible attractions in Paris. His room was spartan. A small portable closet, a simple desk with one center drawer, a single bed, and two straight-back chairs. On the wall, a wooden crucifix, hung beneath a wall lamp fixture and a ceiling smoke detector.

Ben had little to unpack. Some reading material. A Paris map he found in the travel section of the airport bookstore. His cell phone. He was assured by an AT&T clerk that his phone would work with the European system. He had no one to call, but it felt comforting next to him, just in case. Underwear, pajamas, and a toothbrush. An extra black shirt. Bob Reynolds told Ben that he would not be in Paris long enough to require more.

A knock on his door. His door? Who knew he was here? Ben had been in borderline panic mode from his first steps on French soil. He had read spy novels but never the how- to-be-a-spy manual. His courier role didn't come with an instruction sheet.

The second set of knocks was accompanied by a voice.

"Clement."

Ben resumed breathing. He opened the door.

"Comfortable, Brother Ben?" asked Clement.

"Oh yes," said Ben. Instinct discouraged him from saying more, anything that could be overheard to give away the charade. Pride discouraged him from admitting how jumpy he was.

"The others and I have some duties to attend elsewhere," said Clement. "We'll return in a few hours. Brother Foster will remain at the hotel for any help that you might need."

"What kind of help might that be?"

"Oh," said Brother Clement, after a moment's hesitation, "Brother Foster speaks excellent French and can help with translation. Also, Brother Foster will remain in telephone contact with the rest of our group. Just make yourself comfortable."

Clement smiled and disappeared down the short hallway.

Ben wanted to ask about security, about the rest of the schedule, about so many things he hadn't been told and didn't yet understand. But his brain didn't engage quickly enough. Perhaps he wasn't being told for good reasons. Trust. He had to trust Father Bob and whatever plan had been set in motion. In his political world, Ben was always the one devising the strategies, making the plans, assuring others with his take-charge manner. His record of success was his counseling credential. But now and then he miscalculated, as he did about Zach Bowman's campaign. It wasn't the first time he had been outwitted by clever adversaries. But those were just campaigns. Losing here, the stakes would be much higher. Possibly his life.

Ben stood at his now closed door feeling exposed and uncomfortable. He studied the four walls of his bare room. Nothing there. Blank walls. Plenty of space to hang his sense of fear. Too little space to defeat a wave of claustrophobia. Was there a camera in that smoke detector? A listening device? Who else had keys to his room? Strange how he had never considered such things before, not ever during years of living out of suitcases and trusting strange bedrooms. Brother Clement had not asked him to remain in the hotel, but that obviously was implied. The small eating area off the lobby, did they serve lunch? The thought immediately triggered hunger. He opened his door, studied the hallway, and found it empty. Overcoming dread that he might make a wrong move in unfamiliar terrain, he locked his room's door, boarded the empty elevator, and headed for the lobby.

Brother Foster was waiting in one of the lobby's guest chairs. A welcome sight. Foster rose as Ben exited the elevator. Apparently, he had been on guard, watching the lobby.

"Lunch?" Foster asked.

"Definitely," said Ben.

They entered the small dining room together. Few others were dining at the Ephrem. When in Paris, it's a sin not to scope out irresistible French cooking, found on just about every *rue*, large and small. But Ben was a hostage to the mission that brought him here. Fine dining was for another day. Today, hotel food would have to do. He was relieved to have company. Company interested in his safety.

"Let me answer any questions that people might ask," said Foster.

"What kind of questions?"

"Parish, retreats, things of that sort."

Ben had not thought about his dress, how others at the guesthouse would see him as a Jesuit priest and expect priestly answers in conversation. Any questions from strangers related to the church would expose him as a fraud. Foster was here to make sure that didn't happen.

Ben and Foster had talked little on the overnight flight from

Baltimore to Paris. Now Foster introduced himself as an actual priest, currently assigned to Saint Mark's Parish in Burlington, Vermont.

"Where are you from originally?" Ben asked. "Vermont," Foster replied. "I haven't moved far. Born and raised in Rutland. Now I'm in Burlington. It's my French. Living so close to the French part of Canada, it's helpful to know some French. So after I was ordained, they just sent me back home."

"Is being a priest all you expected?"

"Different than I expected, but still satisfying. I understand you're in politics. Well, in a way, so am I. I guess it comes with big organizations."

"So, if you don't mind me asking, why did you decide to become a priest instead of, say, a pro football player?"

Foster smiled. "Funny you would think of that. In fact, I played a lot of football in high school and college. Got awards, even a scholarship. And like so many of us who do that, dreamed of the big bucks and the big stadiums and the adoring crowds."

"Well, you look the part of a football guy. Lineman?"

"Tackle. Yeah, I was good. Just not that good. So, after college I knocked around aimlessly a bit, doing construction, thinking about maybe going back for a business degree or something. I was in love, or at least thought I was, and got anxious about making money."

"That's a long way from being a priest."

"I know. My girlfriend, Jenny, was Catholic, and she talked me into taking classes for people thinking about joining the church. I wasn't too interested in that, but I was interested in Jenny. So, I indulged her and went to those classes. And you know, suddenly it all just felt right. My dad was an alcoholic. My mother had mental problems. My home life was really chaotic. With the church I found serious comfort."

"And Jenny?"

"She was really surprised that instead of converting to marry her, I married the church."

Ben could feel the sharper edges of his tension wearing smoother with this conversation. Finding a human inside the robotic way this mission had been organized around him. He had appetite for more. More understanding of who these assigned guardians actually were. Maybe Foster had the answers.

"Tell me, Foster, why are you here? Who are the others?"

"I don't really know. They didn't give me much notice or much information. I guess it's my size, my football past. I'm supposed to look out for you; that's all I was told. I don't even know what to look for."

"Neither do I," said a disappointed Ben. "Neither do I."

43

The American Embassy compound in Paris faced Avenue Gabriel and the gardens of the Champs-Élysées. Two hundred yards to its east was the Hôtel de Crillon, a building whose history dates to 1758. Benjamin Franklin and his French diplomatic counterparts signed the first treaties between the two countries here, even while the colonists were still fighting for independence. To the south, the US ambassador's office looked out upon the Place de la Concorde, its fountains reminiscent of

Rome's Saint Peter's Square with its gilded lamp columns and Luxor Obelisk, the oldest monument in Paris, a relic of the reign of Ramesses II in the thirteenth century BC. During the French Revolution, King Louis XVI was guillotined directly in front of what was now the American Embassy.

Benjamin Franklin, John Adams, Thomas Jefferson, and James Monroe all served as ministers or ambassadors to France and walked these streets. A bronzed statue of Ben Franklin, seated serenely reading a book, greeted Ben Sage and the nine others in clerical dress as they walked the cobblestone path to enter the chancery. In the building's marble-columned foyer they strode past the busts of Washington, Lafayette, and Frédéric-Auguste Bartholdi, sculptor of the Statue of Liberty. Waiting in the large atrium behind the grand staircase were members of the embassy staff, including Ambassador Harold Thompson. As each visitor reached the ambassador, he shook his hand, a warm and friendly handshake, and leaned close to say a few words.

Ben was sixth in the line of ten. Hal shook hands with him no differently than with the others, showing no particular recognition, even after a lifetime of friendship and political partnership. But when he leaned in intimately, rather than asking Ben's name he said softly, "Wait ten minutes and then go to the woman in the green dress and ask loudly enough to be heard where you might find the bathroom." Hal smiled at Ben, nodded, and then moved on to the next.

When the visitors were all seated, an embassy staff member began discussing the embassy's history, the architectural details of the building, the mission of the embassy staff. Ten minutes into the lecture, Ben followed the script as Hal had instructed. The woman in the green dress escorted him to a door marked "Bureau of Diplomatic Security." She motioned to him to enter, turned, and left him.

Inside, Hal was standing, waiting with a greeting more appropriate for an old friend. "You old sinner! How much did you have to confess to feel comfortable in these clothes?" Hal turned to two other men who flanked him. "You never saw two bigger cutups than we were in high school," he said, hugging Ben tightly around the waist.

The two men smiled. Anxious smiles, Ben noted. Men who didn't look as if they smiled easily.

"High school. College. He got me elected mayor of LA and governor of California. I don't know about the priest outfit, but for me, this guy's a saint." Hal held Ben's shoulders and smiled at him.

"Look," said Hal, "we only have a limited amount of time. No time to tell war stories about us. In a few minutes they'll show a fifteen-minute film to your group. The lights will go out. Before they go on again, be back and seated. Go quietly so no one notices how long you've been gone."

"You don't trust your own staff?"

"Hell, I don't know most of them. I've only been here four months. Can't take any chances. Let's get at it." He motioned to one of the two other men. "Bill, fill him in. Oh, sorry," said Hal, "this is Bill Scully. We're in his office. He heads up security for us."

"Here's what we have," said Scully. "The diplomatic mission has offices in Marseilles, like most other countries. Marseilles is really important for trade around the Mediterranean, the Middle East, and Africa. A lot of stuff goes through Marseilles, and not just business stuff. The Israelis also have a Marseilles office. We stay tight with them because they've got one of the best intelligence operations, and when it's something we should know, they tell us. Well, last week they told us that the Chinese

MSS approached them with information they thought, we, the US, ought to know but they didn't want to pass on directly."

"MSS?" asked Ben.

"Sorry. Ministry of State Security, like the Chinese CIA. They have a lot of different divisions. Usually when they pick up stuff in Marseilles, it's through their political and economic division. But this was unusual. It came through their enterprises division, the one that runs their front organizations; you know, like fake import-export companies, finance companies, places that operate like legitimate businesses but whose main purpose is to stay on top of what other countries are doing that might affect Chinese security, mainly commercial security."

Hal interrupted him and picked up a folder from his desk.

"What we got from them is pretty spectacular," said Hal. "We can't be entirely sure it's authentic, but if it is it means there's a worldwide conspiracy to take over key governments, including ours. The Chinese say they'd feel threatened if these conspirators took over the US, and they want us to know about it and stop it."

"The Chinese told this to the Israelis?" Ben asked.

"They used the Israelis to get to us," said Hal, "and the Chinese did it with unusual urgency. Bowman apparently is part of the plot by whoever's behind it, and if he becomes president, he becomes a big piece of whatever they have in mind."

Scully took the folder from Hal. "Inside this is everything we have. Names, operational plans, timelines, a disc of images from secret correspondence. It looks like the agenda for a major operational meeting, likely connected with Bowman's election. Tenny can give this to Ken Kloss at NSA and Birch at Justice, and they can verify what's here, or not, and they can do it pretty quickly, probably still in time to go public and kill off Bowman's support."

"How about Kyle Christian at the CIA? I sort of filled him in vaguely on what I knew weeks ago."

Hal and the others exchanged quick looks.

"Ben, a few names in this folder are CIA. CIA's one of the agencies they seem to have infiltrated."

"You think Kyle is part of this?" Ben was incredulous.

"We don't know. We just don't know. And since we don't, we leave him out for now."

"Hard for me to believe."

"All of this is hard to believe," said Hal. "We're late to this party, and there's literally, excuse the expression, a drop-dead date. Election Day. If Bowman wins, they win. We lose. We have to go with what we have and a lot of trust that we're right."

Hal pointed to the folder Bill Scully was holding. "That folder will be in your room when you return to the hotel. That's what you have to deliver to Tenny, and only Tenny," said Hal.

"Do the bad guys know we have this?"

"They might."

"Does that mean they might try to kill me to get it?"

"They might try. That's why we're adding more people to your traveling party. More priests who will be going to the US with you tomorrow. And because there's so many of you, the diocese has chartered a flight. The cover story is that you're not going commercial because a charter from Parisian Holidays Air is cheaper."

"Never heard of Parisian Holidays Air," said Ben.

"It's one of those front companies we run," said the third man in the room who had to this point said nothing.

"This is Herve Coriton," said Hal. "Herve's with the DGSE, the French CIA."

"I'll be traveling with you," said Coriton. Four others in our party will be DGSE agents. We'll see that you get there."

"You'd better get back to the group now," said Hal. "After all this is over, come back to Paris and we'll spend time together. I'll show you Paris like you've never seen it."

"If I am still around," said Ben.

44

A private room at London's exclusive East India Club. Five diners share a table.

Tahir Badem, chairman and CEO of Fertile Crescent Industries, had arrived in London from Istanbul a day earlier, traveling separately from Imam Musa Kartal, who tonight dresses in a blue business suit, white shirt, and tie, the image of a successful businessman, rather than his usual tunic. Gilbert Adonis arrived just hours ago, making the trip from New York in his private Dassault Falcon 2000. Boris Bobbinsky, a member of the East India Club who arranged for this dinner and for its privacy, lives in London. London is the hub of Bobbinsky's worldwide import-export business.

The fifth member of the dinner party and the last to arrive is Mariana Lee. She traveled the farthest of all, from Singapore. Lee has no official title, no business or government role. But the others know why she is here.

Once all are seated and wine is poured, Bobbinsky loses no time relaying unwelcome news, the reason for summoning the others. "There's a strong possibility we have been compromised, seriously compromised," he says. "Ugo has missed two separate security calls. No contact in six days. And regrettably, the timing correlates to days when he was entrusted with our most sensitive information."

"Do you suspect he's been turned?" asks Lee.

"Not likely, Mariana. He's one of our best operatives. Very veteran. Very strong. I believe he was taken," Bobbinsky replies.

"By who?"

"We can only suspect. There were an unusual number of Israelis in Marseilles the last few days. Top people. That would indicate some type of mission. Either an exercise they're planning or one they've discovered. It could be related to Ugo's disappearance."

"If it's the Israelis, that usually means martyrdom," said Imam Kartal.

"Martyrdom before or after our information was disclosed?" Lee asked.

"No way to know that answer unless we detect reaction from the other side," said Bobbinsky. "That's why I felt we should risk meeting to discuss our options. I believe it is urgent that we alert all of our sources to be sensitive to any unusual movements or actions that indicate we've been compromised."

"Boris," said Adonis, "if the Israelis do have Ugo's information, do you believe they would share it? The Israelis wouldn't mind Bowman winning the American presidency if they assess he would be friendlier to Israel."

"The Israelis give the Americans everything," said Bobbinsky. "They can't help themselves."

"So how would they do that?"

"Well, they could go directly to US intelligence. That would be the most logical route. But if they have reason not to be so direct, since whatever happened occurred in France, they most likely would confide in the DGSE."

"I have strong commercial contacts in Israel," said Tahir Badem. "I can find out rather quickly if the Israelis have Ugo and if they passed on any intelligence from him to the French or the Americans."

Conversation paused while a waiter delivered menus and refilled wine glasses.

"This is very disturbing," said Lee. "You all know how well the Project is succeeding, lately with important acquisitions in Russia and Korea. We simply cannot tolerate premature disclosure, not with the American election so near." Lee turned to Gil Adonis. "Your assessment of the United States situation, Mr. Adonis?"

Adonis had met before with the others at this table except for Mariana Lee. Now, seated across the table from her, he immediately sensed alpha, pack leader, a command quality he recognized in himself early in life but rarely encountered in others. It was reassuring to know the Project had such leadership. He replied with his own assurance.

"Our election is not that far away. Our candidate is leading in public opinion surveys, and we are confident he will succeed. If we avoid detection for the next three weeks, any disclosure after that will be considered politically suspect, and we will be able to turn it to our advantage."

"And if the stories come out after the election?" she asked.

"The election will be over. We will have won. There will be no possibility of overturning the result."

"Then it appears that the success of our Project depends upon our actions during the next three weeks," said Lee. "Until we know otherwise, we must assume Ugo has been taken. That does not necessarily mean we are in jeopardy. Ugo may have died before revealing our plans and our identity. And even if that information has fallen into unfriendly hands, we all know that it takes time to verify the authenticity of intelligence and that all organizations are slow to act on new information. Boris and Tahir, you must discover as quickly as possible the level of threat to us so that we know how we should respond appropriately."

Both men nodded as if being given assignments by a stern superior. None of the four men at the table knew anything of Lee's background or even her role in the Project. Perhaps she was one of the Project Managers, the small, mysterious group that directed the Salvation Project. Possibly even the chief Manager. They knew there were others, like themselves, directing what amounted to incipient government coups elsewhere. And they knew there was a hierarchy that gave direction and authorized targets and resources. But identities and roles were vigilantly masked. Except for Mariana Lee's. Hers was the face of the Project for all operatives, the conduit for passing information, receiving instructions, recruiting allies, and issuing death warrants.

Lee turned to Adonis. "Mr. Adonis, may we count on you to be alert to any sign that the Americans have Ugo's intelligence?"

"Absolutely," said Adonis.

"We don't live in a world of absolutes, Mr. Adonis. We live in a world of probabilities. And if such information does reach higher American authorities, can you assure us that you will have contingencies in place to prevent our candidate from losing the election?"

"You have my assurance," said Adonis. "We have people in the US intelligence agencies and in the White House itself. We can protect ourselves at a number of levels."

"I understand your president is in poor health," said Lee. "Is one of those protections a means for seeing to it that her health declines precipitously before Election Day?"

"If that's necessary, that can be arranged," Adonis responded.

Waiters entered the private room with the evening meals, bringing a pause to the planning. They ate quickly and in relative silence. Before they went their separate ways, Lee turned to Bobbinsky.

"To lose a trusted and experienced agent such as Ugo means he either was purposely or unwittingly outed. Do you have a sense how that may have happened?"

Bobbinsky took a long moment to carefully consider his answer.

"The only member of our group who knew about Ugo was Javier Carmona. Carmona was in Marseilles on business last week."

"Of course," said Badem. "Carmona is well connected in Marseilles."

Lee turned to Imam Kartal. "I believe Carmona is your responsibility?"

Kartal nodded, fully understanding the reason for Mariana Lee's question.

45

Every exterior noise seemed to waken him. A passing motor scooter straining to climb the steep cobblestones toward the Sacré-Cœur Basilica. The laughter of young people emerging from a nearby Montmartre café. Even the sound of an ancient air-conditioning system clicking to life. His body was drained of energy, but his mind was on full alert. Once awake, a return to sleep required a supreme act of willpower.

"Might they try to kill me to get it?" he had asked his old friend, Ambassador Hal Thompson. "They might try," said Hal. The "it" was beneath the covers of his bed. The folder's surfaces rubbed hard against his body each time he rolled over. Where else could this radioactive package of evidence be but within arm's reach? Not in a drawer of the hotel room's dresser where a knowing thief could barge in, grab it, and run. On a chair beside his bed? Under the bed? The small closet in this sparely furnished room? No. If he was to be the custodian of files that might save or bring down the US government, those files could be in only one place—next to his body, where at least he could fight trying to save them. Unless they found him asleep.

Dawn was a blessing after such a restless night. So was the knock on the door and the now familiar and comforting, "Foster." Foster entered with a breakfast tray.

Orange juice so flavorful it announced itself as being squeezed just that morning. Croissant still warm from the oven, a work of bakery magic one would expect from a French kitchen. Café au lait, rich and jarring.

The darkness was forgotten, the sense of danger eased. A continental French breakfast with a 250-pound former college football lineman looking out for your safety will do that.

So will travel in private aircraft. Ben was no stranger to flying. Decades of political campaign work meant a million miles of air travel, some at the controls of his own single- engine Piper Cherokee. But in all those years he had never flown like this. The bus that transported the group of twenty similarly dressed "clerics" from their hotel rolled directly onto Le Bourget Airport's tarmac, a few steps from the waiting Airbus ACJ319. Before construction of Charles de Gaulle and Orly, Le Bourget was the principal Paris airport. Now it served as the area's private aviation hub. Customs and passport control moved quickly, the aircraft door closed, and they were airborne in what seemed to Ben a matter of minutes. Air travel with no long security lines, no metal detectors, no crowds to maneuver one's way through. A traveler could easily be spoiled by such service.

Once in the air, Ben marveled at the plane's open seating arrangement configured for their group in space that easily could have held twice their number, the beverage cart's sumptuous selection of pre-lunch hors d'oeuvres, and the smiles of Parisian Holidays Air's flight attendants who served them, a crew obviously trained to elevate holiday spirits.

So, this is how it works when you have the money to charter private jets, Ben thought. A world apart, and not just the thirty thousand feet between cruising altitude and earth. Seated next to him, Foster, his protector. Across the aisle, Herve Coriton, French intelligence. Somewhere among the unfamiliar other faces were Herve's trusted agents. His mission wasn't yet over, but for the few hours of this flight he felt secure. He allowed himself the luxury of settling into his seat, the strain of tension easing, sleep overtaking a body he didn't realize was so weary.

A chartered bus was waiting for them when Ben and his fellow travelers disembarked at Signature Flight Support, a private aviation terminal at Washington, DC's Dulles Airport. To his surprise, Father Bob Reynolds was in the bus. Bob occupied a forward seat and motioned for Ben to take the empty seat next to him. He placed a finger to his own lips as a warning against too friendly a greeting. The remainder of the traveling party boarded, and the bus rolled through the airport gate.

"Should I worry even about these guys?" said Ben in a low, nearly whispered voice.

"Worry about everyone right now," said Bob. "It's good to see you. It all went well?"

"How would I know?" said Ben. "I'm just the delivery boy and I have my package, so I guess we're still on target." Ben nodded toward the leather satchel at his feet, then asked, "Where are we going?"

"Georgetown University. You're going to hang out there this afternoon. Tenny's flying in from Florida around dinnertime. You're scheduled to see her and deliver the package about nine."

"Who else is coming?"

"Not sure. Apparently, others in the US intelligence chain. They don't give me all the details."

"You know a helluva lot more than I do," said Ben.

"You're doing fine," said Bob.

"I'm scared shitless," said Ben.

After an hour navigating the twenty-seven miles between Dulles and Georgetown University, the bus came to a stop at a large building at the western edge of the campus.

"This is Wolfington Hall. My home, so to speak," said Bob. "The Jesuit residence. You'll stay with me in my room until it's time to go to the White House. They tell me many of those aboard the bus will take posts as extra security. It should be safe enough."

Foster appeared from the row behind Ben and Bob. He nodded to the bus driver, a signal to open the door, then stepped off the bus and glanced quickly around in a practiced 180-degree arc. He turned back to Ben.

"Let's go," he said.

Ben found Foster's need to check for danger even here, on campus, at a Jesuit residence hall, more disturbing than comforting.

46

In 1789, the year the United States officially was born as a nation, Georgetown was born as a university. The timing was not a matter of historic coincidence. Under British rule of the American colonies, Catholic schools were illegal. With the birth of the nation, the Jesuits wasted little time testing the Constitution's promise of religious liberty.

Revolutionary-era Jesuits not only were early to plant their flag in higher education, they also knew their real estate. The Georgetown University campus occupies 104 acres, bordered on the west by verdant Foundry Branch Valley Park and on the south by the Potomac River, some of the most valuable property in the Washington, DC, area.

A translucent gold painted the evening's clouds as the sun dipped in the western sky. Hints of fall appeared in the leaves of the park's ash groves, among the first trees to sense the end of summer. A tour boat floated past Three Sisters Island, likely on a dinner cruise. Cars clogged Canal Road just below and Key Bridge, the route to Virginia, as workers headed home and others sought the nightlife of commercial Georgetown.

Ben and Bob watched all of this from Wolfington Hall's outdoor patio, after-dinner whiskeys in hand, counting down the moments when they would set out for the White House to complete their delivery mission. They had spent hours in Bob's small apartment. Now it was liberating to be outside on this pleasant October evening.

"Marriott would kill to build a luxury hotel here, with this view," said Ben.

Father Bob Reynolds sipped his drink. "It's really the best thing about living here. You've seen my room. Not much there. The food's passable, not great. I love the campus life, the kids, the energy, the challenge of making my classroom worth attending and my topics worth knowing. But when the day's done, I love just sitting here, alone or with friends, watching the sunsets and just thinking."

"If you don't mind my asking," said Ben, "what do you think about? I've always been curious about life in the clerical world. It seems so rigid, every move ordained, excuse the pun."

"It can be, but it doesn't have to. I believe we're Christ's church and that he is the son of God and I believe in his resurrection. But for me, all of that's a wider window to the contemplation of life. For instance, look down the hill. What do you see?"

It was growing darker, but Ben could still distinguish activity on the roads and river. "The most obvious thing I see is the setting sun. A gorgeous setting sun. And then there's the car traffic."

"Yes. I see that, too. But below the concrete and asphalt there's Earth. That was here well before us and eons before this university. And it will be long after we're gone. Why? Why is this round rock of a planet here? And the molten inferno inside at Earth's core? That's life, too. A different form of life. A life no one, not the physicists or the chemists or the philosophers, truly understand. Yes, we can count the atoms and molecules and detect gasses and measure wavelengths. We can test for elements. We can count the stars. But what is it? What is life? How did it begin? Where did it begin? Where do we, you and I, fit into a cosmos of thousands of galaxies and uncounted trillions of life-forms inside us we call bacteria? For me, religion allows me to consider all of this. Not just allows it but challenges me to consider it."

Ben let Bob's words marinate in his own thoughts for a few moments.

"I apologize, Bob. I guess I've looked at all this too narrowly. One election at a time. One client at a time. You've been thinking big thoughts while I've been the one with tunnel vision."

"Oh, I doubt you have tunnel vision," said Bob. "I've read your letters. Very moving. Very beautiful. Your late wife?"

The events of past weeks had dimmed Ben's embarrassment at the release of the letters implying he was romancing Tenny. He swallowed all the suspicion, the jokes, even the FBI questioning, all without admitting to anyone that he had been writing love letters to his wife for more than a decade after her death.

"How did you guess?"

"Not hard, knowing you," said Bob.

"I met her when she was a graduate student here at Georgetown," said Ben. "She was going for a doctorate in English. I spoke to one of her seminars about the elements of persuasive language. She came up to me afterward and asked me a few questions. That's how it began. I'd meet her for lunch or dinner. We'd go for long walks on the campus. If we had time we might slip through the gate, right here, next to Wolfington Hall, and hike down the park trail to the Potomac and into Georgetown. Some irony, isn't it, that I'm at one of the scariest times of my life in nearly the same location as some of the most beautiful."

Darkness had fully settled in now. With sunset came the buzz of a million creatures that inhabited the nearby park's flora and fauna.

"She's still at your side, so many years later."

"It seems like yesterday. I don't know why. I used to think I wrote the letters so I wouldn't forget her. But there's no danger of my forgetting her. Maybe I wrote as a release of grief. I've never cared to look for a psychological reason."

"You're not alone, Ben. I can't tell you how many parishioners have told me the same story. Many people say they write letters to loved ones in heaven. If you didn't feel the need, you wouldn't be doing it. No reason to be embarrassed or to have self-doubts."

Ben sat back quietly and allowed Bob's counsel to make a full circuit of his thoughts.

"Do you think she knows, Bob? Do you think somewhere, by some means, Almie hears me when I speak about her, that she captures my thoughts when I think about her? Is there some type of forwarding address that allows us to communicate? You think a lot about the mystery of life. What's your best guess?"

Before Bob could answer, Ben's cell phone rang. He answered, listened for a moment, and said, "Yes."

The conversation quickly ended. He turned to Bob. "That was Clement," said Ben. "Tenny's ready for us. But I don't want this to be the last of our conversation about life and death."

"After our meeting at the White House," said Bob, "your package will be out of your life, my mission to get you there will be over, and we'll be free to talk the rest of the night if you like."

They both rose to leave.

"Thank heaven this is almost over," said Ben. "Thanking heaven is what we do here at Wolfington Hall," said Bob. "Let's go finish the job."

47

Clement, Coriton, and Foster were waiting at Wolfington Hall's main entry door.

"We're going to do this by private car so we won't attract attention," said Clement. "Bob, we've registered your car with the White House. They'll be expecting us. You'll drive. Herve and I will go with you to the garage to get the car. Foster, in five minutes' walk Ben to the bus turnaround. We'll pick you up there and head straight down Canal Road. Ben, the satchel's been with you at all times?"

"Look at my white knuckles. I've been gripping it so hard and so long I've practically lost all feeling in my hand."

Clement, whoever he was, whatever intelligence service he worked for, was still dressed as a cleric and obviously was team leader for this mission.

"Then let's go," he said.

Ben and Foster waited silently as Bob, Coriton, and Clement disappeared for the short walk to the underground parking garage.

Georgetown University operated a free student bus service between the main campus and other places where students, faculty, and staff often go: the Georgetown University Hospital, the off-campus Georgetown University Law Center, nearby Metro stations, and other locations. The turnaround adjacent to Wolfington Hall served as the outdoor bus station. A driveway to Canal Road allowed the buses to avoid driving onto the campus itself.

As soon as Ben and Foster stepped outside the hall, they realized they were not alone on what normally was a quiet street. Music, laughter, and milling students surrounded the McDonough Arena not fifty yards away. It was a festive scene, noisy, lively, but not rowdy, a rock concert just getting underway.

The scene drew Ben's attention, distracting him so that he did not fully focus on Bob's car as it pulled up to the curb. Suddenly, Foster pulled a handgun from his jacket and shoved Ben hard in the chest.

"Run, run, run!" yelled Foster. Ben froze, trying to relate to what was happening. Was Foster going to shoot Bob?

Out of the passenger side of the car jumped someone Ben had never before seen. A stranger in a black turtleneck and black pants. There was a gun pointed in his direction.

Then a volley of gunfire.

"Run to the crowd. Run, you idiot!" yelled Foster. A pool of blood suddenly appeared on Foster's chest, and he began sinking to the ground.

Only then did Ben run. He ran to the crowd milling outside the McDonough Arena, as Foster had commanded. Get lost in the crowd. Find security people there. Yell for others to help protect him. No one else apparently reacted to the exchange of gunfire, all from weapons with silencers. The music and ambient noise had drowned out the sound of the shooting. This was a weekend night on a college campus. Anyone watching the gunplay would likely see it as a goofy student stunt connected with the concert.

From his peripheral vision, Ben could see the man with the gun running toward him and whoever was at the wheel of Bob's car driving to block his access to the arena. His line of escape cut off, Ben could only run toward the narrow opening at the west wall of the arena and the campus heating and cooling plant behind it. Ben ran as only fear can run, faster than he ever imagined himself running. Behind him he could hear the squeal of tires as the car's driver maneuvered to get access to the narrow opening. Behind that, footsteps.

From his long-ago walks with Almie, Ben remembered a gate somewhere nearby, a gate in the chain-link fence separating the campus from the wooded Foundry Branch Valley Park. That memory was so faint—was it real or wishful thinking? Without a gate there would be no escape.

Security lights from the heating and cooling plant cut

through the shadows as he ran, giving him blurred images of the fence. He looked wildly for an opening. He no longer heard the car's engine. It had been blocked by dumpsters narrowing the space between the building and the fence. The car was no longer chasing him. But the footsteps were.

Then, just as he remembered, the opening to the park. The blackness beyond. Ben hesitated. What was worse, dropping the satchel and running into the forest to save himself or hanging on to it, trying to elude what was surely a professional hit man?

A flash of light appeared in the darkness. A volley of muffled gunshots. Steps getting closer.

Into the park and the darkness Ben plunged, the canopy of limbs nearly invisible against a moonless sky. The path forward also was barely visible. But he remembered. He remembered the path where he so often walked with Almie, exploring Japanese honeysuckle or standing silent so not to spook feeding deer. Other times, taking foolish risks with their naked bodies under a favorite oak. So many promises made, here, in this park. Now, a park that could also mark his grave.

As if directed by a long-dormant compass, Ben ran past the maples and the elms. He splashed through a rivulet, slightly swollen by recent rain. He flushed two short-tailed shrews and a bevy of wood thrushes. The path leading down to the river was straight and steep, but because he remembered it, Ben ran with confidence, certain that he was outdistancing his pursuer. Until an unexpected tangle of ivy grabbed his ankle.

Ben fell hard to the ground, his speed sending him into an uncontrolled slide, momentum increasing with the descent. Helplessly, he flailed for a handhold, the hard dirt path scraping his chest and legs. Finally, where the path took an elbow turn to the east, Ben crashed hard into a cottonwood tree, his fall stopping as suddenly as it had begun.

Ben lay stunned in the damp underbrush, surrounded by a pungent colony of turkey-tail fungus. A sharp pain traveled through his body, starting where his leg had smashed against the tree trunk. His ribs were on fire, scoured during the long skid. He heard himself panting like a dog that had been too long on a chase.

Ben had to clear his head. Chase. Had they, whoever they were, given up the chase? He had outrun them, he was sure of that. But by how much? Had they turned back? Ben lay quietly, listening for footsteps. With the turn of the path Ben realized he was near the bottom of the trail. From here, the path would go east, toward Canal Road. Not far beyond that, the Georgetown wharf. Restaurants. Nightlife. Safety. How much farther did he need to go? He mentally calculated. Maybe another thousand feet until Canal Road. Still no sound from his pursuers. Where were Coriton, Clement, and Bob? Foster clearly had been shot. What in the hell had happened?

Ben felt his pants pocket. Yes, his cell phone was still there. He could call for help. But who? Then he noticed his hand was sticky. He raised it to his mouth. Blood. *My God*, he thought, *I've been shot*. That volley of bullets as he ducked into the park. He hadn't realized.

Ben forced himself to his feet, took a firm handhold on his satchel, and quietly brushed away dead leaves and crushed ivy clinging to his face. He strained to listen for sounds from the darkness. All remained quiet.

He felt the impact before he heard the gunshot. This time there was no mistake. Another bullet in his side, near the first wound. Like a frightened animal in hunting season, Ben bolted for the trail. His pursuer had shot from higher up, before the trail turned, giving Ben just a few moments head start to get out of the gunman's line of sight.

Shit, thought Ben, *I'm being chased by a guy with night-vision goggles. He can see and I can't.*

Hiding in the woods would be pointless. Even in his wounded condition, he had no choice but to try to run. But his leg was all but useless. He felt himself weakening from loss of blood. He fell forward, stumbling for a few yards, holding his side, trying to ignore his leg pain, grasping his bullet wound, hoping to stem the blood flow, feeling energy ebb from his body.

His pursuer would no longer need to shoot at him from a distance. Now, he could be caught and properly executed rather than brought down like prey in flight.

Waves of pain crashed through his body. An instant before Ben fell to his knees and passed into unconsciousness, he heard the now familiar sound of gunshots and was enveloped by an aura of intense white light.

Not an hour ago, he was asking Father Bob Reynolds about the mystery of life. Could Almie somehow still hear him, sense him, feel his love? We can talk about that the rest of the night, Bob had said.

There would be no rest of the night. He would never know. Or maybe, if there was heaven, he would join her there. Now.

48

It began as if a whisper. Softly, distant. "Ben. Ben."

With growing urgency.

"Ben, can you hear me? Ben, open your eyes!"

He forced his eyelids to move and was immediately blinded by white light. Confusing. He seemed to remember his fall, the pain, a diminishing claim to his passage through life. Then the light, the brilliant light. Now, again the light.

"Ben, it's me. Kyle. Kyle Christian."

Christian could see Ben struggling with the bright medical lights over the gurney. He turned toward one of two nurses in the room. "Turn off the overheads. Just go with room light for a few minutes."

The room dimmed. Ben's eyes opened. He tried to move his arms, without success. This was all so strange. Consciousness was returning, but not familiarity. All he felt was disorientation.

"Can you hear me, Ben? It's Kyle Christian."

Ben turned his head and saw the familiar face of the CIA director, his longtime friend from political wars. Ben nodded. "Kyle?" The name was spoken much weaker than Ben had intended. He was surprised that he could speak at all. Surprised that the bright light above did not mean he was in some form of afterlife. "Kyle?" he repeated.

"Are you in pain? We can help that if you are."

Ben shook his head, ever so slightly.

"You're banged up. Nothing that can't be fixed, they tell me.

They're about to operate on your gun wounds. Looks like you were damned lucky. You took four bullets and lost a lot of blood, but no vital organs were hit."

"Where? Where am I?"

"CIA infirmary. Good docs here. They're used to fixing gunshot wounds and plenty of other stuff that comes through the door in our business."

"But I'm alive. How?"

"We had a sensor in your satchel. As soon as things went to hell up at the bus stop, we could track you on the run. We sent a team into the woods after you, but they got too late a start to do you any good. We sent another team to Canal Road to go up the trail the other way."

"You did that to save me?"

Kyle laughed. "We didn't think we could save you. You were up against real pros. We wanted to save your satchel. By going in both ways, we had the guy trapped. He wasn't getting out."

"Thanks."

"Hey, in this business we do what we have to do. We couldn't save you. You saved yourself."

"But I didn't. Last thing I remember was passing out and then all that white light."

"Oh yeah, the white light. An old trick of the trade. We figured the guy chasing you was wearing night-vision goggles. He was right behind you, maybe ten, twenty yards, when our guys showed up. They blasted him with spots. When you have night-vision goggles on, it's like getting dilated at the eye doc's. So, when bright lights hit, your eyes take time to adjust. That gave us time to wrap him up."

"You've got him?"

"Sure do. Being interrogated right now. A real valuable catch. Thank you."

"What happened, Kyle? Why were they in Bob's car?

Where are the others?"

"Sorry to tell you, Ben. They're all dead. The best we can make out, one of Herve's traveling team, one of the guys who made the trip from Paris with you, was a plant. They must have infiltrated French intelligence, learned about you and your package, and somehow got a guy assigned to the team to take you out and snatch the package."

"He could have killed me anytime during the trip. At the airport, on the plane, even at Wolfington Hall."

"Yes, and no. Clement was one of ours. He had you pretty well covered with his people. But the plant knew how they were getting you to the White House. Apparently had a local accomplice. They waited in the garage, gunned down Clement, Herve, and Bob, and took the car."

"My God!"

"It would have worked. They would have killed or snatched you at the bus stop. But Foster was really alert and quick and spotted them just in time to save you."

"Foster. Is Foster...."

"Dead? No. The docs operated on him a while ago at Georgetown University Hospital. He'll pull through."

"Is Foster one of yours, too?"

"No. He's on loan. We needed a real French-speaking priest for your trip. Foster's worked with us before. A real cool head.

Like we talked about long ago at my house, Ben, we work with the Vatican."

A woman in a white medical gown came into Ben's field of vision.

"It's time," she said.

"Okay," said Kyle. "Ben, if you hadn't come to me with your suspicions, God knows what would be going on now. We've been on this ever since. I'll tell you more about it when you get past surgery. By the way, the president wants to see you then."

"She knows?"

"She's been calling me every ten minutes to check up on you."

"The satchel?"

"I'm heading there right now with the FBI guys and others to go through it with her. Mission accomplished, Agent Sage."

Two orderlies moved Ben's gurney toward the operating room. Ben was now fully awake, trying to process all that Kyle had told him, everything that had happened, the realization that the delivery mission was over, the personal danger likely past, and that he had survived.

But Bob hadn't. Bob. The hurt suddenly swept his body. Hours ago, he and Bob began to explore eternal truths. Bob. So good. So wise. He had become such an important part of Ben's life. They called him "Father Bob," but Ben felt him a brother. To die so suddenly. So senselessly.

Ben could feel the hot anesthetic mixture flow through his vein in symmetry with the tears that began to flow from his eyes. Bob's laughing, loving image was the last he had before consciousness dissolved.

49

The late Ugo Schola had the misfortune of attracting the interest of a fellow export agent by the name of Wu at the worst possible time. Only that morning, Ugo had consolidated coded information from various network sources and was about to transmit the file to Singapore. The organization was scrupulous about keeping such information segmented to prevent security catastrophe. In this instance, however, an exception was made. With the US election so near and the prospects for a favorable outcome so strong, an update of the worldwide strategic plan was required. The Project Managers planned to assess assets, provide postelection guidance for key operatives, and launch initiatives made possible by control of the US government. Ugo's admirable record of penetrating intelligence organizations throughout the Mediterranean and, when required, disposing of troublesome apostates made him an obvious choice for the Project's most sensitive tasks.

Before Ugo could transmit his files, Wu, a Singapore export agent he had known for years and in whom he had developed a trusting relationship, invaded his apartment, accompanied by four others he had never met, and quickly bound his arms and legs, covered his head with a black hood, and carried him to an unknown location. Ugo, a professional who in earlier life had been trained well by the AISI, the Italian intelligence agency, managed to constrain his fear and listen carefully for ambient sounds that might allow him to identify his location for rescuers. If he found an opportunity to contact rescuers.

That opportunity never came. His captors also were professionals, agents of China's intelligence agency, the MSS. They not only knew how to prevent Ugo from summoning help, but they had the training and the tools to unravel the code on his laptop, secure the Project's most sensitive material, and persuade Ugo to be cooperative in answering their many questions. They also were skilled in ways to dispose of bodies so that they were never found.

Now, after a circuitous trip through the MSS office in Marseilles, a Mossad shipping company front nearby, the American Embassy in Paris, and a harrowing chase in Georgetown's woods, Ugo's cache of information was being revealed to a small group of US intelligence leaders in a secure office at the Langley, Virginia, headquarters of the US Central Intelligence Agency. Unfolding before the eyes of those viewing the files was an advanced plan for a worldwide coup involving trusted military and intelligence counterparts, religious leaders, scientists, and familiar names in worldwide finance, business, and the arts and entertainment. Regime changes in three countries over the previous twelve months were shaded in green, for "accomplished." A number of countries, chillingly, the United States among them, were listed as "immediate targets."

Kyle Christian presented this information, each slide and description more baffling to its audience than the one before it. So many questions. Too many. The buzz in the room faded to puzzled silence.

As he concluded his presentation, Christian turned to President Tennyson.

"Madam President," said Christian, "our agency is convinced that this information is authentic, and we have no doubt that we are confronted with a subversive cabal far along on a plan to capture control of our government."

"There's another explanation," interrupted General Forest Grimm, chief of army intelligence. "It's a hoax. I've been in this business for more than thirty years, and there's no way anyone could have pulled together all of these resources without our knowing about it. We all know how difficult it is to keep secrets. The more people who know, the less secure the secret. How could all of these people be recruited, and a plan of this magnitude be so far along without someone, many people, giving it away?"

"Are you saying we should disregard all of this?" said Christian, motioning to the screen.

"Not at all," said Grimm. "We need to check authenticity before taking any other action. I recognize a number of names in those files. No way they would sign up for coups in their countries. I would personally confront them and ask flat out."

"If what we've just seen is real," said NSA director Kenneth Kloss, "letting them know that we know sends them diving underground, erasing their tracks."

"Is that bad?" Grimm asked. "End the threat, if there is one."

"Delays it, postpones it, maybe," said Attorney General Robin Birch. "Then there's an election. President Tennyson loses. Bowman wins, and whatever they have planned reemerges."

"They already know, don't they?" said Sam Vellman, FBI director. "They know we got their guy, which means we have this information."

"Not necessarily," said Christian. "Maybe their guy didn't talk. Someone trusted with this kind of information would be tough to break. Maybe he destroyed the information before he was grabbed. Maybe we have it but don't believe it. If this is what it looks like, there are years of planning behind it. Years of recruitment. It's not easy to give up on a plan like this unless you're dead sure you have to."

"Do you believe it, Mr. Director?" asked President Tennyson.

"Yes, the CIA is convinced this is authentic. We were alerted to something of this nature months ago and have been working it since. But we couldn't be absolutely sure until we saw this package."

"What was in it that convinced you?"

"The names of three of our own agents who we suspected and had been watching. All three are on the list of agents working for this so-called project."

"Have you confronted them?"

"No, Madam President. We've stepped up our monitoring, hoping these people point us to others and that we can identify communication channels that lead to the coup's leadership."

"Madam President," said Attorney General Birch, "it's fairly clear from these documents that a key to their planning is the election of your opponent. I suggest we consider going public right away. Otherwise they could implement their plan through Bowman. Defeating him may be the only way to stop them."

Tenny thought for a moment. "This is very difficult, Robin, and all of you. Yes, not revealing what we know could result in Bowman winning the election, with all that could mean for the future. The polls are very close, and I have no idea how the election will turn out if we do nothing publicly about this. On the other hand, making a public issue of it now runs the risk that the opposition will attack it as a last-minute political gambit, and it could very well cost me the election. They'll accuse me of politicizing our intelligence agencies and, to the extent you confirm the threat, hurting your agencies and the reputations of all of you personally."

"Then what do you suggest we do, Madam President?" asked Birch.

"Find the bastards and clean out the rats' nests. That's your job as professionals. Let me handle the politics. Kyle, you coordinate an action plan, and I'll leave you all to figure it out."

Tenny left the agency heads to consider their next steps. Director Vellman followed her out the door. "May I talk to you privately for a moment, Madam President?" he asked.

"What do you have, Sam?"

"Madam President, the FBI, of course, is neutral in elections. We serve at the pleasure of whoever is president."

"That's the way it should be, Sam."

"But what we just saw is terrifying. If you lose, we've just seen a plan that poses radical risk for the country."

"Well, I hope I don't lose."

Vellman touched Tenny's back, steering her toward a far corner of a room where they were not likely to be overheard.

"A number of weeks ago, our Chicago agents arrested a small-time extortion artist by the name of Buddy Rufus," said Vellman. "The guy's been in and out of trouble for years. This time we nailed him for things that could send him to prison for ten years or more. When he met with the people in the US Attorney's Office, he offered to expose something that he hoped would make the prosecutors go easier on him. It turned out that he had photos of your opponent in some very compromising positions with a woman, not his wife, while he was campaigning in Illinois. I'm sure that if those photos and that story were published, it would really hurt his chances of being elected."

"You've seen the pictures?"

"Seen the pictures and seen the video interview with the woman. She says she was paid to keep quiet about it."

"Bowman knows?"

"Apparently. His campaign paid her off."

Tenny thought for a moment. "Sam, you and I did not have this conversation, did we?"

"No, Madam President, we didn't."

"So, if those photos somehow make their way into the newspapers, I had nothing to do with it, did I?"

"No, Madam President."

"Neither did you or anyone in your agency or the Department of Justice have any role in leaking the story, did they?"

"Not a thing, Madam President. But we can't stop the media from being enterprising, particularly when covering presidential campaigns."

Tenny turned to leave the room.

"How's your family, Sam? Your son Charles must be near graduation from Arizona State."

"Next year. Thank you for asking."

"You must be very proud of him."

50

Ben had been awake for about an hour. Enough time for his brain to clear the anesthesia. Enough time for him to assess the IV in his arm and two tubes of uncertain purpose in the lower part of his body, one he guessed to drain his urine. The other, no one was around to explain. He wasn't in pain. That was a surprise. He had seldom used even an aspirin for a headache, so Ben wasn't familiar with the power of modern analgesics.

A woman in a white doctor's coat entered the small, private room, speaking on her cell phone.

"Yes, he's awake," the doctor said to whoever was on the other end of the conversation. "I'm looking at him now. Just a minute, I'll check."

"Ben," she said, "How are you feeling? You look good."

"Not bad. Alive," said Ben, a bit surprised at how haltingly he spoke the words. A sign he might not be physically as strong as he felt.

"Up to having a visitor?" said the doctor, belatedly introducing herself. "I'm Dr. Crenshaw."

"Why not?" Ben answered. "I don't have any other appointments."

Dr. Crenshaw returned her attention to the cell phone. "He's being a smart-ass," she said. "It's fine." She disconnected and lifted the sheets covering Ben.

"The operation went well. No vital organ damage. Clean wounds. A few more days to let the incisions heal, watch for infection, and we'll have you out of here."

"Where am I?"

"CIA infirmary. Post-op. You'll feel a bit of discomfort in a while as the heavy-duty pain killers dissipate, but we'll try to let you down easy. Other than that, it's just bed rest, a few assisted walks, and you'll be back in business."

"Who's my visitor?"

"This is the CIA. Can't tell you."

"That's bullshit."

"Sure is," said Dr. Crenshaw. She patted his arm and left. A moment later, two nurses entered. With practiced expertise, they replaced his bedsheets and pillowcases while gently repositioning Ben's body. They removed his IV and hooked him to a new full bag. One of the nurses ran a comb through Ben's hair and patted his cheek.

"Got to look your best," she said. "Can't make it look like we're not taking good care of you."

She smiled at Ben as the door opened and Tenny and CIA director Kyle Christian entered.

Tenny said nothing for a moment, just ran her eyes over his face like a finely calibrated laser checking for imperfections.

"You know," she finally said, "the last time we talked I fired you to keep you from getting shot or poisoned or thrown off a ten-story building. What the hell are you doing here?"

"Sorry," he said. "But you can't fire me again. You already did that."

"Ben, you are such an idiot."

"You've come here to tell me that?"

"Yes, and I mean it" she said, her smile indicating she didn't.

"I also came to thank you."

Tenny walked to the side of the bed and took Ben's hand. "In much pain?"

"No," said Ben. "I don't know what they gave me, but I feel fine."

"No, you don't," said Tenny. "I can hear it in your voice. You don't have to talk. I can't stay long. Kyle's brought me up to date. His people have analyzed all the material you brought back from Paris. We've met with the whole security team to decide how to respond."

"Just so you know," said Kyle Christian, "after you came to my home, passing on the warning you got from your Vatican source, I put some of our top people on it. Actually, what you had fit with stuff we were picking up from the field. It helped us narrow the search."

"If you had it, why'd you need me?" Ben asked. "I was probably the weakest link. Why not a real agent to carry that package? And by the way, everyone cautioned me about talking to you again. They thought the agency might have moles."

Christian smiled and shook his head.

"The agency did have moles," he said. "They showed up in the files you brought us. Why you? I felt I needed to act fast once I learned about the package in Paris. I leaped a lot of protocol by sending you. But I knew you and Hal Thompson were buddies and that I could trust you. That gave me a flimsy excuse to put together that traveling priest thing. It's one of the advantages of being a Knight of Malta. The Vatican connection. What blew us away was how quickly the bad guys got onto all of this and how they managed to infiltrate French security."

That reminded Ben his mission had resulted in three

murders—one, his close friend Father Bob Reynolds. "And kill really three people you sent to protect me."

"One day, Ben," Christian said, "we'll be able to recognize Bob as a real hero. For now, all this has to stay under the blanket. This is still an active operation. Still plenty of danger out there. You can't tell anyone where you were or what's happened."

"Lee knows. He was with me when I got the call from Bob. What do I tell him? What do I tell people in my office? What do I tell anybody?"

"I'll handle Lee," said Tenny. "I'll tell him I was planning to appoint Hal to the cabinet and asked you to make a quick trip to Paris to see if he was interested."

"He won't believe that."

"Of course not. But it gives him a story to tell your staff and anyone else who asks."

"And when I show up with bullet wounds?"

"You won't," said Christian. "When you get out of here, you'll be able to walk. You'll be sore. Appendix operation, if anyone asks. Emergency surgery in Paris."

Tenny motioned to Christian, a time-to-go signal.

"When you're strong enough, I'll expect you back in the campaign," said Tenny. "Remember the campaign? It's not over yet, and I'm behind in the polls."

"I'll be there," said Ben.

Tenny took Ben's hand, squeezed hard, and kissed his cheek. As she and Christian turned to leave, Ben had one more thought.

"Will I need a bodyguard? Will they still be after me?"

Christian smiled. "No worries," he said. "You're damaged

goods. They don't care about you anymore."

51

Groupo Aragon's corporate Gulfstream G550 arrived at dusk. Nine hours had elapsed since Javier Carmona boarded in Buenos Aires. A long and tiring flight, even though Carmona napped for a few hours in a private compartment. He often traveled by air but had never mastered the ability to sleep soundly on long-distance flights. This flight was no different. Too much going on in his head to easily shut down. The business that took him to Argentina was well worth his time. Very profitable. He was glad to have made the trip. Now he was more than ready to go home, to sleep in his own bed, to return to his normal routine in an environment where he knew he would be comfortable and safe.

Before that horrible night when his security chief, Soto, was murdered, Carmona had little concern about personal threats. True, he had many enemies, accumulated during years managing the affairs of Groupo Aragon. Competitors whom he destroyed. Employees and associates who required banishment or punishment. Soto would always see to Carmona's safety. When more security was required, he could always outsource jobs to the cartels. Quite efficient, the cartels. They would not want such a lucrative client as Javier Carmona harmed.

Soto's murder, and the leash Imam Musa Kartal had attached to him, had changed all that. Now he was personally in bondage to foreigners for whom murder was merely another task on a to-do list. Was he, Carmona, on the next page of that list? They said no. They assured him that he was a valuable partner in their enterprise. Only a fool would believe that.

It was even more foolish to believe that their so-called project would ever succeed. Take over the world? Indeed! Inevitably, they would be unmasked and most likely hanged by the very government leaders they plotted to overthrow. Carmona was confident he could survive disclosure. He certainly could not be accused of trying to replace leaders of the Mexican government, his own people. He had purchased those leaders with generous outlays of cash, stock in his enterprises, and other valuables. And if any of them did show signs of straying despite his generosity, well, then Carmona had his own secret files and leashes to tug.

Until he could rid himself of the plotters in Istanbul, his safety was paramount. He could not afford to be surprised a second time. Four security men were aboard this airplane, traveling with him. One of the four was Araya, his new security chief. He liked Araya. He liked the fact that the man had been on his payroll for a dozen years. Very trustworthy. And he liked the idea that Araya came from Basque people. Basque people were very strong. They lived up to the Spanish concept of macho, *machismo*, tough guy. Araya had demonstrated on many occasions that he was a very tough guy.

The plane's cabin door opened to reveal the clear night sky above Toluca's airport, home base for Groupo Aragon's air fleet. Araya disembarked first, the new security arrangement. Two of Araya's men waited at the bottom of the stairs. After a brief conversation with them, Araya waved to a Carmona aide standing in the doorway, the signal that it was safe for Carmona to descend. Carmona hurried down the stairs and into his limousine, just steps away. Araya joined the driver in the front seat while the other two security men settled in on each side of Carmona in the back. Now, tightly secure, Carmona headed to his home in Mexico City's Polanco neighborhood.

Some of Mexico's most luxurious homes were in Polanco, none more noteworthy than Carmona's Spanish colonial revival villa, a rare architectural monument, with its sprawling, artfully landscaped entry court, sweeping marble stairway, and oversize arched windows that even on cloudy days washed most interior rooms with brilliant natural light. Above the hand-painted tiled patios, sculpted balconies glowed with flaming red bougainvillea. An eight- foot wall surrounded the entire property, dotted with sensors to detect anyone who might attempt an unwanted entry. Kalashnikov-carrying guards stood sentinel, protecting front and rear entrances. Javier Carmona had turned this showpiece of a home into a personal fortress.

His journey finally at an end, Carmona emerged from his limousine and was met by Nicholas, his manservant.

"Welcome home, Senor Carmona. May I get you anything? Food? Drink?"

"Perhaps some brandy, Nicholas. That bottle of Tesseron that I favor. Set it beside my bed. Anything we need to discuss?"

"A few household details, sir. Nothing that won't keep until morning, or later. Your luggage arrived a few moments ago and has been taken to your room and sorted. Will you require a bath or shower?"

"No. That will keep until tomorrow, too. I'm very tired and will go straight to bed."

"Should I instruct your breakfast and car to be available at the usual time in the morning?"

"Nicholas, I've had a very tiring trip. I believe I will allow myself the luxury of sleeping a bit longer. Just have everyone stand by, and I'll call you when I'm up."

"Very good, sir. Good night."

Carmona slowly climbed the marble staircase to the sleeping quarters. A weary climb. He had often considered installing an elevator. An extravagance. But lately, his visits with doctors had increased. Age was announcing itself ever more prominently in his body. Thank heaven his mind was still clear. Maybe tomorrow he would discuss the elevator once again with Groupo Aragon's maintenance people.

Carmona shed his travel clothes for his pajamas and poured a small amount of the Tesseron from the carafe Nicholas had set out. Sitting by the side of the bed, he swallowed it quickly, a sacrilege for such a rare and expensive cognac. No matter. All he really wanted was to place his head on his pillow, bury himself deeply between his satin sheets, and finally fall into deep sleep.

52

Nicholas was reluctant to disturb Javier Carmona. His instruction was to wait for a morning call. But it was now well past the usual breakfast hour, and Carmona's private secretary had called, anxious to confirm an important scheduled luncheon meeting.

Nicholas approached Carmona's door and called to him gently. No response. Carmona had looked so tired last night. If he was still asleep, perhaps it was because his body required it. He decided to give Carmona more time.

Another hour passed. Another urgent phone call from Carmona's office. That settled the matter for Nicholas. He knocked on Carmona's bedroom door. No response. With a growing sense of concern, Nicholas entered the still- darkened room.

Under normal circumstances, as soon as he saw Carmona's body, sprawled face down on the bed, one foot dangling in space, Nicholas would have summoned medical assistance. But it was evident there was no life left in Javier Carmona to save and no point calling for help. Nicholas was aware that his employer did not lead a normal life; otherwise, why would he insist on so much security? There could well be arrangements that required handling before authorities were notified.

Nicholas backed out of the bedroom, closed the doors tightly, and hurried downstairs to find Araya, who had been waiting in the kitchen to accompany Carmona. It was their morning routine.

Araya had seen much death in his work. In fact, he occasionally was the cause of death. He knew what to look for. Alerted by Nicholas, Araya went to the bedroom and with a professional's eye inspected Carmona's body. Gun wounds? Knife? Blood traces of any kind? Signs of suffocation? No marks or bruises. No one could have entered the home during the night without being seen by his men. Nicholas was the only other person on the premises. Clearly, natural causes.

"Wait for one more hour. I need some time before you call anyone else," Araya told Nicholas. Time for what? Nicholas knew better than to ask.

The medical people arrived first. Heart failure, they said. Carmona had a history of heart problems. He even wore a pacemaker to regulate his heartbeats. Given Carmona's business and political importance, and the sudden nature of his death, the police placed a hold on removal of the body. Two hours later, an investigative team from Policía Federal arrived and fanned out through the home. Two detectives and a police cameraman headed for the bedroom. Two other detectives began questioning the staff: a cook, two maids, a driver, the security guards. The chief inspector, Rinaldo Herrero, motioned to Nicholas to join him at the dining room table, where Nicholas related the events of the past evening.

"Nothing at all unusual?" asked Herrero. "Think hard, Nicholas. Anything you recall could be helpful." Nicholas lowered his head into his hands, as if trying to squeeze out a thought that he missed during his first review of Carmona's homecoming.

"Nothing. Absolutely nothing," Nicholas finally replied. "Just that he was tired after such a long trip. He didn't complain of any specific ailment."

"Not a headache? Chest pain? Upset stomach?"

"Nothing. Although I did notice he drank very little of the cognac I delivered to him."

"Was that cognac from an open bottle? Any chance it was tampered with?"

"Tampered with?" Nicholas didn't understand.

"Could anyone have dropped poison or other substance into the bottle?"

Nicholas was startled at the suggestion. "Of course not. I opened the bottle myself and poured it into the carafe, as he requested."

"We'll have the lab check it out anyway. I'm not accusing you, Nicholas. It's my job."

"And it's been my job to manage this household," said Nicholas. "A very good job. Now I have no idea what I will do. Senor Carmona was a kind and generous employer."

Herrero wrote notes on a pocket pad and then returned to his questions.

"Anyone here who might have reason to do Senor Carmona harm? An employee he argued with? Someone who didn't like him? Anyone recently fired?"

"No one. No one at all. This is a very harmonious household. The medical people said it was his heart. Why would you suspect anyone?"

Before Herrero could reply, he was interrupted by one of his investigators.

"Something in the bedroom you need to see," said Detective Pineda.

Herrero motioned to Nicholas to join him. They climbed the stairs and entered the bedroom. Coroner aides were waiting for approval to remove Carmona's body for autopsy or the funeral home, whichever Herrero decided. They already had placed the body on a gurney.

Pineda walked to the now empty bed and pulled back the fitted bottom sheet to reveal a five-foot-long square cotton pad positioned where Carmona's body had been found. Herrera studied the object and turned to Nicholas.

"How do you explain this?"

"Oh," said Nicholas, "that was something Senor Carmona ordered. It was delivered while he was away. I had the household help place it under his sheets as instructed."

"Who instructed you?"

"The man who delivered it. He said Senor Carmona had it custom made to his specifications."

"Did Senor Carmona have bed-wetting problems? What were you told?"

"No. He often complained of body aches. This pad had something to do with that, relieving soreness while he slept."

"Who told you that?"

"The representative from El Palacio de Hierro who delivered it."

"Did this 'representative' show you any credentials? An order form? A bill for the merchandise? An identification card?"

Nicholas could hear accusation in every question. He hesitated before replying, searching his memory to recall an incident that at the time seemed unremarkable. Carmona often ordered personal items and had them delivered to his home. Hierro was Carmona's favorite department store. Expensive jewelry, fine clothes. The store never sent bills or asked for payments. All that was settled at the Groupo Aragon business office.

"Think hard before you reply," said Chief Inspector Herrero. "Why would you accept this item?"

"Why wouldn't I?" said Nicholas, trying hard not to sound defensive. "Maybe once a week, sometimes more, deliveries would arrive from that store. It was not uncommon."

"By the person who delivered this?"

"No, he was new to me."

"How would you describe him?"

"Very proper. He wore a dark suit. A turtleneck sweater, I believe. Black also. My first thought upon seeing him was that he looked Middle Eastern. And he did have an accent I found hard to place."

Nicholas leaned over the bed to observe the pad in question more closely. "Why are you asking these questions? It seems like a normal mattress pad. I thought little of it when it was delivered and asked one of our housekeepers to see that it was placed properly on Senor Carmona's bed before he returned home. I knew he would be exhausted from his trip and that if he purchased this pad to help relieve his pains, it would be good to have it here for his first night home. Why are you so interested?"

"Because," said Herrero, fixing his eyes tightly on Nicholas to see his immediate reaction, "the pad killed him."

Nicholas responded the way one might when clubbed between the eyes with a police nightstick.

"How is that possible?" he gasped.

"It's a magnetic mattress pad," said Herrero. "It's filled with strong magnets. The idea is that they send radiation and electric signals to your body while you sleep, and that's supposed to increase your blood flow and make you feel better."

"So the deliveryman was correct about the purpose."

"Oh yes. Quite correct. He just left out one small detail. That much magnetism next to a person's pacemaker turns the pacemaker into a killing machine. It might just turn off the pacemaker completely or send the heart into wild fluctuations."

Nicholas could feel ice-cold fingers of terror creeping from his stomach to his extremities, catching his throat so it was difficult to speak, driving water out of his body through his facial pores.

Herrero just watched as Nicholas transformed from a confident manservant to someone who realized he had been responsible for his patron's death.

"Did this delivery person leave a card?" asked Herrero. "No, never mind. Murderers never leave calling cards. How about a name? Did he introduce himself with a name?"

Nicholas had retreated to a bedroom wall, leaning hard against it, trying his best not to faint, to pass out, to fall. Words came hard.

"Odd name. I remembered it as one I had never heard before. 'Melek,' I think he said. Melek."

53

The memorial service for Father Bob Reynolds was conducted at the Dahlgren Chapel, capacity three hundred. If held elsewhere, double or triple the number of mourners likely would have attended. Much thought was given to moving the service to the Cathedral of Saint Matthew the Apostle, seat of Washington, DC's archdiocese, but an ad hoc group of those who knew Reynolds best felt that since their friend's life had been devoted to Georgetown, so should the final passage of his soul, the place where he had conducted so many marriages, baptized so many children, and heard so many confessions. The Dahlgren Chapel was located at the geographic center of the Georgetown University campus, its religious heart. For many, so was Father Bob Reynolds.

Father John Wycoski celebrated the mass. Others, priests and laity alike, spoke of Reynolds's importance to the church, the university, and to their lives. Loudspeakers broadcast the ceremony to the adjacent quadrangle, where hundreds of fellow faculty and students gathered in silence. The media was well represented, its coverage anchored in campus safety and the university's plans to tighten its security.

Ben was in awe of how quickly and smoothly the intelligence services had spun the deadly events of that night into a case of simple car hijacking. Reporters were told that as Bob and two friends arrived at his car, they encountered someone trying to steal it. In attempting to stop the thief, the three men were shot and killed. Then the hijacker drove quickly out of the garage to escape down the bus ramp to Canal Road. A visiting priest was at the bus stop, recognized Bob's car, and attempted to flag him down to get a ride to town. The gunman stopped and fired at the priest, identified as Foster Compte from Burlington, Vermont, a friend of Bob's. The gunman sped away and the car was found later, abandoned, in nearby Virginia.

The men who died with Father Bob Reynolds were identified as Clement Augustine from San Antonio, Texas, and Herve Coriton, from Paris. Bob had met Augustine while assigned as a priest in a minor parish near San Antonio before moving to Georgetown. Coriton had arrived that very day from Paris. He served as an active laity member of his church in Paris and had taken the opportunity to travel with a group of American priests returning to the US on a charter flight.

Police officials rolled out this story in a series of press conferences. One reporter said he had spoken to a number of people who described mysterious lights and what sounded like gunfire in the woods near Canal Road about the same time as the murders. A police spokesman said that they investigated but determined that the noise and lights all were associated with the concert.

Ben surprised himself that he could shed so many tears. Not

since Almie's death, so harsh, so unexpected, so unfair, had Ben felt such a wrenching sense of loss.

"We were so involved in talking about an afterlife," said Ben as he and Lee walked toward Lee's car. "So involved. We were going to talk more later. About how Bob viewed immortality. About what I still felt about Almie. Just minutes before he died."

"Tough to take," Lee agreed. "He lived preaching what he saw as eternal truths, and his death was reported as part of a phony cover story."

"It is amazing how fast the intelligence guys moved in with that story," said Ben. "They make us look like amateurs."

"I'm not sure the story will stick," said Lee. "Too many witnesses at the arena, too many on Canal Road, and a lot of guys in the traveling party. Even reporters in France may tie that intelligence director's death to an operation rather than bad luck."

"Could be," said Ben. "But the way Kyle Christian described it to me, they're playing for time. The longer the bad guys have doubts about what our guys know and what they intend to do about it, the better the chance there is of stopping whatever is going on."

"What *is* going on?" said Lee.

"Damned if I know," said Ben. "I was just the UPS guy for the delivery of a keg of dynamite."

"Since it blew up in your face, you deserve an explanation."

"Above my pay grade," said Ben. "Not cleared for the details."

"Well, it's good to have you back. And not a day too soon. There's still an election coming up, and so far, we're not winning it."

54

The first indication of trouble to come for the otherwise flawless Bowman for President campaign appeared in a local Springfield, Illinois, TV news report. A Springfield air charter service fired one of its pilots for what was termed "irregularities" during a campaign charter. The company refused to describe the incident. A personnel matter, the company said.

Two days later, Blue State Illinois, a partisan Democratic Party website, published the following item:

No wonder Mid-State Air Charter of Springfield didn't give a reason for firing veteran pilot Anthony Cribbens. If it had, the incident would have been X-rated. "Family Man" Zach Bowman was caught with his pants down in a back- seat tryst with a woman we are told was most definitely not part of his family. And instead of keeping his eyes respectfully on the road, so to speak, Cribbens used the moment to record the event on his cell phone and attempted to blackmail the Bowman campaign.

Three weeks before Election Day, such a news item, even on a little-trafficked partisan website, was bound to draw interest. It took less than twenty-four hours for the national media to be on the trail of the story. Campaign manager Crystal Kranz initially dismissed it as "last-minute campaign garbage from a desperate losing candidate" and refused to say more. Bowman would not comment on it. Denials and stonewalling lasted only until the video showed up on YouTube.

Kranz and her media team tried to convince reporters that the video was a cleverly edited hit piece. They were having some success until Chicago attorney Bruce Canby produced his client, Amy Renson, who identified herself as the woman in that movie and said she had been invited by Bowman to join him on the campaign trip and he had sexually attacked her.

The Bowman campaign had been light on issues and heavy on Zach's character. A handsome, earnest leader with a picturesque and devoted family. A new face for America to replace a president deeply scarred by controversy. Now, a hard-to-dismiss muddying of that image suggesting that Bowman was a fraud deeply undercut many voters' reasons for voting for him.

The reversal of fortune happened quickly. Most scandals have short media shelf lives. News, by definition, is a perishable commodity. But in the brief period while stories are hot, the fire can be intense. So, it was with this one, with control of the White House at stake and the election just weeks away. And, as these types of stories do, they prompted a number of women in his home state of Pennsylvania and two former staffers to call reporters and describe their own unwanted attention from Zach Bowman.

Zach inspired little loyalty among Republican Party leaders and elected officials. Now, put to an extreme test, few rushed to his defense. Some found it politically useful for their own careers to call for him to resign from the ticket and allow his running mate, Ohio governor Lester Bowles, to replace him. Privately, Bowles encouraged that idea.

Despite the uproar, Bowman remained outwardly calm and confident, denying everything, vowing to prove the charges were fabricated, and refusing to cede his place at the head of his

party's presidential ticket. When it became clear that Bowman
intended to remain the party nominee until the end, Lester
Bowles quietly sent his own letter of resignation to the
Republican Party chairman and went home to Columbus, Ohio.

55

Gil Adonis was in New York when he first heard the news, a call
from Crystal Kranz.

"The son of a bitch quit," she said.

"Zach?" asked Gil hopefully.

"No, your other guy, Bowles."

Adonis couldn't believe it. Lester, quitting without letting
him know in advance? After all they had been through together?
Knowing what was at stake in this election? Adonis called
Bowles's cell phone. No answer. He left an urgent message on
Bowles's voice mail. No response. He tried again. Again, no
response. Lester clearly was avoiding him. That left just one
alternative. Adonis boarded his private plane, flew to Columbus,
Ohio, and drove to Lester Bowles's home.

"What the fuck, Les? You quit without talking with me. You
don't take my calls. You go home to hide. You can't do this!"

Bowles was a man for whom everything in life had come
easily—wealth, political office, and this, the possibility of
becoming president of the United States. Nothing in his career
had prepared him to handle the Bowman scandal.
Uncharacteristically, he unloaded his frustration on his lifelong
friend, Gil.

"Can't do this? Can't do what? Make a bigger fool of myself than I already have? Humiliate myself even more than I've done by defending that idiot you picked to run for president? You planned to kill him off in a year. Well, you've killed me off right now. I don't know how to show my face in public. Half the Republican Party wants my head for not coming to Bowman's defense. The other half will never forgive me for giving him credibility in the first place. Politically, I'm dead. And I'll tell you another thing. Emotionally I am, too. Every day of this campaign has killed something inside me. Integrity. Common sense. Trust in my own judgment. My own sense of worth. I don't hate you for what's happened, Gil. I hate myself for listening to you."

Gil Adonis had assembled his financial empire by understanding all factors of a given deal, adjusting to them, and using the weight of his understanding to wear down others. He called on all of that skill now to try to talk Bowles off the political ledge.

"Pour me a drink, Les."

Bowles was taken aback by Gil's reaction. No screaming, bullying, pleading. He walked to his liquor cabinet and poured Gil a glass of his favorite Scotch whiskey.

"Have one yourself," said Gil.

"It's not even eleven in the morning."

"Doctor's orders," said Gil.

Bowles smiled and did as Gil asked.

"One helluva fine mess, isn't it?" said Gil.

"Incredible. But maybe it's a blessing that jackass showed the world who he is before the election. My God, think of what the country would be like if he started screwing around like this out of the White House. You don't think he can still win, do you?"

"Hard to tell," said Gil. "You jumping off the ticket could be strike three. You on the ticket, I think he still could make it."

"And then where'd we be?" asked Lester. "Let's be honest— Tennyson can be a real pain in the ass, and she'd give away the store if she could, but she actually runs a pretty good ship. Good people around her."

"Don't forget her own sex problems," said Gil. "All that stuff with that Sanchez woman, and what was up with Sage, her consultant? And during impeachment, all the news about her whoring around. If this is a morality contest, I'm not sure she wins."

"But it isn't a morality contest, Gil. It's about competence. And we both know which one is the idiot."

Lester went to the liquor cabinet and poured another drink for each of them. An aide came into the den where Gil and Lester were talking and ran down the list of media and political calls waiting for response.

"I'm busy," said Lester. "Just tell them I'm out of the campaign."

"Wait a minute," said Gil. "For me. For my protection, not yours, can you hold back a bit? The rumble about your resignation's out there, but until you confirm it it's not real. The party guys haven't gone public with it yet. They don't know what to do with it. How this gets done makes a big difference to me because of how tightly I'm wrapped into it. And it makes a big difference to you, too. For the rest of your career. It's worth taking the time to figure it out."

Bowles hesitated. "But it won't change my mind, Gil. I'm done. You make a good point, though."

Bowles turned to his aide. "Do what I'm doing, which is nothing. No callbacks, and don't answer the phone again until I tell you."

The bewildered aide wasn't sure he heard the instruction correctly. "Don't even answer the phone?"

"Just because a phone rings doesn't mean you have to answer it," said Bowles. "Now, get out of here and let me and my friend get properly drunk."

Bowles's mood was definitely lighter and calmer because of the alcohol and Gil's presence. He poured them both another drink. Gil took his glass and fist-bumped Bowles, a thank-you gesture. Gil was determined to stay at Lester's side until he himself decided on a next move. For now, his strategy was just to let Les talk it out.

"Gil, face it, Zach's a loser. He's always been a loser. And despite your big talk about getting rid of him early in the term, I know you too well to think you would actually be involved in anything like that. It's best this way. I face the press, tell them how disappointed I am and just don't want to serve with someone I can't respect. Maybe I get back a bit of credibility. Maybe I can look in the mirror and not see something awful. I'm in my last term as governor. I won't run again for anything. I'm saving myself and the country from a huge mistake."

While Lester spoke, Gil's mind was not so much absorbing Lester's logic as considering possible consequences from the other team he had joined, the Salvation Project. He had assured them delivery of a US president. He already had spent hundreds of millions of dollars of his own fortune on the campaign, and as recently as a week earlier, in London, he had guaranteed a victory. He didn't know all the details of the Project, but he did know that wheels were in motion for coups and other forms of takeover in many target countries, all dependent on having compliant US leadership.

Gil also knew that his associates would kill to achieve their goals. Would they try to kill him for his failure? The possibility could not be discounted. And then there was the matter of the intelligence breach. From the London meeting he was aware that something serious had happened. A key person had disappeared, likely taken by some hostile security people. How much had been divulged? Was his name on any lists? No sign yet that US agencies were onto it or that they wanted any part of a case that could affect the US election.

What were Gil's options? He could try to force Lester back onto the ticket. He would certainly try persuasion, but should he use heavy weapons available to him? He could offer Zach Bowman a financial fortune to quit, but knowing Bowman, the ego and power trip of the campaign likely weighed more than a financial bonanza. He could warn his associates in the Project that they were about to lose and urge them to adapt as quickly as possible, whatever that meant.

In creating the presidential team of Bowman and Bowles, it was obvious now that Gil had made the wrong decision. At minimum he had to talk Lester into not doing anything more than he already had to cripple Bowman's chances. Maybe pretend he had some kind of ailment that kept him from public appearances. Maybe a family emergency. Bare minimum, Les had to say he was just taking time to consider the situation while Bowman worked it out for himself. If by some chance Bowman were to win, Bowles would still be vice president. That could still happen. Gil had made too large an investment to give up on it now.

Then Gil remembered. At first, he had considered it a crazy

idea, a needless risk. But in his financial career he had always built in a plan B, and occasionally it was plan B that made the difference between success and failure. He had once thought, why not build in a plan B here, just in case. And so, months ago he had arranged for one last fail-safe option if the Bowman campaign were to go south. Luckily, he just remembered it. He still had time to pull the trigger on it. He could still win this sucker.

56

Mariana Lee waited patiently for the last of the Project Managers to link to the private network. She knew how difficult it was for some to find a safe and secure way to connect when a meeting was called. Meetings ran the risk of exposure, so they were rarely called.

The Salvation Project had remained successfully underground for years because security had been so sternly enforced. Most Project Managers did not even know the identity of the others. Each had his or her own assignment, a region or nation to bring under the Project's umbrella. Some already had been successful and were in a maintenance stage. It was commonly understood that until the US, Russia, and China were in friendly hands, no individual triumph would be revealed. The effort to control the powerful nations, and most others, still dominated Project strategy. The organizational hive was a wide-ranging compendium of operations, directed by individual local Managers who understood the need to clandestinely segregate responsibility and identity. Like a reverse human block chain, if one piece was compromised, or failed, others did not fall. Those involved were experienced professionals—military, intelligence, business, science, government—well aware of the risks and the reasons for working in restricted environments, where being too inquisitive about things one was not expressly told could be dangerous for the Project and perilous for one's own safety.

At the top of the organizational chart was an executive group of five Managers, three of whom had been guiding strategy since the Project's founding in Singapore. They were responsible for the appointment of others, a flexible ruling body whose size grew or diminished depending on individual nation projects and shifts in operational fortune. On today's virtual meeting call, eighteen elite Managers were summoned to participate. When a woman's voice announced herself, "Number Sixteen here," Lee started the meeting.

"As you know," she began, "our last planning meeting was abruptly canceled. The reason for that cancellation was the disappearance of our key operative who temporarily was in possession of our most sensitive information. I now have learned that our operative was taken by unfriendly intelligence sources and that the information he possessed was exposed. I also have learned that the information has reached the president of the United States and the United States intelligence agencies and that they are beginning to deploy counterintelligence operations against us."

A male voice responded. "This is Eight. That would explain the arrests of some of our people in Japan. We had no idea how their identities were revealed."

"That's why I have called this meeting," said Lee. "To make all of you aware of the threat. Existing information channels to you and other key people must be destroyed immediately."

"Are you suggesting that our Project is finished?" asked

another male voice, who identified himself as Fourteen.

"Not at all," said Lee. "As on a submarine that begins to take on water, we need to secure all of our hatches. I expect we will suffer some losses, but there is no need to panic about survival of the Project itself."

"Mariana, how can you be certain American intelligence will act on the information? Might they not consider it a setup of some kind to distract them?"

"Who is this?" asked Lee.

"Sorry. Ten."

"That's an excellent question. Our operative inside the CIA is the source of our information. He says he personally has not been questioned, as you would expect with this type of information breach. He is making arrangements to protect himself if he feels he is about to be discovered. Nevertheless, I recommend that you respond as if we are facing mass discovery and isolate yourselves from all questionable contacts until we have more information."

"Eleven here." A woman's voice. "Thank you for this warning, Mariana. Can you give us an assessment of the American election? I understand we have had a setback there as well."

"Yes, we have," said Lee. "Most unfortunate. We have worked for many years to arrive at this moment. But our American contact told me just this morning that he has arranged for countermeasures. I remain confident."

"Mariana, this is Number Two. You and I have worked together for many years, and we both understand that to win the American election is to all but ensure the success of our Project. We may never again have the opportunity we have now, and we simply cannot allow ourselves to be defeated. We cannot allow it. Am I understood?"

"Yes, Two, I understand."

"Number Four, Mariana. To underscore Two, winning the American election means that our person gets control of the American intelligence apparatus and can minimize any damage the security breach might cause. Failure could mean the destruction of everything we have accomplished and any chance of future success. What's at stake here is what we call in Catalonia *tot o nadares*, or in English, 'all or nothing.' We are counting on you, Mariana. You and your American Manager."

For a few moments there was silence on the network. No one else spoke. No other words were needed.

Mariana broke the silence. "We will succeed," she said confidently. "We will succeed."

57

Today's Tennyson campaign meeting in New York was more optimistic than those of recent weeks, but given the stakes, it was just as tense, and longer than most. Media was being reedited to adjust to the new political environment. Schedules needed to reflect new political opportunities. Tens of thousands of door-to-door and phone volunteers were waiting for final messaging instructions. Before scandals overtook the Bowman campaign, millions of votes had been cast in early-voting states. Those votes could not be changed. News continued to be brutal for Bowman, but political opinion seldom changes radically or overnight. Support once given could be difficult to dislodge. Even though momentum now was on her side, Tenny could not be sure of reelection. Polls continued to show a close race.

As a rule, Tenny didn't participate in campaign meetings. She was the candidate. She knew her role and trusted Ben's experience and judgment. But this was likely the final and decisive strategic session of the campaign. Ben insisted that she participate, and she reluctantly agreed.

It had been a long and exhausting campaign for Tenny. More physically wearing than any that preceded it. Age and injuries had drained her stamina and lowered her threshold for pain. Her clandestine visits with traveling White House medical staff were increasingly frequent. Tenny was relieved when she could finally say her goodbyes and let others continue to work out operational details.

Leaving the meeting also meant she could be with Andres. Thank heaven for Andres. They had been together in the months since their reunion in San Diego. A surprising development in her life and a surprisingly welcome one. He was charming and so much fun to be with. How much easier the past few weeks had been because of Andres. They had not slept together. There had not even been a suggestion of sexual contact between them. But she thought about it. Often. How could she not? Her body had aged, but with Andres a part of her life now, her mind often reminded her of the giddy, sexy, self-absorbed young woman she once was.

Carmie, always so perceptive, took notice. "Pre- Andres. Post-Andres. He's like a miracle tonic for you." Tenny could almost feel herself blush.

But. There already had been too much talk of sex in this campaign. The embarrassment of Ben's diaries. The suggestions that she, Carmie, and Ben were a threesome. The opposition continued to dredge up old affairs that had been such a titillating sideshow of her impeachment trial. Already there had been questions about Andres. His reappearance could not have been more public than it was that day at San Diego's Hotel del Coronado. So far that reunion had been helpful to her image. A love story never hurt. *Let's not make it messier*, she thought. *Keep the separate rooms. At least until we see how the election turns out.*

Tonight, though, they would have dinner. Just the two of them. A rare break in nonstop campaign appearances. After that, she would be the centerpiece for a high-dollar campaign reception, then star attraction of a rally at Madison Square Garden. Twenty thousand were expected. But for the next two hours....

Tenny relished the thought as she stepped off the elevator at the Sherry-Netherland Hotel and into her hotel apartment. She headed for the kitchen and found Andres there, the table set with a steaming chicken dish, mashed potatoes, tossed salad, a spinach casserole, red wine, and candlelight Andres had artfully arranged.

"What's this?" she asked, pleasantly surprised.

"Well, we planned to have dinner, and I felt like preparing it. Actually, I'm a very good cook, and since my only job these days is serving as your traveling companion, I decided to make myself useful. Hope you don't mind."

"Mind? A home-cooked meal? By you? Surprised? No, I'm delighted."

"How much time do we have?" asked Andres.

"For dinner? Maybe a long hour. Then I have to do a bit of work and change before the next event."

"Well, the food is warm. Let's go for it."

The conversation was warm, too, recalling their earlier days together, each day then a joy to live, with tomorrows of exciting anticipation. When the marriage collapsed, Tenny vowed never again to lose herself through love. She created an emotional control panel, one where she could regulate the knobs to assure that expectation never rose too high, nor disappointment drag her too low. With Andres, even for brief encounters during an impossible schedule, she sensed those controls being disabled. Tenny needed love. It had been so long.

Then she heard Andres speak the words that were on her own lips. "I love you, Tenny. I didn't mean to say it, and I don't want to complicate our lives, but...."

She rose from her chair, took two steps to be beside him, reached down with both hands, and held his face for a moment, staring into eyes that many years ago had made her crazy with desire. Whatever sensible notions she might have harbored about Andres's return into her life had no chance against the intoxication of his breath in hers, her lips now gently widening with his.

As they kissed, he reached around her legs. Through her wool skirt she could feel his strong hand on her thigh, his grip tightening with the tension between them. He rose from his chair, still locked in their embrace.

"Come," he whispered, "just for a few moments. Just like before."

It was what? A suggestion? For her body it was more of a command, an irresistible command.

He steered her to the bedroom, kissed her hard beside the bed, and gently lowered her until they both were lying prone, his lips on hers, his hand now between her legs, stroking her stockinged inner thigh.

"God, Andres, lover," she whispered, waiting for him to undress her, wanting to be naked with him, forgetting the time, the campaign, oblivious to who she was or where she was. Wanting only this. Him. Now.

He removed his hand from her leg for a moment. "Don't stop, please don't stop." She was his, desperate to be transported to wherever ecstasy resides.

His hand returned between her legs gently, softly, each touch adding a level of excitement she had not experienced for a time beyond recent memory.

Then, an unexpected touch, a stick, as if the point of a needle.

Surprised and confused, she called out, "Andres?" Andres abruptly stood and walked to the bathroom. "I can't. I can't," he kept repeating.

Tenny sat up. Thinking Andres was embarrassed by being unable to sustain an erection, she gently called to him. "It's okay. It's okay, Andres. It's okay."

Then through the light of the bathroom door, she saw the syringe in his hand.

The softness of passion instantly transformed into recognition of betrayal.

"What did you do, Andres?"

"It's what I didn't do, Tenny. I'm so sorry. It was unforgivable. I'm so sorry."

"I don't understand."

"I started to inject you with a drug that would put you into a coma."

Tenny was now on full alert. Back on earth from wherever Andres momentarily had transported her. "Put me into a coma? Andres!"

"I didn't push the plunger on the needle, Tenny. I couldn't. I couldn't do it to you."

Tenny jumped to her feet. Unbelievably, her lover had become her enemy, maybe even her assassin. "Why would you even consider it?"

"You would have come out of it. The idea was that you would collapse, be rushed to the hospital unconscious. It would have taken a while to diagnose. The media would have revived stories about your health, how you wouldn't be able to govern. It likely would have cost you the election."

"Andres! Well, I'm not in a coma. And I can see clearly what a fool I was to think you just showed up in my life to keep me company. An even greater fool to believe we could go back decades and re-create what you threw away. How could I have trusted you again?"

"Tenny," he said, "they're holding my daughter hostage. I lied when I said she married a Japanese man and was living in Osaka. She really is in Japan, but the truth is some people, I don't know who, grabbed her, took her God knows where. Months ago, I was contacted by a woman, a stranger, who told me that the people who had my daughter would kill her if I didn't do exactly what they told me to do. All they asked was that I reconnect with you. And they said that might be the end of it. Well, the other day I was told to do more to save my daughter. I was told to inject you and kill you. I knew I couldn't. But I agreed, thinking I would administer a nonfatal dose. I had to decide between your political future and my daughter's life. But when it came time to push the plunger on the needle, I couldn't do it."

Tenny stared at Andres silently. Stared at a face she had loved since the moment they met. A face that had haunted her through a lifetime. A face that this very night, moments ago, drove her to wild and lustful passion. All she felt now was fury, at Andres for his complicity with people so determined to defeat her they were willing to kill her. Fury at herself for reverting to a gullible schoolgirl, letting sex rule her brain.

"Come with me," she ordered.

Tenny walked to the entry door of the apartment and summoned the Secret Service agent who was standing guard.

"Agent Wells," she said, "please have one of your men escort Dr. Navarro to his room and place a guard at the door so he cannot leave."

"Are you in trouble?" asked Agent Wells. "Are you charging him?"

"No. Just do as I say, please, and have your supervisor talk with me."

"Madam President, we can't just confine someone without a charge, a reason."

"The reason is that I'm telling you to do it. Dr. Navarro will not resist."

She turned to Andres. "Will you, Dr. Navarro?"

Andres, completely unsettled by the crime he came so close to committing, merely shook his head.

58

Election night in the United States.

By 11:00 p.m. eastern standard time, as polls closed on the West Coast, those results confirmed what already was evident: President Isabel Aragon Tennyson had been elected to a second term in the White House.

At 11:20 p.m., in a crowded ballroom at the Washington Hilton Hotel, President Tennyson emerged from her suite and spoke to the world's media, grateful for the opportunity to continue serving, thanking everyone who worked on her behalf, and promising progressive change in the years ahead.

At midnight, Ben Sage, Lee Searer, and Susan Cipriani were the center of a boisterous victory party Susan had arranged, a party that lasted until dawn and drew three separate visits from hotel security.

Halfway around the earth, in Singapore, midnight in Washington, DC, was noon in Singapore, the time Mariana Lee had scheduled a meeting of Project Managers to assess results of the US election.

"We've lost," she began simply. "We all knew this would be difficult. Our candidate failed us. Our American contact failed us. Furthermore, we have confirmed that US intelligence agencies are aggressively following up on our security breach. A number of our operatives already have been detained. I see no alternative now but to initiate deep cover, erase all previous lines of contact, and await our next opportunity."

A Scandinavian voice spoke. "This is Twenty-Two. That may not be possible in Sweden. My closest contacts have been arrested. If I do not appear at the next convening, it will be because I have been betrayed."

"Twelve here. Mariana," said a Spanish-accented speaker, "at our last meeting you assured us we would win. The American Manager assured us. This is shocking news."

"Our Manager failed," Lee responded. "We have been unable to reach him.

An English speaker, French Canadian, spoke next.

"Sixteen. Do we still have the option to disable Tennyson before she resumes office?"

Lee replied, "If she is assassinated now, her vice president will become president. She is younger, stronger, and has no different outlook than Tennyson. There would be no purpose. Our only option now is salvage what we can and regroup for another time."

"How much of our plan has been revealed?" asked a thickly accented Middle Eastern voice. "Are we all at risk?"

"Who is this?" Lee asked.

"Sorry. Number Seven."

"They know our plan, and they know many of our subordinates. We will need to rebuild portions of our network. Whether you personally are at risk depends upon how successful you have been in removing all communications that lead to you. I do not believe your identities have been revealed as yet, although I suggest you all designate trusted successors so in the event you are taken the Project will continue."

"Our greatest risk is you, Mariana. You are the only one who knows who we all are and how to find us," said the Middle Eastern voice.

"I am aware of that," she replied. "I will arrange for another person to serve in this capacity."

"Even if another has that information, there is still you, and you are a risk to us all. You know the consequences of failure or betrayal."

"I agree," said Lee. "But you should not be concerned."

"How can we be certain?" asked the man.

"Because," said Lee, "once this meeting is concluded I will kill myself."

59

Four years earlier, Tenny had celebrated her election as president of the United States with a mixture of disbelief and unrestrained joy. How had she, a Mexican American woman who had spent most of her life viewing politics from a distance, and with marginal interest, now become the most powerful person in the world?

Her political life was born when Ben Sage convinced her to run for Congress in a district that always elected Democrats. At the time, she hardly knew one political party from another. She had devoted years and a considerable amount of her personal fortune to helping those on the other side of the wealth divide. The hungry. The homeless. Newly arrived immigrants. Neglected children. The disabled. Over time, Tenny's works became local legends. Her public profile grew.

"You can easily win this congressional seat," Ben had said.

"Why would I want to be in Congress?" she protested.

"To elevate your work for the people you care about to a higher level," he insisted.

That seemed a lifetime ago. She woke this morning as the winner of a second four-year term as president. The first four years had cost her the life of the brother she dearly loved and body wounds that almost certainly would shorten her own life. This campaign the casualties included her lifelong friend, Carmie, and her political mentor, Ben Sage. Andres, the love of her life, had reappeared only to betray her.

Yes, she had won. Physically and mentally exhausted, she had somehow prevailed against a worldwide conspiracy. A stronger opponent would have defeated her. She had no doubt about that. But she had survived, and the Congress elected with her was one she believed she could work with. All good. The good feeling, though, carried with it little joy. Her morning would be consumed with calls to key congressional winners, campaign supporters, and staff. Then, an afternoon and evening of public appearances and media events to promote bipartisanship and heal inevitable campaign wounds.

Carmie didn't wait for the day's schedule to begin. She appeared early in the White House living quarters with a bottle of Dom Pérignon and two Waterford crystal champagne flutes.

"Champagne before breakfast?" said Tenny. "I'll be drunk by noon and impeached as a sot and slut by dinner."

She hugged Carmie, took one of the glasses, and filled it from the already uncorked bottle.

"Congratulations, lady," said Carmie. "I guess this means we'll have to postpone getting back to all our fun and games for four more years."

"Oh, we'll figure something out before then," said Tenny. "I'll never run for anything again, so there's no political price to pay for being a bit wild."

They clinked their glasses without naming their toast. They knew what they were celebrating and what winning meant. More difficult political years. More strain on Tenny's already weakened body. Tenny ordered food for them both, and they rehashed the vote and other events of election night.

"I guess I'd better get out of here and let the rest of the world in," Carmie finally conceded.

"Not yet," said Tenny. "I need to ask you a question. You spent all those years working on Wall Street. What do you know about Gil Adonis?"

"Gil Adonis? To tell you the truth, not much. I know he was the biggest money behind the Bowman campaign. In finance, hard to tell. He was hugely successful, more feared than loved, but mostly private. Operated in seclusion. Almost a man of mystery. Why? You want to beat up on him for supporting Bowman?"

"I'm going to have dinner with him next week here at the White House."

60

In less than a year, the Tennyson campaign had grown from a plan scribbled on a few notebook pages into a billion- dollar coast-to-coast organization that employed more than ten thousand workers and managed nearly two million volunteers. It enlisted some of the most creative and experienced talent in the United States to produce media, manage huge databases of information, provide logistics worthy of UPS, and mobilize enough skilled researchers to populate a midsize university.

Now this vast enterprise would be reconfigured to sell not a candidate but her second-term agenda. Four years earlier, Ben had failed to convince Tenny she needed such a postelection organization. She was finished with campaign politics, she insisted at the time. All her energies would be focused on policy. For a while she succeeded beyond expectations. Ultimately, though, the opposition dragged down her popularity and left her agenda in shreds. She didn't intend to make that mistake again. Tenny wanted Ben to build and manage a privately funded public relations firm with her agenda as the only client.

Four years earlier, Ben would have relished such an assignment. Now he had other plans.

"I didn't think I'd ever see the day when you'd hang it up," said Lee. I've never met anyone more competitive or quicker to size up situations and develop creative strategies. You're like an artist in your peak years, packing up all your brushes."

Ben laughed.

"Lee. Do you have any idea how many cities and towns in the United States are named Washington? Let me tell you. Eighty-eight. There are eighty-eight Washingtons. Forty-one Springfields. Thirty-five Franklins. And you know what? I think I've been to them all. After a while, most everywhere we go to campaign looks the same. I'm staying at a Holiday Inn, or a Best Western, or a Double Tree and look across the highway at an IHOP, or a McDonald's, or an Olive Garden. It's gotten so I wake up and haven't a clue where I'm at. In the hospital, after I was shot, I had more time to think about my life than I've had in years. What I thought, mainly, was that somewhere along the line I lost my sense of adventure. My life has become an accumulation of yesterdays. I'd like to wake up excited about what I'm going to do tomorrow."

"So," said Lee, "what I'm hearing is electing a president of the United States and being the key figure in an international spy conspiracy and being chased like a rabbit with guns blazing behind you isn't enough adventure to satisfy you."

"Well, now that you put it in context, I do sound stupid, don't I? Let me tell you something else that sounds stupid. When I came out of surgery after being shot, the very first sensory experience I had was the smell of burning toast. Burning toast? That's going to be my last thought before I die? I hate the smell of burning toast."

They were in their Washington, DC, office, sorting paperwork debris accumulated during the campaign's closing weeks and unwinding tensions often hard to release after months of tightening uncertainty.

"I talked with Tenny, and she's fine with you and Susan taking on the job of selling her agenda," said Ben. "Susan's willing?"

"Yes, she is," said Lee. "She says she's ready for a change, too. More security, less time living out of suitcases, just like you. We worked pretty well together."

"Then why don't you change the name of the firm to Searer and Cipriani? My name took a pretty big hit this year, so get rid of it before it scares any clients away."

"And you? Where do you plan to go to lose the smell of burning toast? I don't see you becoming a full-time beach bum back in your Lewes home."

"A clean break, Lee. A clean break. An old friend of mine owns a small daily newspaper near Poulsbo, Washington, an old town on the water near Seattle settled by Norwegian fishermen. He's retiring, and I'm buying the paper and moving there to run it. It's been on my bucket list to do something like that."

"Really? Back to your roots? Print journalism in the digital age?"

"I'm an old softie when it comes to newspapers," Ben admitted. "I started there and never really left it. You know, I got into journalism in the first place because I thought it was really noble and important to translate what was happening into words regular people could understand. How are people going to know how to vote and who to elect if they don't understand what's happening? That still appeals to me."

"In Poulsbo, Washington?"

"It's like everywhere else I've ever been. They elect school boards and city councils and put people on library boards and make decisions that affect jobs and people's incomes. I like the idea that I can be part of that."

"I'm going to miss working with you," said Lee. "But you should like being around so many Norwegians. How can you not like a country where the king's guard has a brigadier who's a penguin?"

"A penguin?"

"Nils Olav. He has a knighthood in the Norwegian army and lives at the Edinburgh Zoo. You didn't know? Ben, you're going to miss me being around to do your deep research."

61

For three weeks, Andres Navarro had been held in what amounted to informal house arrest. No charges had been filed against him. No word of his confinement appeared in any court case or legal document. His accommodations weren't at all unpleasant, a spacious suite at New York's Sherry-Netherland Hotel. Meals brought to him with regularity. His rooms serviced by hotel staff, just as any guest's would be. That's how he officially was listed, as a hotel guest. But an unobtrusive twenty-four-hour guard outside his door assured that he would not leave. That was the president's direct order. Andres offered no resistance or complaint. He expected worse.

Five days after the election, with no prior notice, he was told to pack his belongings. A Secret Service agent escorted him to New York's Pennsylvania Station and sat next to him on the Acela high-speed Amtrak train to Washington, DC, where he was driven in a government car to the White House.

There had been no contact between Tenny and Andres since the night that began with passion ended with Andres's unrecorded arrest. On arrival at the White House, he was escorted into the Oval Office, where Tenny greeted him with grim formality and instructed him to take a seat on one of the room's two gold-toned sofas. She did not sit down, however. She walked to one of the windows facing the Rose Garden and stared out silently. Finally, with her back still to Andres, she said, "It's not good to have all the power I have as president. I was tempted to do so much more to you, I was so furious. Fortunately, I've had time to consider our situation."

This was a Tenny he had never seen. Their time together

during the campaign was end-of-the-day meals and hurried conversations on whatever transportation the campaign arranged to get them from here to there. He was just one of many in the traveling campaign entourage. Now she was President Tennyson, in the Oval Office, the seat of world power, the place she would govern from for the next four years.

Still with her back to him, she continued. "Andres," she began, "I've got three things to say to you."

She turned and took a seat on the matching sofa directly across from him.

"First, I'm not going to charge you with any crime, although what you planned to do was unspeakable."

Andres started to speak, to apologize, but Tenny raised her hand and stopped him.

"As far as the world is concerned, Andres, it didn't happen. I won reelection, and that's that. Punishing you now would serve no purpose."

Again, Andres started to react, but before he could speak, Tenny moved on to her second message.

"Second, I've arranged for the release of your daughter. She is in the hands of Japanese intelligence now. After we've finished here, our communications people will connect you so that you can have a video talk with her."

Andres was startled at this news. "How—" he began. She cut him off.

"I have resources," she said, a slight smile crawling across her lips. "I'm told she's unharmed and that the people who kidnapped her are in custody."

Andres was visibly moved by the news. Despite himself, his

voice choked as he tried to say, "Thank you!"

Tenny rose and moved to sit on the sofa next to Andres. Without looking at him, she said, "Finally, Andres, I want to marry you. I'd suggest living together. Marriage is rather pointless at our age. But I'm president and can't just cohabitate without consequences. So, marriage is the only alternative. If it was all an act, if what I thought we had in the weeks we were together was just you performing as you were told to do by your daughter's captors, then be on your way. The show's over. But if it was real, if you felt what I felt, what we felt for one another that night, and long ago when we first married, I want you in my life. I suppose I always have wanted you in my life."

Andres, who had entered the Oval Office expecting to leave in handcuffs, finally found his voice. "You can't mean this, Tenny," he said finally. "Not after I abused your trust. Not once, but twice. Why would you ever want to see me again, let alone marry me?"

"I can't explain it, Andres. Chemistry? Emotion? Maybe this is foolish. But it wouldn't be the first foolish thing anyone ever did for love. People kill for it. They give up fortunes for it. They abandon their own children for it. When I was young, Andres, you were my future. Now I'm old, and here you are again, my past. All I know is that I want you in my present."

She turned to face him. Andres's cheeks were wet with tears. Tenny quickly read his look. To her, it seemed real.

62

Gil Adonis managed to avoid much public notice during the campaign, but among financial and political insiders, his support for Zach Bowman was well known and now would be universally derided. He had little appetite for facing even temporary humiliation. More motivating, the loss would not sit well with the Project Managers who entrusted him to win. These were not people accustomed to failure. He could not discount the possibility that he could be in mortal danger. And not only from the Project. He had not directly ordered the president's execution, but the idea was his, and he was certain Mariana Lee had arranged for it. What had happened? The information void was ominous, and the consequences for Gil could be devastating if the wrong people were in custody and talked freely.

His first instinct was to leave the US while he still could. Saint Bart's seemed appealing. His Caribbean villa there was secluded and with enough personnel could be made secure. For years he had cultivated a reputation for disappearing without prior notice, reachable only by a few trusted staff. His absence from New York would hardly be noticed.

On the other hand, he might be safer in his New York penthouse, both legally and physically. If the US government came after him, certainly a distinct possibility, he would be within a legal system he knew how to manipulate, near his legal team who had proven often in the past that they could protect his interests. And if anyone wanted to do him bodily harm, well, they would need to overcome a lot of armed gatekeepers already on his payroll to get to him.

A phone call interrupted these considerations. The

president's personal secretary. Would Mr. Adonis join the president at the White House for dinner next Tuesday? Nine o'clock.

The president's personal secretary? What kind of sick joke was this? The woman he'd spent two years trying to defeat? Worse, the woman he'd ordered killed? Adonis disconnected the call and called back through the White House switchboard to the president's scheduling office. Startled, he was connected with the same person who had made the initial call. The president was, indeed, inviting him to dinner.

"Who else will be there?" Adonis asked, still skeptical of the invitation.

"No one else has been invited," said the secretary. "The president informs me it will be just the two of you. She also asks that you mention this invitation to no one and use the Seventeenth Street entrance, where you will have less chance of being recognized. Please arrive at 8:30 p.m. to leave ample time for security. One of the president's assistants will be there to escort you. What is your date of birth and your Social Security number, please? I will need to provide these to the Secret Service for clearance."

Was this a ruse so that they could arrest him? Should he inform his lawyer? Should he bring his lawyer with him? Was this invitation related to the election or to the Project? These were questions he could not ask. If he were a wanted man, they would find him no matter where he might be. There was no point in running and little value in declining. His entire career had been built on being straightforward, even when truth came hard. Whatever this was about, he would face it up front and directly.

63

Two members of his security staff accompanied Gil on his flight to Washington. His regular driver, Hughes, was waiting for him at National Airport with a black Escalante and drove him to the Hay-Adams Hotel. The president had asked him to tell no one about their meeting, and that was fine with him. Gil had every reason to avoid attention. He arrived at the hotel with just enough time to shower, change clothes, and take the brief walk across Lafayette Park to the White House. A drenching rain foreclosed the possibility of walking. Instead, Hughes drove Gil to the White House entrance he was instructed to use.

Despite his concerns, no armed posse of federal agents was waiting at the gate to arrest him. Just a pleasant young aide who met Gil and escorted him through security to the second-floor residence quarters.

Tenny was at a desk in the Treaty Room, alone, reading from a neatly stacked group of documents. As Gil entered, she rose to greet him, then asked him to give her a few moments to finish up. As she skimmed some papers, made notes, and signed others, Gil surveyed the room. A modest, well-tended fire in a marble fireplace took the edge of chill off an otherwise cool room. Room thermostats, he already had detected, were kept low in this White House. An embassy-size Heriz Persian carpet covered the parquet floor, a stunning contrast. He loved Persian carpets. The walls were covered with a light-gold sisal paper, giving the room a contemporary feel, even as portraits and photos of former presidents and times past anchored the room in White House history. It was a mix of eras and styles, and it seemed to work.

Tenny finally left her desk and joined Gil in a seating area arranged in the middle of the room, four almond-colored leather chairs, two on either side of a walnut coffee table. She chose a seat directly facing him.

"Thank you for coming, Gil. May I call you Gil? Consider this an informal dinner."

"Yes, please call me Gil. That's my preference as well, Madam President."

"Since this is informal, then let's make it Gil and Tenny. Please join me in a glass of cabernet before dinner. I've opened a very good bordeaux."

Without waiting for a reply, she turned to an end table next to her and filled two glasses. They toasted. "To your next four years," Gil offered.

"Yes. To the next four years," she replied. "But before we go there, Gil, I've asked you here tonight to clear up a matter unresolved by the elections results. I'm naturally curious as to why you tried to kill me."

Stunned by the question, Gil began to reply, but she interrupted him.

"Before you try to deny it, if that's what you intend to do, you should know that our intelligence people have proof that you were the principal American contact in something called the Salvation Project, which apparently intends to overthrow a number of democratically elected governments. I also am well aware of your role in creating the Zach Bowman campaign, which logically was somehow tied in with the Salvation Project's agenda. And since this Project tried to kill me, and you were its American leader, I naturally conclude it was you who signed my death warrant. I can't prove it. I'm told we can't even bring charges against you for your involvement with the Salvation

Project. I'm not asking you to disclose names, nor am I recording this conversation, in case that's a concern. I simply want to know why so many accomplished people like yourself would want to overthrow democratically elected governments, and even kill to do it. I'm being as open as I can be about my concern, and I would appreciate your doing the same with me. I genuinely want to understand."

Tenny leaned forward, shortening the space between him, and focused intently on his reaction.

Gil lived in the ruthless world of international finance. He was a black belt master in successfully navigating ploys and deception. He could deceive as well as anyone when the occasion required. But his negotiating preference was not to play mind games but rather to be straightforward—my position against yours, and let's see where that goes. He was stunned by Tenny's accusation, and in other circumstances he would have responded in kind: "Yes, Madam President, I moved heaven and earth trying to defeat you, even kill you, because I consider you a menace to the future of life on earth." But to do that would violate an oath he took when he joined the Salvation Project. Violation would almost certainly have its consequences. Besides, he still believed in the mission. If not this year, perhaps in two or four or six years. The future of civilization was too important a cause for him to betray.

Tenny filled the silence that followed her question.

"You seem to be struggling with what should be a simple answer, Gil. Take your time. We have the evening."

Gil hesitated a few seconds longer before replying.

"Tenny, let me answer your question with a question. What do you hope to accomplish with all your power in the next two years?"

"Four years," she corrected him.

"Two years," he repeated. "You and I know that in the last two years you will be a lame duck with limited power to change anything."

"Possibly," she said. "But to answer your question. My priorities. Trying to avoid anyone's use of nuclear or other devastating weapons here or anywhere on earth. Rebalancing the economy to correct the inequality that you captains of capitalism have created. Dealing with the dislocations climate change already is causing and trying to limit the damage. Harnessing the output from scientific developments to make them useful, not threatening. Those will be my main interests."

"And what do you think your chances are of accomplishing any or all of that?"

"I expect to make progress on all of it. How much, who can say?"

"Is that good enough?" said Gil. "You've just mentioned developments that are literally threatening the future of human civilization. Is it good enough to make just a bit of progress in avoiding calamity?"

"Where are you going with this, Gil?"

"My point is that your good intentions and your persuasive skills are no match for the system you're trying to manage. You've got a Congress that's erratic and lacking in quality control. You've got political power lined up against you backed by tens of billions of dollars of self- interested wealth. And maybe the highest obstacle of all, you have the indifference and prejudice of the uninformed and the misinformed voters who can so easily be played. You've just gone through four years of that. You think the next two or four will be any different?"

Now it was Tenny who hesitated to respond while she considered the message he was delivering.

"I see, Gil. You obviously have a problem with our system of government," she finally said. "No surprise there. So do I. So should any thoughtful person. I don't disagree. We certainly need some fundamental change to make it all work better."

Gil struggled to find words that would make his point without breaking his oath to the Project.

"Tenny, I live in a real world. If I succeed in a deal, I make millions, sometimes billions. If I don't, I lose. There's little margin for spin, or false hope, or self-deception. And in that real world I look at our system of government and say it needs more than the kinds of change that are politically possible. The system itself is obsolete."

"That's where you lose me, Gil. I buy the system's weaknesses. Elections aren't particularly effective either for civic participation or for government accountability. Lord knows we have all the proof we need of that. But all this is inherent in the system. Democracy's a self-correcting mechanism, with lots to correct. It just takes time and patience."

"But you're out of time. That's what makes now so much more treacherous than before. During your next term, or certainly not much longer, a dozen or more countries and nonstate actors like ISIS will have nuclear weapons. We're less than a generation away from technology obsoleting tens of millions of jobs, with all the political unrest that will create. The climate change migration's already started. The artificial intelligence era is just ahead. God knows what's happening in labs where they're messing with DNA and genetic editing. Who knows what's coming out of there? The disruptions of the next few years will unleash monumental political and cultural instability. Even with what we've seen already, the political blowback's fierce."

"If our system is obsolete, what do you suggest we should do to replace it?"

Now Gil hesitated. He had said too much. But his beliefs were too strong to hold his passions in check.

"Isn't it obvious to you?"

"From what you say, I hear dictatorship. You want a system like China's or Russia's, where the leader says do it and it gets done or else?"

"Well, those systems have their own inherent problems. But it definitely needs to be top-down."

"Yes," said Tenny, "top-down would be about as radical a change as one could imagine. It also is the system that most people have lived under for ten thousand or more years. A king, or emperor, or tribal leader, or tsar, whatever you want to call it. Have you ever studied the origin of World War I? I have. I've always been puzzled why the assassination of a member of the Austrian royal family led to a war that involved half the planet and killed millions. You know why that war began? Ego. Pride. Rivalry among the few who ran those countries, many of them blood relatives. They created a black hole and pulled a big part of civilization in with them. I'll take the problems of managing a country like the United States with all its system inefficiencies and maddening roadblocks any day over one where a few ruling idiots can snap their fingers and make everyone else either dead or miserable."

A steward emerged from the kitchen and motioned that their dinner was ready. As they walked into the dining room, Gil could not let her last comment pass untested.

"You know, Tenny, you just won an election where only half the eligible voters went to the polls, and little more than half of those voted for you. That means you're the choice of maybe twenty-five percent of the people you're governing. And the people you have to deal with in Congress got their party nominations with much less support than that. We already have a system where a few people decide who governs. And most of those people who do vote do it because they're wedded to a political party."

They settled into their dining room chairs, where an endive and tomato salad awaited them, but Tenny took little notice of the food, still trying to understand the forces Gil had helped unleash in the election.

"I believe you've answered my question without explicitly answering it, Gil. You and your friends think a ruling class should replace what we have and that my election just perpetuates what you consider dangerous obsolescence. We both recognize that the current system isn't up to the new challenges. I don't have the power of a queen, but I am powerful. You've obviously given a lot of thought to this, even willing to risk murder and treason to make changes. What changes?"

Gil smiled. He was genuinely beginning to like this woman, this president. She was strong enough to survive a campaign that should have brought her down. She was perceptive enough to try to understand her enemies, even those who tried to kill her. Perhaps there was the potential here for a deal. Tenny sounded like a woman with whom he could do business. Maybe the Project wasn't finished after all.

64

It was after midnight. They had spoken for three hours, through courses of a rich potato soup, sea bass, and lemon pie. But Gil Adonis was not thinking food. He had hardly noticed the food, so consumed was he with the possibilities the conversation with President Tennyson promised. Here was someone who understood, with more clarity and knowledge than anyone he had ever met outside the Project. He should have been here years ago, in the White House, having this conversation. The entire Bowman campaign was needless. The Salvation Project itself might have been needless.

No, she was not an authoritarian. But she understood the need for authority, and for process that led to action. The forces the Salvation Project had been assembling could yet be deployed, with adjustments in goals, plans, timing. The promise was still there.

After her inauguration, she said, they would meet again. Meanwhile she would test thoughts and ideas in discussions with her policy people and key political figures. She would consider building a case for fundamental change and aim for her next State of the Union speech as a platform for advancing it.

Three hours earlier, Gil Adonis had approached the West Wing entrance unsure whether he might leave in shackles. Instead, remarkably, he was leaving with an injection of hope and promise. Years of traveling the world, meeting leaders and scientists, economists and philosophers, had convinced him of the depth and immediacy of humanity's peril. Now he could see a path to its salvation.

The rain had not stopped. Walking back to his hotel was not

an option. Retrieving his cell phone from the security desk, he
called Hughes and told him to meet him at the same White
House entrance where he had dropped him off. Too exhilarated
to go back to the hotel, Gil said they would take a drive around
the National Mall to see the monuments, so elegantly lit at night.
Washington. Lincoln. Jefferson. The Capitol building.

His car pulled up to the White House entrance. Gil hurried
through the pouring rain and quickly jumped into the back seat
of the Escalante. He was so engrossed in wiping rainwater from
his eyes that he was taken completely off guard when the driver
of the limo turned and shoved a cloth against his face, a cloth wet
with a substance so strong it immediately made his eyes tear.
Struggling to free himself, Gil realized that his assailant was not
Hughes, nor anyone he had ever seen.

"No! No!" Gil yelled, or tried to yell, his voice muffled by the
firmly held cloth.

"No! You don 't u n der s t a n d. W e w o n..." Each word,
each syllable, slower, as his world turned dark and his brain shut
down.

Characters

Adonis, Gilbert; Gil rich financier; based in NYC; member of the Salvation Project

Aragon, Federico priest, murdered by Soto on Carmona's orders; older brother of Isabel, grandson of Miguel Aragon

Aragon, Miguel founder of Groupo Aragon; deceased

Araya Soto's replacement as Carmona's security chief; Basque

Augustine, Clement CIA operative; tall, muscular, close-cropped graying hair

Badem, Tahir CEO of Fertile Crescent Industries; Turkish

Birch, Robin attorney general under Tennyson

Bobbinsky, Boris wealthy London-based import-export businessman

Bowles, Lester Republican governor of Ohio; Republican candidate for vice president; old friend of Adonis; trim, gray hair

Bowman, Zach congressman from Pennsylvania, Republican candidate for president; trim, blue eyes

Cabrillo, Chub guard at Soto's tenement in Tepito

Carmona, Javier chairman of Groupo Aragon; Mexican

Christian, Kyle CIA director, former congressman; a Knight of Malta

Cipriani, Susan political consultant, Ben Sage's successor in Tennyson campaign

Compte, Foster Catholic priest; muscular, former football player

Coriton, Herve DGSE (French CIA) agent

Deacon President Tennyson's chief of staff

Durazzo, FBI agent

Earl, Cadance conservative TV network CEO; member of the Salvation Project

Egert, Kevin tech billionaire, Democratic presidential candidate

Etok, Kiloonik; Nikky Sheila Fishburne's mother; former teacher; Inupiaq

Fishburne, Clyde Sheila Fishburne's father; former high school math teacher

Fishburne, Sheila; Fish congresswoman from Alaska; Divorced

Galen, Petra Carmen Sanchez's chief of staff

Grimm, General Forest chief of US Army intelligence

Herrero, Rinaldo chief inspector with Mexico's Policía Federal

Kartal, Musa imam; member of Salvation Project; youngish, neatly trimmed beard, dark eyes

Kloss, Kenneth; Ken director of the US National Security Agency

Kranz, Crystal political strategist based in Chicago working for Bowman

Larson, Jake former Republican governor of Wyoming and losing presidential candidate

Leary, Marcelle White House physician

Lee, Mariana high-ranking member of the Salvation Project; based in Singapore

Lincoln family TV characters; Cathy and Lyle, teen daughters Geraldine/Gerry and Kelly, preteen son Scott, Cathy's sister Marion

Melek associate of Musa Kartal

Navarro, Andres Tennyson's ex-husband; retired surgeon; wealthy; blue eyes; second wife Catherine, deceased; two grown daughters Amy and Beth

Nicholas personal servant to Carmona

Pine, Charlene office manager at Sage, Searer Political Consulting Agency

Reynolds, Bob; Father Bob Jesuit pastor and professor at Georgetown University; friend of Federico's

Rufus, Buddy old-school Chicago political operative

Rusher, Roderick former vice president of the US; former senator from Virginia; secret ally of Carmona

Sage, Ben President Tennyson's chief political consultant; wife Almie deceased ten years (car crash)

Sanchez, Carmen; Carmie Tennyson's childhood friend and secretary of commerce; USC graduate

Schola, Ugo operative for the Salvation Project working undercover as an export agent; former AISI agent

Scully, Bill security chief, US Embassy in Paris

Searer, Lee Sage's political consulting business partner

Soto, Bernard Carmona's personal security chief

Tennyson, Isabel Aragon; Tenny president of the US; sister of Federico Aragon; former congresswoman and senator from California; Mexican American; divorced; walks with a cane; wealthy

Thompson, Harold; Hal former mayor of Los Angeles and governor of California; Tennyson's political mentor and former lover; appointed ambassador to France

Vellman, Sam director of the FBI

Wu Singapore export agent, actually an MSS operative

Author's Notes

I am very grateful to you for selecting *The Salvation Project* among all the many fine books available.

In writing *The Salvation Project* I drew upon extraordinary episodes from my three decades at the center of the turbulent world of elective politics. As it is lived in real life, politics is the stuff of great drama. Those who run for political office subject themselves to intense public scrutiny and, quite often, personal humiliation. Their finances, their love lives, their most private life's secrets, all become fair game for public review. Careers, marriages, life savings and long-time friendships are at risk. The campaigns are a blur of daily decisions, any one of which, on any given day, could win or lose the election. Election day itself is a one-day sale. Finishing with 49.9% of the vote may not be a winning number. There are no prizes for second best, only disappointment, heartbreak and often huge financial deficits. The process unfolds in a vice of tension, ratcheting tighter with each new poll, each favorable or unfavorable news cycle, each day closer to electoral judgment.

In my 30+ years living through all of this, I've been involved in more high wire adventures than I can recall, and I've met countless people I can never forget. Some of my experiences are repurposed in my writing. But my fictional individuals are what they seem, fictional. They are inventions from my imagination, composites from my experience.

That includes my principal protagonist, Isabel Aragon "Tenny" Tennyson. I first introduced Tenny in my novel, *The Latina President and The Conspiracy to Destroy Her*. She proved of such compelling interest to me I felt I had to stay with her to see what happened next. What did happen next is told in *The*

Salvation Project. Will there be a third Tenny novel? After all she's been through already, I'd feel remiss if I didn't allow her to serve four more years. If you have enjoyed reading *The Salvation Project*, I invite you to return to Tenny's origin story in *The Latina President*. Each novel was written to stand-alone on its individual merits, but reading both provides a more complete story.

If you would like to know when book three in the Tenny trilogy will be ready for publication, or if you would like to contact me about anything at all, you can reach me at jrothstein@rothstein.net.

No writer reaches the finish line without help, and I certainly could not have completed *The Salvation Project* without the assistance of a small army of friends and acquaintances who, through the process, advised me about content, made important suggestions, and corrected spelling and grammatical errors. Thank you, one and all.

As always through our four decades of marriage, I owe more than I can ever acknowledge to my extraordinary wife, Sylvia Bergstrom, for her advice and continuing support and encouragement. As a small token of repayment to that debt I dedicate *The Salvation Project* to Sylvia.

—Joe Rothstein
   Washington, D.C.
   www.joerothstein.net

About The Author

For more than thirty years, through over two hundred campaigns, Joe Rothstein was at the center of U.S. politics. Rothstein was a strategist and media producer for United States Senators Tom Daschle of South Dakota, Patrick Leahy of Vermont, Don Riegle of Michigan, Bob Kerrey of Nebraska, Tom Harkin of Iowa, and many others in the campaigns that brought each of them to the U.S. Senate. His TV commercials have won many national awards, including the gold medal at the Houston Film Festival. In addition to his work for candidates, Rothstein has consulted and produced media for dozens of commercial and non-profit clients and he has been a featured political analyst on network television and radio.

Rothstein is a former editor of the Anchorage, Alaska Daily News, and he is currently chairman and editor of the international news aggregation and distribution service EINNEWS.com. His political opinion columns are published at www.uspoliticstoday.com. Joe Rothstein lives in Washington, D.C., with his wife, Sylvia Bergstrom.

Praise for *The Latina President*:

"If John Grisham wrote political thrillers instead of legal ones, they'd feel like this."

"An unusually deep plot for a political thriller...An enthralling protagonist at the heart of a gripping tale. A suspenseful--and topical--tale of White House intrigue."

—*Kirkus Reviews*

"For intrigue and suspense *The Latina President* rivals anything I've ever read about campaign politics."

—*U.S. Senator Tom Daschle, founder and CEO, The Daschle Group and former Senate Majority Leader.*

"Joe Rothstein spent decades living in the real world of political drama. Now he's packed all of that experience into a riveting political work of fiction that is a guaranteed page turner."

—U.S. Senator Byron Dorgan, former chairman, Senate Democratic Policy Committee and best-selling N.Y. Times author.

"Powerful fiction, directly relevant to growing risks now facing us as individuals and the stability of our entire global financial system."

—U.S. Senator Don Riegle, former Chairman, Senate Banking Committee."

"A gripping tale about our country's first Latina president and her unbelievable rise and fall. Couldn't put it down. How does one say 'spell-binding' in Spanish?"

— Dick Lobo, award-winning journalist and broadcast executive.

How would you rate *The Salvation Project*? 1,2,3,4,5 stars? Let us (and other readers) know by posting a grade and review on your favorite book store's web site.